THE KLARKASH-TON CYCLE

Clark Ashton Smith's Cthulhu Mythos Fiction

Edited and Introduced by Robert Price
Cover Art by Stephen Gilberts

A Chaosium Book
2008

More Titles from Chaosium
Call of Cthulhu® Fiction

The Antarktos Cycle
The Book of Eibon
The Disciples of Cthulhu, 2nd Ed.
Disciples of Cthulhu II
The Ithaqua Cycle
The Necronomicon
Singers of Strange Songs
Song of Cthulhu
Tales Out of Innsmouth
The Tsathoggua Cycle
Lin Carter's The Xothic Legend Cycle
R. W. Chambers' The Yellow Sign *(his complete weird fiction)*
Arthur Machen's The Three Impostors & Other Stories
Arthur Machen's The White People & Other Tales

Miskatonic University® Archives

The Book of Dzyan

Contents

This book is printed on 100% acid-free paper.

FIRST EDITION

10 9 8 7 6 5 4 3 2 1

Chaosium Publication 6046. Published in 2008.

ISBN 1-56882-160-3

Introduction to
The Klarkash-Ton Cycle

The Atlantean High Priest Klarkash-Ton

In a number of Cthulhu Mythos stories we read over the naive narrator's shoulder as he peruses some ancestor or predecessor's notebook or grimoire. Usually the excerpt from the book is a broad enough hint as to what is to come around the next bend in the plot, though the narrator is not yet in the position to see that. And just in case the reader is similarly dense, some Mythos scribes, especially August Derleth, like to supply marginal notes on the notebook like "Same as Ithaqua?" Or "Check Alhazred." It's almost like the answer to a puzzle printed upside down on the bottom of the same page. Well, once I had a real-life Mythos moment of exactly this type. I was paging through a new sorcerous specimen I had added to my collection of talismans and periapts. The item in question happened to be an ancient tome called *The Dunwich Horror*, Armed Forces Edition. I saw that a previous owner of the book, coming upon the passage in "The Whisperer in Darkness" which mentions "the Commoriom myth-cycle preserved by the Atlantean high priest Klarkash-Ton," had scribbled in the margin "Clark Ashton Smith?" Bingo!

Smith first signed his letters to his new friend Lovecraft simply "C.A.S." Next he signed himself "Tsathoggua the Primordial," just as HPL sometimes used the signature "Cthulhu" or "Grandpa Cthulhu." Soon he made of his initials a kind of mystery-cult name, "Ci-Ay-Ess," subjoining his titles as "the evangelist of Tsathoggua, and the archivist of Mu and Antares." And then, starting with his letter of June 27, 1930, he is "Klarkash-Ton." He would even initial his sculptures "KA," having forgotten, I guess, that it was "Klarkash-Ton," not "Klark-Ashton"! (Similarly, Lin Carter used to abbreviate himself not as "L.C." but as "L.X." When asked why, he'd say the X stood for "excellent"!) Thus it is obvious that HPL's fictive characterization of Smith as Klarkash-Ton, preserver of the Commoriom myth-cycle is drawn from Smith's own nickname plus his self-designation as archivist of lost civilizations.

Have you ever wondered what sort of a priest Klarkash-Ton was? What eldritch entity it was before whom he groveled? Why, Tsathoggua of course! HPL mentions him in this and that letter as "high priest of Tsathoggua" and such. He even makes him the seventh incarnation of the sorcerer Eibon! It makes sense, since Klarkash-Ton preserved the myths of Hyperborea (Commoriom) and presumably the fragments of the *Liber Ivonis* which the Averoni brought with them from foundering Atlantis to Gaul.

The Clark Ashton Smythos

Will Murray ("The Clark Ashton Smythos" in *The Horror of It All: Encrusted Gems from The Crypt of Cthulhu*, pp. 68-70) coined this happy phrase for Smith's unique contribution to and understanding of the Cthulhu Mythos. In an exchange of letters with August Derleth after the death of their friend Lovecraft, Smith replies to Derleth's trial balloons in which the younger man, the first Mythos buff, I suppose, set forth his notorious theology of the Mythos, making the Old Ones evil foes of the blessed Elder Gods as well as elemental forces of earth, air, fire and water. Smith, like Robert E. Howard, seems to have shared Lovecraft's outlook to a great degree, so his reactions to the emerging Derleth Mythos are especially worthy of note.

"As to classifying the Old Ones, I suppose that Cthulhu can be classed both as a survival on earth and a water-dweller; and Tsathoggua is a subterranean survival. Azathoth, referred to somewhere as 'the primal nuclear chaos', is the ancestor of the whole crew but still dwells in outer and ultra-dimensional space, together with Yog-Sothoth, and the demon piper Nyarlathotep, who attends the throne of Azathoth. I shouldn't class any of the old ones as *evil*: they are plainly beyond all limitary human conceptions of either ill or good. Long's Chaugnar Faugn, the Rhan-Tegoth of Hazel Heald's opus, "The Horror in the Museum", and the Ghatanothoa of her later tale "Out of the Eons", belong, I should venture to say, among the spawn of Azathoth and the brethren of Cthulhu and Tsathoggua. Rhan-Tegoth and Ghatanothoa, I'd be willing to gamble, were created by HPL in what was practically a job of ghost-writing. The first named is a survival and earth-dweller, somewhat analogous to Tsathoggua; while Ghatanothoa is a sea-submerged entity more akin to Cthulhu . . . . I don't think it necessary to enter into quite so much detail in presenting the stories to intelligent readers; but the growth of the whole mythos, the borrowings and contributions by various writers, is certainly an interesting study." (April 13, 1937)

Smith seems to have been willing to accept Derleth's term "mythos" as well as his suggestion (derived in turn from Francis T. Laney) that the Old Ones might have elemental "affiliations," at least if this is what Smith means by "survivals" and "dwellers" in this or that element. The Manichaean good-versus-evil scenario did not much appeal to him in this context, despite the fact that Smith had himself made effective use of it in "The Devotee of Evil." He just recognized that it didn't quite fit Lovecraft's Mythos.

But Derleth did not give up so easily. Smith is later forced to concede him some ground: "I started to read over some of HPL's stories last night, with a critical eye to mythologic references. Certainly some of the variations are puzzling. In "[The Call of] Cthulhu", the Great Old Ones are clearly specified as the builders and inhabitants of R'lyeh, 'preserved by the spells of mighty Cthulhu,' and worshipped through the aeons by obscure and evil cultists. Then, in "The Shadow over Innsmouth", Cthulhu and his compeers are referred to as the Deep Ones; and the Old Ones, whose 'palaeologean magic' alone could check the sea dwellers, are evidently something else again. Certainly these latter references would support your theory as to good and evil deities. In the earlier story, it might be argued that Castro was making out a case for his own side and ignoring the true Old Ones or confusing the evil gods with them. In "The Dreams in the Witch House", Nyarlathotep seems clearly identified with the Black Man of Satanism and witchcraft; since, in one of his dreams, Gilman is told that he must meet the Black Man and go with him to the throne of Azathoth." (April 29, 1937)

Indeed, as Tani Jantsang has pointed out in the case of Old Castro, it is the most elementary error to identify the utterance of a character with the narrative truth as imagined by the author, especially when the author has done everything possible to discredit the character as a witness: Old Castro is a degenerate half-breed (definitely a strike against him in HPL's mind!), who kidnaps children and sacrifices them in the noxious orgies of a murder cult in the depths of the bayou! Not exactly Mr. Credibility! Of course, Smith has rightly grasped HPL's implication: Old Castro only makes Cthulhu's ways "beyond good and evil" as an excuse to justify evil. And there can be no doubt that, e.g., in "The Dunwich Horror" and "The Case of Charles Dexter Ward" the reader, through Lovecraft's narrative rhetoric (Wayne Booth) is invited to identify with Dr. Armitage and Dr. Willett, not, for God's sake, with Wilbur Whateley and Joseph Curwen! And does not the final horror of "The Shadow over Innsmouth" reside in the fact that Robert Olmstead, the narrator, has at length succumbed to the horror he seemed to have escaped? The ending is something on the order of Bloch's "Yours Truly, Jack the Ripper." Or like the Donald Sutherland remake of *Invasion of the Body Snatchers*, in which the Kevin McCarthy analogue finally gets taken over by the pods after you thought he'd managed to prevail.

An unwitting innovation on Smith's part is the relegation of Nyarlathotep to the role of Skarl the Drummer to Azathoth's Mana-Yood-Sushai. Lovecraft did indeed borrow this Dunsanian mytheme, though Smith has made the correspondence between the Lovecraftian adaptation and the Dunsanian prototype more exact.

As for Smith's own contribution to the Mythos, he is equally explicit: "Tsathoggua, Eibon, and the *Book of Eibon* are . . . my own contributions to the mythos of the Old Ones and their world; and I first introduced Tsathoggua in "The Tale of Satampra Zeiros", written in the fall of 1929 but not printed in *W.T.* till Nov. 1931. Eibon made his debut in "The Door to Saturn" (*Strange Tales* Jan. 1932), where Tsathoggua was also featured under the variant of Zhothaqqua [*sic* for Zhothaqquah]. Tsathoggua is again mentioned in "The Testament of Athammaus" (*W.T.* Oct. 1932); and is linked with the Averoigne legendry under the variant Sadagui [*sic*: actually "Sodagui"], in "The Holiness of Azedarac" (Nov. 1933, *W.T.*). I think my only mention of Yog-Sothoth is in "Azedarac", where he is given the Gallicized form, Iog-Sotot. [CAS also cites him as "Yok-Zothoth" in "Ubbo-Sathla"]. The *Book of Eibon* is first mentioned and quoted in "Ubbo-Sathla" (*W.T.* July 1933); and Eibon also enters indirectly another Averoigne tale, "The Beast of Averoigne" (*W.T.* May, 1933). Tsathoggua plays an important part in "The Seven Geases" (*W.T.*, Oct. 1934) and my still unpublished tale "The Coming of the White Worm", purports to be Chapter IX of *The Book of Eibon*. This summary seems to exhaust my own use of the mythology to date." (to Derleth, April 13, 1937). For the record, Tsathoggua is also briefly mentioned in "The Ice-Demon."

Is this really the extent of Klarkash-Ton's Cthulhuvian creations? I think not. What of Atlach-Nacha the spider god? How about Vulthoom? Abhoth the Unclean? Xexanoth the Lurking Chaos? The tentacled Dweller in the Gulf? Quachil Uttaus the Ultimate Corruption? Here is a whole new pantheon of Old Ones! And may we not place *The Testaments of Carnamagos* alongside the *Book of Eibon* on our sorcerous shelf? I think so. And speaking of books . . . .

Rightly Dividing the Word of Truth

The manner in which I have apportioned Clark Ashton Smith's Cthulhu Mythos fiction among three volumes, *The Tsathoggua Cycle*, *The Klarkash-Ton Cycle*, and *The Book of Eibon*, requires some elucidation. On the one hand, it is natural that the Eibonic chapters of Smith and Lin Carter should be published as Lin Carter had outlined. Only two Smith tales, "The Coming of the White Worm" and "The Door to Saturn," appear amid Carter's various "posthumous collaborations" with Smith, written up as more chapters of Eibon. It is natural, too, that the Tsathoggua tales of Smith ("The Tale of Satampra Zeiros," "The Seven Geases," "The Testament of Athammaus") should appear together, along with subsequent Tsathoggua stories by other writers, following the format of our other Cycle Series volumes collecting the lore of each Old One.

But on the other hand, how dare we pretend to present Smith's Lovecraftian fiction in this volume as if it were a comprehensive collection of it? How can it be worthy of the name if it excludes the stories of Eibon and Tsathoggua? Here's how.

First, as I argue in the Introduction to *The Tsathoggua Cycle*, it is not at all clear, once you read Smith's Tsathoggua tales on their own, refraining from linking them in your mind with the Lovecraft Mythos, that they are really tales of the Cthulhu Mythos at all. Of course Lovecraft borrowed Smith's Tsathoggua and adopted him into his pantheon. But Lovecraft's tales of Tsathoggua are quite different. I believe it is by no means going too far to say that Tsathoggua counts as a Lovecraftian Old One *only in Lovecraft's own stories, not in Smith's*. Though that may scorch the ears of some as blasphemy, remember that Smith conceived Tsathoggua along quite different lines from Lovecraft's conceptions of Cthulhu or Yog-Sothoth, and he continued to write about Tsathoggua as a quaint and sardonic godling, more like Lovecraft's "mild gods of earth" than his terrible Other Gods. Thus I see no problem in cutting the Tsathoggua tales loose here. Smith surely did write Lovecraftian tales, Mythos tales, but they do not include the fanciful drolleries of Hyperborea. Those should be filed in the Dunsanian drawer. Smith had the same three categories of stories as Lovecraft: Dunsanian, Cthulhu Mythos, and traditional spectral tales. The present volume collects his Lovecraftian Cthulhu Mythos tales.

Second, the same holds true for Eibon. "The Coming of the White Worm" is Dunsanian in flavor, as is "The Door to Saturn." But is it not inconsistent to include "Ubbo-Sathla" and (a stray version of) "The Beast of Averoigne" here? Why not relegate them, too, to the *Book of Eibon*? Simply because these are not droll and lyrical tales of Eibon's ancient age of fable. No, in "Ubbo-Sathla" and "Averoigne," Eibon figures, as he does in Lovecraft's Mythos tales, as an ancient source of mystic erudition and baleful necromancy. A story told by Eibon or told about Eibon belongs in Smith's Dunsanian canon. A story which employs the *Book of Eibon* as an Elder Grimoire is a Cthulhu Mythos tale.

You will have noticed that I observed the same distinctions in Lin Carter's case. His "Dunsanian" episodes of the *Necronomicon* appear in our *Necronomicon* collection. His *Eibon* chapters, relegated to our *Book of Eibon*, are similarly "Dunsanian," but I collected his Mythos tales proper, so to speak, in *The Xothic Legend Cycle*.

Welcome, then, to the Testaments of Klarkash-Ton, the tales of the Clark Ashton Smythos.

— *Robert M. Price,*
Assistant Archivist of Mu and Antares

The Ghoul

During the reign of the Caliph Vathek, a young man of good repute and family, named Noureddin Hassan, was haled before the Cadi Ahmed ben Becar at Bussorah. Now Noureddin was a comely youth, of open mind and gentle mien; and great was the astonishment of the Cadi and of all others present when they heard the charges that were preferred against him. He was accused of having slain seven people, one by one, on seven successive nights, and of having left the corpses in a cemetery near Bussorah, where they were found lying with their bodies and members devoured in a fearsome manner, as if by jackals. Of the people he was said to have slain, three were women, two were traveling merchants, one was a mendicant, and one was a gravedigger.

Ahmed ben Becar was filled with the learning and wisdom of honorable years, and withal was possessed of much perspicacity. But he was deeply perplexed by the strangeness and atrocity of these crimes and by the mild demeanor and well-bred aspect of Noureddin Hassan, which he could in no wise reconcile with them. He heard in silence the testimony of witnesses who had seen Noureddin bearing on his shoulders the body of a woman at yester-eve in the cemetery; and others who on several occasions had observed him coming from the neighborhood at unseemly hours when only thieves and murderers would be abroad. Then, have considered all these, he questioned the youth closely.

"Noureddin Hassan," he said, "thou has been charged with crimes of exceeding foulness, which thy bearing and lineaments belie. Is there haply some explanation of these things by which thou canst clear thyself, or in some measure mitigate the heinousness of thy deeds, if so it be that thou art guilty? I adjure thee to tell me the truth in this matter."

Now Noureddin Hassan arose before the Cadi; and the heaviness of extreme shame and sorrow was visible on his countenance.

"Alas, O Cadi," he replied, "for the charges that have been brought against me are indeed true. It was I and no other, who slew these people; nor can I offer an extenuation of my act."

The Cadi was sorely grieved and astonished when he heard this answer.

"I must perforce believe thee," he said sternly. "But thou has confessed a thing which will make thy name hence forward an abomination in the ears and mouths of men. I command thee to tell me why these crimes were committed, and what offense these persons had given thee, or what injury they had done to thee; or if perchance thou slewest them for gain, like a common robber."

"There was neither offense given nor injury wrought by any of them against me," replied Noureddin. "And I did not kill them for their money or belongings or apparel, since I had no need of such things, and, aside from that, have always been an honest man."

"Then," cried Ahmed ben Becar, greatly puzzled, "what was thy reason if it was none of these?"

Now the face of Noureddin Hassan grew heavier still with sorrow; and he bowed his head in a shamefaced manner that bespoke the utterness of profound remorse. And standing thus before the Cadi, he told this story:

The reversals of fortune, O Cadi, are swift and grievous, and beyond the foreknowing or advertence of man. Alas! for less than a fortnight agone I was the happiest and most guiltless of mortals, with no thought of wrongdoing toward anyone. I was wedded to Amina, the daughter of the jewel-merchant Aboul Cogia; and I loved her deeply and was much beloved by her in turn; and moreover we were at this time anticipating the birth of our first child. I had inherited from my father a rich estate and many slaves; the cares of life were light upon my shoulders; and I had, it would seem, every reason to count myself among those Allah had blest with an earthly foretaste of Heaven.

Judge, then, the excessive nature of my grief when Amina died in the same hour when she was to have been delivered. From that time, in the dire extremity of my lamentation, I was as one bereft of light and knowledge; I was deaf to all those who sought to condole with me, and blind to their friendly offices.

After the burial of Amina my sorrow became a veritable madness, and I wandered by night to her grave in the cemetery near Bussorah and flung myself prostrate before the newly lettered tombstone, on the earth that had been digged that very day. My sense deserted me, and I knew not how long I remained on the damp clay beneath the cypresses, while the horn of a decrescent moon arose in the heavens.

Then, in my stupor of abandonment, I heard a terrible voice that bade me rise from the ground on which I was lying. And lifting my head a little, I saw a hideous demon of gigantic frame and stature, with eyes of scarlet fire beneath brows that were coarse as tangled rootlets, and fangs that overhung a cavernous mouth, and earth-black teeth longer and sharper than those of the hyena. And the demon said to me:

"I am a ghoul, and it is my office to devour the bodies of the dead. I have now come to claim the corpse that was interred today beneath the soil on which thou art lying in a fashion so unmannerly. Begone, for I have fasted since yester-night, and I am much anhungered."

Now, at the sight of this demon, and the sound of his dreadful voice, and the still more dreadful meaning of his words, I was like to have swooned with terror on the cold clay. But I recovered myself in a manner, and besought him, saying:

"Spare this grave, I implore thee; for she who lies buried therein is dearer to me than any living mortal; and I would not that her fair body should be the provender of an unclean demon such as thou."

At this the ghoul was angered, and I thought that he would have done me some bodily violence. But again I besought him, swearing by Allah and Mohammed with many solemn oaths that I would grant him anything procurable and would do for him any favor that lay in the power of man if he would leave undespoiled the new-made grave of Amina. And the ghoul was somewhat mollified, and he said:

"If though wilt indeed perform for me a certain service, I shall do as thou askest." And I replied:

"There is no service, whatsoever its nature, that I will not do for thee in this connection, and I pray thee to name thy desire."

Then the ghoul said: it is this, that thou shalt bring me each night, for eight successive nights, the body of one whom thou hast slain with thine own hand. Do this, and I shall neither devour not dig the body that lies interred hereunder."

Now was I seized by utter horror and despair, since I had bound myself in all honor to grant the ghoul his hideous requirement. And I begged him to change the terms of the stipulation, saying to him:

"Is it needful for thee, O eater of corpses, that the bodies should be those of people whom I myself have slain?"

And the ghoul said: "Yea, for all others would be the natural provender of myself or of my kin in any event. I adjure thee by the promise thou hast given to meet me here tomorrow night, when darkness has wholly fallen or as soon thereafter as thou are able, bringing the first of the eight bodies."

So saying, he strode off among the cypresses, and began to dig in another newly made grave at a little distance from that of Amina.

I left the graveyard in even direr anguish than when I had come, thinking of that which I must do in fulfillment of my sworn promise, to preserve the body of Amina from the demon. I know not how I survived the ensuing day, torn as I was between sorrow for the dead and my horror of the coming night with its repugnant duty.

When darkness had descended I went forth by stealth to a lonely road near the cemetery; and waiting there amid the low-grown branches of the trees, I slew the first passer with a sword and carried his body to the spot appointed by the ghoul. And each night thereafter, for six more nights, I returned to the same vicinity and repeated this deed, slaying always the very first who came, whether man or woman, or merchant or beggar or gravedigger. And the ghoul awaited me on each occasion, and would begin to devour his provender in my presence, with small thanks and scant ceremony. Seven persons did I slay in all, till only one was wanting to complete the agreed number; and the person I slew yester-night was a woman, even as the witnesses have testified. All this I did with utmost repugnance and regret, and sustained only by the remembrance of my plighted word, and the fate which would befall the corpse of Amina if I should break the bond.

This, O Cadi, is all my story. Alas! For these lamentable crimes have availed me not, and I have failed in wholly keeping my bargain with the demon, who will doubtless this night consume the body of Amina in lieu of the one corpse that is still lacking. I resign myself to thy judgment, O Ahmed ben Becar, and I beseech thee for no other mercy than that of death, wherewith to terminate my double grief and my two-fold remorse.

When Noureddin Hassan had ended his narrative, the amazement of all who had heard him was verily multiplied, since no man could remember hearing a stranger tale. And the Cadi pondered for a long time and then gave judgment, saying:

"I must needs marvel at thy story, but the crimes thou has committed are none the less heinous, and Iblis himself would stand aghast before them. However, some allowance must be made for the fact that thou hadst given thy word to the ghoul and was bound as it were in honor to fulfill his demand, no matter how horrible its nature. And allowance must likewise be made for thy connubial grief which cause they to forfend thy wife's body from the demon. Yet I cannot judge thee guiltless, though I know not the punishment which is merited in a case so utterly without parallel. Therefore, I set thee free, with this injunction, that thou shalt make atonement for thy crimes in the fashion that seemeth best to thee, and shalt render justice to thyself and to others in such degree as thou art able."

"I thank thee for this mercy," replied Noureddin Hassan; and he then withdrew from the court amid the wonderment of all who were present. There was much debate when he had gone, and many were prone to question the wisdom of the Cadi's decision. Some there were who maintained that Noureddin should have been sentenced to death without delay for his abominable actions though others argued for the sanctity of his oath to the ghoul, and would have exculpated him altogether or in part. And tales were told and instances were cited regarding the habits of ghouls and the strange plight of men who had surprised such demons in their nocturnal delvings. And again the discussion returned to Noureddin, and the judgment of the Cadi was once more upheld or assailed with divers arguments. But amid all this, Ahmed ben Becar was silent, saying only:

"Wait, for this man will render justice to himself and to all others concerned, as far as the rendering thereof is possible."

So indeed, it happened, for on the morning of the next day another body was found in the cemetery near Bussorah lying half-devoured on the grave of Noureddin Hassan's wife,

Amina. And the body was that of Noureddin, self-slain, who in this manner had not only fulfilled the injunction of the Cadi but had also kept his bargains with the ghoul by providing the required number of corpses.

A Rendering
from the Arabic

I had been out of work for several months, and my savings were perilously near the vanishing point. Therefore I was naturally elated when I received from John Carnby a favorable answer inviting me to present my qualification in person. Carnby had advertised for a secretary, stipulating that all applicants must offer a preliminary statement of their capacities by letter, and I had written in response to the advertisement.

Carnby, no doubt, was a scholarly recluse who felt averse to contact with a long waiting-list of strangers; and he had chosen this manner of weeding out beforehand many, if not all, of those who were ineligible. He had specified his requirements fully and succinctly, and these were of such nature as to bar even the average well-educated person. A knowledge of Arabic was necessary, among other things; and luckily I had acquired a certain degree of scholarship in this unusual tongue.

I found the address, of whose location I had formed only a vague idea, at the end of a hilltop avenue in the suburbs of Oakland. It was a large, two-story house, overshaded by ancient oaks and dark with a mantling of unchecked ivy, among hedges of unpruned privet and shrubbery that had gone wild for many years. It was separated from its neighbors by a vacant, weed-grown lot on one side and a tangle of vines and trees on the other, surrounding the black ruins of a burnt mansion.

Even apart from its air of long neglect, there was something drear and dismal about the place — something that inhered in the ivy-blurred outlines of the house, in the furtive, shadowy windows, and the very forms of the misshapen oaks and oddly sprawling shrubbery. Somehow, my elation became a trifle less exuberant, as I entered the grounds and followed an unswept path to the front door.

When I found myself in the presence of John Carnby, my jubilation was still somewhat further diminished; though I could not have given a tangible reason for the premonitory chill, the dull, somber feeling of alarmed that I experienced, and the leaden sinking of my spirits. Perhaps it was the dark library in which he received me as much as the man himself — a room whose musty shadows could never have been wholly dissipated by sun or lamplight. Indeed, it must have been this; for John Carnby himself was very much the sort of person I had pictured him to be.

He had all the earmarks of the lonely scholar who has devoted patient years to some line of erudite research. He was thin and bent, with a massive forehead and a many of grizzled hair; and the pallor of the library was on his hollow, clean-shaven cheeks. But coupled with this, there was a nerve-shattered air, a fearful shrinking that was more than the normal shyness of a recluse, and an unceasing apprehensiveness that betrayed itself in every glance of his dark-ringed, feverish eyes and every movement of his bony hands. In all likelihood his health had been seriously impaired by over-application; and I could not help but wonder at the nature of the studies that made him a tremulous wreck. But there was something about him — perhaps the width of his bowed shoulders and the bold aquilinity of his facial outlines — which gave the impression of great former strength and a vigor not yet wholly exhausted.

His voice was unexpectedly deep and sonorous.

"I think you will do, Mr. Ogden," he said, after a few formal questions, most of which related to my linguistic knowledge, and in particular my mastery of Arabic. "Your labors will not be very heavy; but I want someone who can be on hand at any time required. Therefor you must live with me. I can give you a comfortable room, and I guarantee that my cooking will not poison you. I often work at night; and I hope you will not find the irregular hours too disagreeable."

No doubt I should have been overjoyed at this assurance that the secretarial position was to be mine. Instead, I was aware of a dim, unreasoning reluctance and an obscure forewarning of evil as I thanked John Carnby and told him that I was ready to move in whenever he desired.

He appeared to be greatly pleased; and the queer apprehensiveness went out of his manner for a moment.

"Come immediately — this very afternoon, if you can," he said. "I shall be very glad to have you, and the sooner the better. I have been living entirely alone for some time; and I must confess that the solitude is beginning to pall upon me. Also, I have been retarded in my labors for lack of the proper help. My brother used to live with me and assist me, but he has gone away on a long trip."

* * *

I returned to my downtown lodgings, paid my rent with the last few dollars that remained to me, packed my belongings, and in less than an hour was back at my new employer's home. He assigned me a room on the second floor, which, though unaired and dusty, was more than luxurious in comparison with the hall-bedroom that failing funds had compelled me to inhabit for some time past. Then he took me to his own study, which was on the same floor, at the further end of the hall. Here, he explained to me, most of my future work would be done.

I could hardly restrain an exclamation of surprise as I viewed the interior of this changer. It was very much as I should have imagined the den of some old sorcerer to be. There were tables strewn with archaic instruments of doubtful use, with astrological charts, with skulls and alembics and crystals, with censers such as are used in the Catholic Church, and volumes found in worm-eaten leather with verdigris-mottled claps. In one corner stood the skeleton of a large ape; in another, a human skeleton; and overhead a stuffed crocodile was suspended.

There were cases overpiled with books, and even a cursory glance at the titles showed me that they formed a singularly comprehensive collection of ancient and modern works on demonology and the black arts. There were some weird paintings and etchings on the walls, dealing with kindred themes; and the whole atmosphere of the room exhaled a medley of half-forgotten superstitions. Ordinarily I would have smiled if confronted with such things; but somehow, in this lonely, dismal house, beside the neurotic, hag-ridden Carnby, it was difficult for me to repress an actual shudder.

Carnby had noted my surprise, and was watching me with a keen, analytic expression which I found impossible to fathom. He began to speak, in explanatory tones.

"I have made a life-study of demonism and sorcery," he declared. "It is a fascinating field, and one that is singularly neglected. I am now preparing a monograph, in which I am trying to correlate the magical practices and demon-worship of every known age and people. Your labors, at least for a while, will consist in typing and arranging the voluminous preliminary notes which I have made, and in helping me to track down other references and correspondences. Your knowledge of Arabic will be invaluable to me, for I am none too well-grounded in this language myself, and I am depending for certain essential data on a copy of the *Necronomicon* in the original Arabic text. I have reason to think that there are certain omissions and erroneous renderings in the Latin version of Olaus Wormius."

I had heard of this rare, well-nigh fabulous volume, but had never seen it. the book was supposed to contain the ultimate secrets of evil and forbidden knowledge; and, moreover, the original text, written by the mad Arab, Abdul Alhazred, was said to be unprocurable. I wondered how it had come into Carnby's possession.

"I'll show you the volume after dinner," Carnby went on. "You will doubtless be able to elucidate one or two passages that have long puzzled me."

The evening meal, cooked and served by my employer himself, was a welcome change from cheap restaurant fare. Carnby seemed to have lost a good deal of his nervousness. He was very talkative, and even began to exhibit a certain scholarly gaiety after we had shared a bottle of mellow Sauterne. Still, with no manifest reason, I was troubled by intimations and forebodings which I could neither analyze not trace to their rightful source.

We returned to the study, and Carnby brought out from a locked drawer the volume of which he had spoken. It was enormously old, and was found in ebony covers arabesqued with silver and set with darkly glowing garnets. When I opened the yellowing pages, I drew back with involuntary revulsion at the odor which arose from them — an odor that was more than suggestive of physical decay, as if the book had lain among corpses in some forgotten graveyard and had taken on the taint of dissolution.

Carnby's eyes were burning with a fevered light as he took the old manuscript from my hands and turned to a page near the middle. He indicated a certain passage with his lean forefinger.

"Tell me what you make of this," he said, in a tense, excited whisper.

I deciphered the paragraph, slowly and with some difficulty, and wrote down a rough English version with the pad and pencil which Carnby offered me. Then, at his request, I read it aloud:

> *"It is verily known by few, but is nevertheless an attestable fact, that the will of a dead sorcerer hath power upon his own body and can raise it up from the tomb and perform therewith whatever action was unfulfilled in life. And such resurrections are invariable for the doing of malevolent deeds and for the detriment of others. Most readily can the corpse be animated if all its members have remained intact; and yet there are cases in which the excelling will of the wizard hath reared up from death the sundered pieces of a body hewn in many fragments, and hath cause them to serve his end, either separately or in a temporary reunion. But in every instance, after the action hath ben completed, the body lapseth into its former state."*

Of course, all this was errant gibberish. Probably it was the strange, unhealthy look of utter absorption with which my employer listened, more than that damnable passage from the *Necronomicon*, which caused my nervousness and made me start violently when, toward the end of my reading, I heard an indescribable slithering noise in the hall outside. But when I finished the paragraph and looked up at Carnby, I was more than startled by the expression of stark, staring fear which his features had assumed — an expression as of one who is haunted by some hellish phantom. Somehow, I got the feeling that he was listening to that odd noise in the hallway rather than to my translation of Abdul Alhazred.

"the house is full of rats," he explained, as he caught my inquiring glance. "I have never been able to get rid of them, with all my efforts."

The noise, which still continued, was that which a rat might make in dragging some object slowly along the floor. It seemed to draw closer, to approach the door of Carnby's room, and then, after an intermission, it began to move again and receded. My employer's agitation was marked; he listened with

fearful intentness and seemed to follow the progress of the
sound with a terror that mounted as it drew near and decreased
a little with its recession.

"I am very nervous," he said. "I have worked too hard
lately, and this is the result. Even a little noise upsets me."

The sound had now died away somewhere in the house.
Carnby appeared to recover himself in a measure.

"Will you please re-read your translation?" he requested. "I
want to follow it very carefully, word by word."

I obeyed. He listened with the same look of unholy absorption as before, and this time we were not interrupted by any
noises in the hallway. Carnby's face grew paler, as if the last
remnant of blood had been drained from it, when I read the
final sentences; and the fire in his hollow eyes was like phosphorescence in a deep vault.

"That is a most remarkable passage," he commented. "I
was doubtful about its meaning, with my imperfect Arabic;
and I have found that the passage is wholly omitted in the Latin
of Olaus Wormius. Thank you for your scholarly rendering. you
have certainly cleared it up for me."

His tone was dry and formal, as if he were repressing himself and holding back a world of unsurmisable thoughts and
emotions. Somehow I felt that Carnby was more nervous and
upset than ever, and also that my reading from the *Necronomicon*
had in some mysterious manner contributed to his perturba-
tion. He wore a ghastly brooding expression, as if his mind
were busy with some unwelcome and forbidden theme.

However, seeming to collect himself, he asked me to trans-
late another passage. This turned out to be a singular incanta-
tory formula for the exorcism of the dead, with a ritual that
involved the use of rare Arabian spices and the proper intoning
of at least a hundred names of ghouls and demons. I copied it
all out for Carnby, who studies it for a long time with a rapt
eagerness that was more than scholarly.

"That, too," he observed, "is not in Olaus Wormius." After perusing it again, he folded the paper carefully and put it away in the same drawer from which he had taken the *Necronomicon*.

That evening was one of the strangest I have ever spent. As we sat for hour after hour discussing renditions from that unhallowed volume, I came to know more and more definitely that my employer was mortally afraid of something; that he dreaded being alone and was keeping me with him on this account rather than for any other reason. Always he seemed to be waiting and listening with a painful, tortured expectation, and I saw that he gave only a mechanical awareness to much that was said. Among the weird appurtenances of the room, in that atmosphere of unmanifested evil, of untold horror, the rational part of my mind began to succumb slowly to a recrudescence of dark ancestral fears. A scorner of such things in my normal moments, I was now ready to believe in the most baleful creations of superstitious fancy. No doubt, by some process of mental contagion, I had caught the hidden terror from which Carnby suffered.

By no word or syllable, however, did the man admit the actual feelings that were evident in his demeanor, but he spoke repeatedly of a nervous ailment. More than once, during our discussion, he sought to imply that his interest in the supernatural and the Satanic was wholly intellectual, that he, like myself, was without personal belief in such things. Yet I knew infallibly that his implications were false; that he was driven and obsessed by a real faith in all that he pretended to view with scientific detachment, and had doubtless fallen a victim to some imaginary horror entailed by his occult researches. But my intuition afforded me no clue fear and oppression to which I had been subjected. to the actual nature of this horror.

There was no repetition of the sounds that had been so disturbing to my employer. We must have sat till after midnight with the writings of the mad Arab open before us. At last Carnby seemed to realize the lateness of the hour.

"I fear I have kept you up too long," he said apologetically. "You must go and get some sleep. I am selfish, and I forget that such hours are not habitual to others, as they are to me."

I made the formal denial of his self-impeachment which courtesy required, said good-night, and sought my own chamber with a feeling of intense relief. It seemed to me that I would leave behind me in Carnby's room all the shadowy fear and oppression to which I had been subjected.

Only one light was burning in the long passage. It was near Carnby's door; and my own door at the further end, close to the stairhead, was in deep shadow. As I groped for the knob, I heard a noise behind me, and turned to see in the gloom a small, indistinct body that sprang from the hall-landing to the top stair, disappearing from view. I was horribly startled; for even in that vague, fleeting glimpse, the thing was much too pale for a rat, and its form was not at all suggestive of an animal. I could not have sworn what it was, but the outlines had seemed unmentionably monstrous. I stood trembling violently in every limb, and heard on the stairs a singular bumping sound like the fall of an object rolling downward from step to step. The sound was repeated at regular intervals and finally ceased.

If the safety of the soul and body depended upon it, I could not have turned on the stair-light; nor could I have gone to the top steps to ascertain the agency of that unnatural bumping. Anyone else, it might seem, would have done this. Instead, after a moment of virtual petrification, I entered my room, locked the door, and went to bed in a turmoil of unresolved doubt and equivocal terror. I left the light burning; and I lay awake for hours, expecting momentarily a recurrence of that abominable sound. But the house was as silent as a morgue, and I heard nothing. At length, in spite of my anticipations to the contrary, I fell asleep and did not awaken till after many sodden, dreamless hours.

* * *

It was ten o'clock, as my watch informed me. I wondered whether my employer had left me undisturbed through thoughtfulness, or had not arisen himself. I dressed and went downstairs, to find him waiting at the breakfast table. He was paler and more tremulous than ever, as if he had slept badly.

"I hope the rats didn't annoy you too much," he remarked, after a preliminary greeting. "Something really must be done about them."

"I didn't notice them at all," replied. Somehow, it was utterly impossible for me to mention the queer, ambiguous thing which I had seen and heard on retiring the night before. Doubtless I had been mistaken; doubtless it had been merely a rat after all, dragging something down the stairs. I tried to forget the hideously repeated noise and the momentary flash of unthinkable outlines in the gloom.

My employer eyed me with uncanny sharpness, as if he sought to penetrate my inmost mind. Breakfast was a dismal affair; and the day that followed was no less dreary. Carnby isolated himself till the middle of the afternoon, and I was left to my own devices in the well-supplied but conventional library downstairs. What Carnby was doing alone in his room I could not surmise; but I thought more than once that I heard the faint, monotonous intonations of a solemn voice. Horror-breeding hints and noisome intuitions invaded my brain. More and more the atmosphere of that house enveloped and stifled me with poisonous, miasmal mystery; and I felt everywhere the invisible brooking of malignant incubi.

It was almost a relief when my employer summoned me to his study. Entering, I noticed that the air was full of a pungent, aromatic smell and was touched by the vanishing coils of a blue vapor, as if from the burning of Oriental gums and spices in the church censers. An Ispahan rug had been moved from its position near the wall to the center of the room, but was not sufficient to cover entirely a curving violet mark that suggested the drawing of a magic circle on the floor. No doubt Carnby had been performing some sort of incantation; and I thought of the awesome formula I had translated at his request.

However, he did not offer any explanation of what he had been doing. His manner had changed remarkably and was more controlled and confident than at any former time. In a fashion almost business-like he laid before me a pile of manuscript which he wanted me to type for him. the familiar click of the keys aided me somewhat in dismissing my apprehensions of vague evil, and I could almost smile at the recherché and terrific information comprised in my employer's notes, which dealt mainly with formulae for the acquisition of unlawful power. But still, beneath my reassurance, there was a vague, lingering disquietude.

Evening came; and after out meal we turned again to the study. There was a tenseness in Carnby's manner now, as if he were eagerly awaiting the result of some hidden test. I went on with my work; but some of his emotion communicated itself to me, and ever and anon I caught myself in an attitude of strained listening.

At last, above the click of the keys, I heard the peculiar slithering in the hall. Carnby had heard it, too, and his confident look had utterly vanished, giving place to the most pitiable fear.

The sound drew nearer and was followed by a dull, dragging noise, and then by more sounds of an unidentifiable slithering and scuttling nature that varied in loudness. The hall was seemingly full of them, as if a whole army of rats were hauling some carrion booty along the floor. And yet no rodent or number of rodents could have made such sounds, or could have moved anything so heavy as the object which came behind the rest. There was something in the character of those noises, something without name or definition, which caused a slowly creeping chill to invade my spine.

"Good Lord! What is all that racket?" I cried.

"The rats! I tell you it is only rats!" Carnby's voice was a high hysterical shriek.

A moment later, there came an unmistakable knocking on the door, near the sill. At the same time I heard a heavy thudding in the locked cupboard at the further end of the room. Carnby had been standing erect, but now he sank limply into a chair. His features were ashen, and his look was almost maniacal with fright.

The nightmare doubt and tension became unbearable and I ran to the door and flung it open, in spite of a frantic remonstrance from my employer. I had no idea what I should find as I stepped across the sill into the dim-lit hall.

When I looked down and saw the thing on which I had almost trodden, my feeling was one of sick amazement and actual nausea. It was a human hand which had been severed at the wrist — a bony, bluish hand like that of a week-old corpse, with garden-mould on the fingers and under the long nails. *The damnable thing had moved!* It had drawn back to avoid me, and was crawling along the passage somewhat in the manner of a crab! And following it with my gaze, I saw that there were other things beyond it, one of which I recognized as a man's foot and another as a forearm. I dared not look at the rest. All were moving slowly, hideously away in a charnel procession, and I cannot describe the fashion in which they moved. Their individual vitality was horrifying beyond endurance. It was more than the vitality of life, yet the air was laden with a carrion taint. I averted my eyes and stepped back into Carnby's room, closing the door behind me with a shaking hand. Carnby was at my side with the key, which he turned in the lock with palsy-stricken fingers that had become as feeble as those of an old man.

"You saw them?" he asked in a dry, quavering whisper.

"In God's name, what does it all mean?" I cried.

Carnby went back to his chair, tottering a little with weakness. His lineaments were agonized by the gnawing of some

inward horror, and he shook visibly like an ague patient. I saw
down in a chair beside him, and he began to stammer forth his
unbelievable confession, half incoherently, with inconsequential
mouthings and many breaks and pauses:

"He is stronger than I am — even in death, even with his
body dismembered by the surgeon's knife and saw that I used.
I thought he could not return after that — after I had buried
the portions in a dozen different places, in the cellar, beneath
the shrubs, at the foot of the ivy-vines. But the *Necronomicon* is
right . . . and Helman Carnby knew it. He warned me before I
killed him, he told me he could return — *even in that condition.*

But I did not believe him. I hated Helman, and he hated
me, too. He had attained to higher power and knowledge and
was more favored by the Dark Ones than I. That was why I
killed him — my own twin-brother, and my brother in the service of Satan and of Those who were before Satan. We had
studied together for many years. We had celebrated the black
Mass together and we were attended by the same familiars. But
Helman Carnby had gone deeper into the occult, into the forbidden, where I could not follow him. I feared him, and I could
not endure his supremacy.

"It is more than a week — it is ten days since I did the
deed. But Helman — or some part of him — has returned
every night. . . . God! His accursed hands crawling on the floor!
His feet, his arms, the segments of his legs, climbing the stairs
in some unmentionable way to haunt me! . . . Christ! His awful
bloody torso lying in wait! I tell you, his hands have come even
by day to tap and fumble at my door . . . and I have stumbled
over his arms in the dark.

"Oh, God! I shall go mad with the awfulness of it. But he
wants me to go mad, he wants to torture me till my brain gives
way. That is why he haunts me in this piecemeal fashion. He
could end it all at any time, with the demoniacal power that is
his. He could re-knit his sundered limbs and body and slay me
as I slew him.

"How carefully I buried the parts, with what infinite fore-thought! And how useless it was! I buried the saw and knife, too, at the further end of the garden, as far away as possible from his evil, itching hands. But I did not bury the head with the other pieces — I kept it in that cupboard at the end of my room. Sometimes I have heard it moving there, as you heard it a while ago. . . . But he does not need the head, his will is else-where, and can work intelligently through all his members.

"Of course, I locked all the doors and windows at night when I found that he was coming back. . . . But it made no dif-ference. And I have tried to exorcise him with the appropriate incantations — with all those that I knew. Today I tried that sovereign formula from the *Necronomicon* which you translated for me. I got you here to translated it. Also, I could no longer bear to be alone and I thought that it might help if there were someone else in the house. That formula was my last nope. I thought it would hold him — it is a most ancient and most dreadful incantation. But, as you have seen, it is useless . . . ."

His voice trailed off in a broken mumble, and he sat star-ing before him with sightless, intolerable eyes in which I saw the beginning flare of madness. I could say nothing — the con-fession he had made was so ineffably atrocious. The moral shock, and the ghastly supernatural horror, had almost stupi-fied me. My sensibilities were stunned; and it was not till I had begun to recover myself that I felt the irresistible surge of a flood of loathing for the man beside me.

I rose to my feet. The house had grown very silent, as if the macabre and charnel army of beleaguerment had now retired to its various graves. Carnby had left the key in the lock; and I went to the door and turned it quickly.

"Are you leaving? Don't go," Carnby begged in a voice that was tremulous with alarm, as I stood with my hand on the doorknob.

"Yes, I am going," I said coldly. "I am resigning my position right now; and I intend to pack my belongs and leave your house with as little delay as possible."

I opened the door and went out, refusing to listen to the arguments and pleadings and protestations he had begun to babble. For the nonce, I preferred to face whatever might lurk in the gloomy passage, no matter how loathsome and terrifying, rather than endure any longer the society of John Carnby.

The hall was empty; but I shuddered with repulsion at the memory of what I had seen, as I hastened to my room. I think I should have screamed aloud at the least sound or movement in the shadows.

I began to pack my valise with a feeling of the most frantic urgency and compulsion. It seemed to em that I could not escape soon enough from that house of abominable secrets, over which hung an atmosphere of smothering menace. I made mistake in my haste, I stumbled over chairs, and my brain and fingers grew numb with a paralyzing dread.

I had almost finished my task, when I heart the sound of slow measured footsteps coming up the stairs. I knew that it was not Carnby, for he had locked himself immediately in his room when I had left; and I felt sure that nothing could have tempted him to emerge. Anyway, he could hardly have gone downstairs without my hearing him.

The footsteps came to the top landing and went past my door along the hall, with that same monotonous repetition, regular as the movement of a machine. Certainly it was not the soft, nervous tread of John Carnby.

Who, then, could it be? My blood stood still in my veins; I dared not finish the speculation that arose in my mind.

The steps paused; and I knew that they had reached the door of Carnby's room. There followed an interval in which I could scarcely breathe; and then I heard an awful crashing and shattering noise, and above it the soaring scream of a man in the uttermost extremity of fear.

I was powerless to move, as if an unseen iron hand had reached forth to restrain me; and I have no idea how long I waited and listened. The scream had fallen away in a swift silence; and I heard nothing now, except a low, peculiar sound which my brain refused to identify.

It was not my own volition, but a stronger will than mine, which drew me forth at last and impelled me down the hall to Carnby's study. I felt the presence of that will as on over-powering, superhuman thing — a demoniac force, a malign mesmerism.

The door of the study had been broken in and was hanging by one hinge. It was splintered as by the impact of more than mortal strength. A light was still burning in the room, and the unmentionable sound I had been hearing ceased as I neared the threshold. It was followed by an evil, utter stillness.

I seemed to know with a loathly prescience the sight that awaited be beyond the sill. But the reality would have put to shame the foulest enormities of the nether pits. Carnby — or what remained of him — was lying on the floor; and above him stooped an unbelievable thing — the nude, headless body of a man, already blue with incipient putrefaction, and marked with earth-stains. At wrist and ankle and hip, there were red sutures where the sundered limbs had been knit together in some hellish fashion, by the power of a will that was more than mortal. The Thing was holding a bloody surgeon's saw in its right hand; and I saw that its work had been completed . . . .

Surely, it would seem, I was viewing the climax of all con-ceivable horror. But even as the Thing knelt with its ghastly tool suspended above the remains of its victim, there came a violent crash from the cupboard, as if something had been hurled against the door. The lock must have been defective; for the door burst open, and a human head emerged and bounded to the floor. It rolled over, and lay facing the medley of human remnants, that had been John Carnby. It was in the same con-dition of decay as the body; but I swear that the eyes were alive with malignant hate. Even with the marks of corruption upon them, the features bore a manifest likeness to those of John Carnby; and plainly they could belong only to a twin brother.

I was beyond horror, beyond terror; and I do not believe I could have stirred again if it had not been for the thing that happened now. As if the animating and uniting power had been removed with the completion of its task, the headless cadaver toppled to the floor, scattered in all its original portions. The life had gone out of the eyes in that terrible head; and there was nothing but a heap of mouldy members, beside the fresh segments of that other.

The spell was broken. I felt that something had withdrawn from the room — the overpowering volition that had held me captive was gone. It had released me, even as it had released the corpse of Helman Carnby. I was free to go; and I fled from that ghastly room and ran headlong through an unlit house, and into the outer darkness.

The Hunters from Beyond

I have seldom been able to resist the allurement of a bookstore, particularly one that is well supplied with rare and
exotic items. Therefore I turned in at Toleman's to browse
around for a few minutes. I had come to San Francisco for one
of my brief, biannual visits, and had started early that idle
forenoon to an appointment with Cyprian Sincaul, the sculptor, a second or third cousin of mine, whom I had not seen for
several years.

The studio was only a block from Toleman's, and there
seemed to be no especial object in reaching it ahead of time.
Cyprian had offered to show me his collection of recent sculptures; but, remembering the smooth mediocrity of his former
work, amid which were a few banal efforts to achieve horror
and grotesquerie, I did not anticipate anything more than an
hour or two of dismal boredom.

The little shop was empty of customers. Knowing my proclivities, the owner and his one assistant became tacitly non-
attentive after a word or recognition, and left me to rummage
at will among the curiously laden shelves. Wedged in between
other but less alluring titles, I found a de luxe edition of Goya's
Proverbios. I began to turn the heavy pages, and was soon
engrossed in the diabolic art of these nightmare-nurtured
drawings.

It has always been incomprehensible to me that I did not shriek aloud with mindless, overmastering terror, when I happened to look up from the volume, and saw the thing that was crouching in a corner of the book-shelves before me. I could not have been more hideously startled if some hellish conception of Goya had suddenly come to life and emerged from one of the pictures in the folio.

What I saw was a forward-slouching, vermin-gray figure, wholly devoid of hair or down or bristles, but marked with faint, etiolated rings like those of a serpent that has lived in darkness. It possessed the head and brow of an anthropoid ape, a semi-canine mouth and jaw, and arms ending in twisted hands whose black hyena talons nearly scraped the floor. The thing was infinitely bestial, and, at the same time, macabre; for its parchment skin was shriveled, corpselike, mummified, in a manner impossible to convey; and from eye sockets well-nigh deep as those of a skull, there glimmered evil slits of yellowish phosphorescence, like burning sulfur. Fangs that were stained as if with poison or gangrene, issued from the slavering, half-open mouth; and the whole attitude of the creature was that of some maleficent monster in readiness to spring.

Though I had been for years a professional writer of stories that often dealt with occult phenomena, with the weird and the spectral. I was not at this time possessed of any clear and settled belief regarding such phenomena. I had never before seen anything that I could identify as a phantom, nor even an hallucination; and I should hardly have said offhand that a bookstore on a busy street, in full summer daylight, was the likeliest of places in which to see one. But the thing before me was assuredly nothing that could ever exist among the permissible forms of a same world. It was too horrific, too atrocious, to be anything but a creation of unreality.

Even as I stared across the Goya, sick with a half-incredulous fear, the apparition moved toward me. I say that it moved, but its change of position was no instantaneous, so utterly without effort or visible transition, that the verb is hopelessly inadequate. The foul specter had seemed five or six feet away. But now it was stooping directly above the volume that I still held in my hands, with its loathsomely lambent eyes peering upward at my face, and a gray-green slime drooling from its mouth on the broad pages. At the same time I breathed an insupportable fetor, like a mingling of rancid serpent-stench with the moldiness of antique charnels and the fearsome reek of newly decaying carrion.

In a frozen timelessness that was perhaps no more than a second or two, my heart appeared to suspend its beating, while I beheld the ghastly face. Gasping, I let the Goya drop with a resonant bang on the floor, and even as it fell, I saw that the vision had vanished.

Toleman, a tonsured gnome with shell-rimmed goggles, rushed forward to retrieve the fallen volume, exclaiming: "What is wrong, Mr. Hastane? Are you ill?" From the meticulousness with which he examined the binding in search of possible damage, I knew that his chief solicitude was concerning the Goya. It was plain that neither he nor his clerk had seen the phantom; nor could I detect aught in their demeanor to indicate that they had noticed the nephritic odor that still lingered in the air like an exhalation from broken graves. And, as far as I could tell, they did not even perceive the grayish slime that still polluted the open folio.

I do not remember how I managed to make my exit from the shop. My mind had become a seething blur of muddled horror, of crawling, sick revulsion from the supernatural vileness I had beheld, together with the direst apprehension for my own sanity and safety. I recall only that I found myself on the street above Toleman's, walking with feverish rapidity toward my cousin's studio, with a neat parcel containing the Goya volume under my arm. Evidently, in an effort to atone for my clumsiness, I must have bought and paid for the book by a sort of automatic impulse, without any real awareness of what I was doing.

I came to the building in which was my destination, but went on around the block several times before entering. All the while I fought desperately to regain my self-control and equipoise. I remember how difficult it was even to moderate the pace at which I was walking, or refrain from breaking into a run; for it seemed to me that I was fleeing all the time from an invisible pursuer. I tried to argue with myself to convince the rational part of my mind that the apparition had been the product of some evanescent trick of light and shade, or a temporary dimming of eyesight. But such sophistries were useless; for I had seen the gargoylish terror all too distinctly, in an unforgettable fullness of grisly detail.

What could the thing mean? I had never used narcotic drugs or abused alcohol. My nerves, as far as I knew, were in sound condition. But either I had suffered a visual hallucination that might mark the beginning of some obscure cerebral disorder, or had been visited by a spectral phenomenon, by something from realms and dimensions that are past the normal scope of human perception. It was a problem either for the alienist or the occultist.

Though I as still damnably upset, I contrived to regain a nominal composure of my faculties. Also, it occurred to me that the unimaginative portrait busts and tamely symbolic figure-groups of Cyprian Sincaul might serve admirably to sooth my shaken nerves. Even his grotesques would seem sane and ordinary by comparison with the blasphemous gargoyle that had drooled before me in the bookshop.

I entered the studio building, and climbed a worn stairway to the second floor, where Cyprian had established himself in a some what capacious suite of rooms. As I went up the stairs, I had the peculiar feeling that somebody was climbing them just ahead of me; but I could neither see nor hear anyone, and the hall above was no less silent and empty than the stairs.

Cyprian was in his atelier when I knocked. After an interval which seemed unduly long, I heard him call out, telling me to enter. I found him wiping his hands on an old cloth, and surmised that he had been modeling. A sheet of light burlap had been thrown over what was plainly an ambitious but unfinished group of figures, which occupied the center of the long room. All around were other sculptures, in clay, bronze, marble, and even the terra cotta and steatite which he sometimes employed for his less conventional conceptions. At one end of the room there stood a heavy Chinese screen.

At a single glance I realized that a great change had occurred, both in Cyprian Sincaul and his word. I remembered him as an amiable, somewhat flabby-looking youth, always dapperly dressed, with no trace of the dreamer or visionary. It was hard to recognize him now, for he had become lean, harsh, vehement, with an air of pride and penetration that was almost Luciferian. His unkempt mane of hair was already shot with white, and his eyes were electronically brilliant with a strange knowledge, and yet somehow were vaguely furtive, as if there dwelt behind them a morbid and macabre fear.

The change in his sculpture was no less striking. The respectable tameness and polished mediocrity were gone, and in their place, incredibly, was something little short of genius. More unbelievable still, in view of the laboriously ordinary grotesques of his earlier phase, was the trend that his art had now taken. All around me were frenetic, murderous demons, satyrs mad with nympholepsy, ghouls that seemed to sniff the odors of the charnel, lamias voluptuously coiled about their victims, and less namable things that belonged to the outland realms of evil myth and malign superstition.

Sin, horror, blasphemy, diablerie — the lust and malice of pandemonium — all had been caught with impeccable art. The potent nightmarishness of these creations was not calculated to reassure my trembling nerves; and all at once I felt an imperative

desire to escape from the studio, to flee from the baleful throng
of frozen cacodemons and chiseled chimeras.

My expression must have betrayed my feeling to some
extent.

"Pretty strong work, aren't they?" said Cyprian, in a loud,
vibrant voice, with a note of harsh pride and triumph. "I can
see that you are surprised — you didn't look for anything of the
sort, I dare say."

"No, candidly, I didn't," I admitted. "Good Lord, man, you
will become the Michelangelo of diabolism if you go on at this
rate. Where on Earth do you get such stuff?"

"Yes, I've gone pretty far," said Cyprian, seeming to disre-
gard my question. "Further even than you think, probably. If
you could know what I know, could see what I have seen, you
might make something really worth-while out of your weird
fiction, Philip. You are very clever and imaginative, of course.
But you've never had any experience."

I was startled and puzzled. "Experience? What do you
mean?"

"Precisely that. You try to depict the occult and the supernatural without even the most rudimentary first-hand knowledge of them. I tried to do something of the same sort in sculpture, years ago, without knowledge; and doubtless you recall
the mediocre mess that I made of it. But I've learned a thing or
two since then."

"Sounds as if you had made the traditional bond with the
devil, or something of the sort," I observed, with a feeble and
perfunctory levity.

Cyprian's eyes narrowed slightly, with a strange, secret
look.

"I know what I know. Never mind how or why. The world
in which we live isn't the only world; and some of the others lie
closer at hand than you think. The boundaries of the seen and
the unseen are sometimes interchangeable."

Recalling the malevolent phantom, I felt a peculiar disquietude as I listened to his words. An hour before, his statement would have impressed me as mere theorizing, but now it assumed an ominous and terrifying significance.

"What makes you think I have had no experience of the occult?" I asked.

"Your stories hardly show anything of the kind — anything factual or personal. They are all palpably made up. When you've argued with a ghost, or watched the ghouls at mealtime, or fought with an incubus, or suckled a vampire, you may achieve some genuine characterization and color along such lines."

For reasons that should be fairly obvious, I had not intended to tell anyone of the unbelievable thing at Toleman's. Now, with a singular mixture of emotions, of compulsive, eery terrors and desire to refute the animadversions of Cyprian, I found myself describing the phantom.

He listened with an inexpressive look, as if his thoughts were occupied with other matters than my story. Then, when I had finished:

"You are becoming more psychic than I imagined. Was your apparition anything like one of these?"

With the last words, he lifted the sheet of burlap from the muffled group of figures beside which he had been standing.

I cried out involuntarily with the shock of that appalling revelation, and almost tottered as I stepped back.

Before me, in a monstrous semicircle, were seven creatures who might all have been modeled from the gargoyle that had confronted me across the folio of Goya drawings. Even in several that were still amorphous or incomplete, Cyprian had conveyed with a damnable art the peculiar mingling of primal bestiality and mortuary putrescence that had signalized the phantom. The seven monsters had closed in on a cowering, naked girl, and were all clutching foully toward her with their hyena claws. The stark, frantic, insane terror on the face of the girl, and the slavering hunger of her assailants, were alike unbearable. The group was a masterpiece, in its consummate power of technique — but a masterpiece that inspired loathing rather than admiration. And following my recent experience, the sight of it affected me with indescribable alarm. It seemed to me that I had gone astray from the normal, familiar world into a land of detestable mystery, of prodigious and unnatural menace.

Held by an abhorrent fascination, it was hard for me to wrench my eyes away from the figure-piece. At last I turned from it to Cyprian himself. He was regarding me with a cryptic air, beneath which I suspected a covert gloating.

"How do you like my little pets?" he inquired. "I am going to call the composition *The Hunters from Beyond*".

Before I could answer, a woman suddenly appeared from behind the Chinese screen. I saw that she was the model for the girl in the unfinished group. Evidently she had been dressing, and she was now ready to leave, for she wore a tailored suit and a smart toque. She was beautiful, in a dark, semi-Latin fashion; but her mouth was sullen and reluctant, and her wide, liquid eyes were wells of strange terror as she gazed at Cyprian, myself, and the uncovered statue-piece.

Cyprian did not introduce me. He and the girl talked together in low tones for a minute or two, and I was unable to overhear more than half of what they said. I gathered, however, that an appointment was being made for the next sitting. There was a pleading, frightened note in the girl's voice, together with an almost maternal concern; and Cyprian seemed to be arguing with her or trying to reassure her about something. At last she went out, with a queer, supplicative glance at me — a glance whose meaning I could only surmise and could not wholly fathom.

"That was Marta," said Cyprian. "She is half Irish, half Italian. A good model; but my new sculptures seem to be making her a little nervous." He laughed abruptly, with a mirthless, jarring note that was like the cachinnation of a sorcerer.

"In God's name, what are you trying to do here?" I burst out. "What does it all mean? Do such abominations really exist, on earth or in any hell?"

He laughed again, with an evil subtlety, and became evasive all at once. "Anything may exist, in a boundless universe with multiple dimensions. Anything may be real — or unreal. Who knows? It is not for me to say. Figure it out for yourself, if you can — there's a vast field for speculation — and perhaps for more than speculation."

With this, he began immediately to talk of other topics. Baffled, mystified, with a sorely troubled mind and nerves that were more unstrung than ever by the black enigma of it all, I ceased to question him. Simultaneously, my desire to leave the studio became almost overwhelming — a mindless, whirlwind panic that prompted me to run pell-mell from the room and down the stairs into the wholesome normality of the common, Twentieth Century streets. It seemed to me that the rays which fell through the skylight were not those of the sun, but of some darker orb; that the room was touched with unclean webs of shadow where shadow should not have been; that the stone Satans, the bronze lamias, the terra-cotta satyrs, and the clay gargoyles had somehow increased in number and might spring to malignant life at any instant.

Hardly knowing what I said, I continued to converse for a while with Cyprian. Then, excusing myself on the score of a nonexistent luncheon appointment, and promising vaguely to return for another visit before my departure from the city, I took my leave.

I was surprised to find my cousin's model in the lower hall, at the foot of the stairway. From her manner, and her first words, it was plain that she had been waiting.

"You are Mr. Philip Hastane, aren't you?" she said, in an eager, agitated voice. "I am Marta Fitzgerald. Cyprian has often mentioned you, and I believe that he admires you a lot.

"Maybe you'll think me crazy," she went on, "but I had to speak to you. I can't stand the way that things are going here, and I'd refuse to come to the place any more, if it wasn't that I — like Cyprian so much.

"I don't know what he has done — but he is altogether different from what he used to be. His new work is so horrible — you can't imagine how it frightens me. The sculptures he does are more hideous, more hellish all the time. Ugh! those drooling, dead-gray monsters in that new group of his — I can hardly bear to be in the studio with them. It isn't right for anyone to depict such things. Don't you think they are awful, Mr. Hastane? They look as if they had broken loose from hell — and make you think that hell can't be very far away. It is wrong and wicked for anyone to — even imagine them; and I wish that Cyprian would stop. I am afraid that something will happen to him — to his mind — if he goes on. And I'll go mad, too, if I have to see those monsters many more times. My God! No one could keep sane in that studio."

She paused, and appeared to hesitate. Then:

"Can't you do something, Mr. Hastane? Can't you talk to him, and tell him how wrong it is, and how dangerous to his mental health? You must have a lot of influence with Cyprian — you are his cousin, aren't you? And he thinks you are very clever, too. I wouldn't ask you, if I hadn't been forced to notice so many things that aren't as they should be.

"I wouldn't bother you, either, if I knew anyone else to ask. He has shut himself up in that awful studio for the past year, and he hardly ever sees anybody. You are the first person that he has invited to see his new sculptures. He wants them to be a complete surprise for the critics and the public, when he holds his next exhibition.

"But you'll speak to Cyprian, won't you, Mr. Hastane? I can't do anything to stop him — he seems to exult in the mad horrors he creates. And he merely laughs at me when I try to tell him the danger. However, I think that those things are making him a little nervous sometimes — that he is growing afraid of his own morbid imagination. Perhaps he will listen to you."

If I had needed anything more to unnerve me, the desperate pleading of the girl and her dark, obscurely baleful hintings would have been enough. I could see that she loved Cyprian, that she was frantically anxious concerning him and hysterically afraid; otherwise, she would not have approached an utter stranger in this fashion.

"But I haven't any influence with Cyprian," I protested, feeling a queer embarrassment. "And what am I to say to him, anyway? Whatever he is doing is his own affair, not mine. His new sculptures are magnificent — I have never seen anything more powerful of the kind. And how could I advise him to stop doing them? There would be no legitimate reason; he would simply laugh me out of the studio. An artist has the right to choose his own subject-matter, even if he takes it from the nether pits of Limbo and Erebus."

The girl must have pleaded and argued with me for many minutes in that deserted hall. Listening to her, and trying to convince her of my inability to fulfil her request, was like a dialog in some futile and tedious nightmare. During the course of it, she told me a few details that I am unwilling to record in this narrative; details that were too morbid and too shocking for belief, regarding the mental alteration of Cyprian, and his new subject-matter and method of work. There were direct and oblique hints of a growing perversion; that even in here most horrifying disclosures she was not wholly frank with me. At last, with some sort of hazy promise that I would speak to Cyprian, would remonstrate with him, I succeeded in getting away from her, and returned to my hotel.

The afternoon and evening that followed were tinged as by the tyrannous adumbration of an ill dream. I felt that I had stepped from the solid earth into a gulf of seething, menacing, madness-haunted shadow, and was lost hence forward to all rightful sense of location or direction. It was all too hideous — and too doubtful and unreal. The change in Cyprian himself was no less bewildering, and hardly less horrifying, than the vile phantom of the bookshop, and the demon sculptures that displayed a magisterial art. It was as if the man had become possessed by some satanic energy or entity.

Everywhere that I went, I was powerless to shake off the feeling of an intangible pursuit, of a frightful, unseen vigilance. It seemed to me that the worm-gray face and sulphurous eyes would reappear at any moment; that the semi-canine mouth with its gangrene-dripping fangs might come to slaver above the restaurant table at which I ate, or upon the pillow of my bed. I did not dare to reopen the purchased Goya volume, for fear of finding that certain pages were still defiled with a spectral slime.

I went out and spent the evening in cafés, in theaters wherever people thronged and lights were bright. It was after midnight when I finally ventured to brave the solitude of my hotel bedroom. then there were endless hours of nerve-wrung insomnia, of shivering, sweating apprehension beneath the electric bulb that I had left burning. Finally, a little before dawn, but with no conscious transition and with no premonitory drowsiness, I fell asleep.

I remember no dreams — only the vast, incubus-like oppression that persisted even in the depth of slumber, as if to drag me down with its formless, ever-clinging weight into gulfs beyond the reach of created light or the fathoming of organized entity.

It was almost noon when I awoke, and found myself staring into the verminous, apish, mummy-dead face and hell-illumined eyes of the gargoyle that had crouched before me in the corner at Toleman's. The thing was standing at the foot of my bed; and behind it as I stared, the wall of the room, which was covered with a floral papers, dissolved in an infinite vista of grayness, teeming with ghoulish forms that emerged like monstrous, misshapen bubbles from plains of undulant ooze and skies of serpentining vapor. It was another world, and my very sense of equilibrium was disturbed by an evil vertigo as I gazed. It seemed to me that my bed was heaving dizzily, was turning slowly, deliriously toward the gulf; that the feculent vista and the vile apparition were swimming beneath me; that I would fall toward them in another moment and be precipitated forever into that world of abysmal monstrosity and obscenity.

In a start of profound alarm, I fought my vertigo, fought the sense that another will than mine was drawing me, that the unclean gargoyle was luring me by some unspeakable mesmeric spell, as a serpent is said to lure its prey. I seemed to read a nameless purpose in its yellow-slitted eyes, in the soundless moving of its oozy lips; and my very soul recoiled with nausea and revulsion as I breathed its pestilential fetor.

Apparently, the mere effort of mental resistance was enough. The vista and the face receded; they went out in a swirl of daylight. I saw the design of tea roses on the wallpaper beyond; and the bed beneath me was sanely horizontal once more. I lay sweating with my terror, all adrift on a sea of nightmare surmise, of unearthly threat and whirlpool madness, till the ringing of the telephone bell recalled me automatically to the known world.

I sprang to answer the call. It was Cyprian, though I should hardly have recognized the dead, hopeless tones of his voice, from which the mad pride and self-assurance of the previous day had wholly vanished.

"I must see you at once," he said. "Can you come to the studio?"

I was about to refuse, to tell him that I had been called home suddenly, that there was no time, that I must catch the

noon train — anything to avert the ordeal of another visit to
that place of mephitic evil — when I heard his voice again.

"You simply must come, Philip. I can't tell you about it
over the phone, but a dreadful thing has happened: Marta has
disappeared."

I consented, telling him that I would start for the studio as
soon as I had dressed. The whole nightmare had closed in, had
deepened immeasurably with his last words; but remembering
the haunted face of the girl, her hysteric fears, her frantic pleas
and my vague promise, I could not very well decline to go.

I dressed and went out with my mind in a turmoil of abominable conjecture, of ghastly doubt, and apprehension all the
more hideous because I was unsure of its object. I tried to imagine what had happened, tried to piece together the frightful,
evasive, half-admitted hints of unknown terror into a tangible
coherent fabric, but found myself involved in a chaos of shadowy menace.

I could not have eaten any breakfast, even if I had taken
the necessary time. I went at once to the studio, and found
Cyprian standing aimlessly amid his baleful statuary. His look
was that of a man who has been stunned by the blow of some
crushing weapon, or has gazed on the very face of Medusa. He
greeted me in a vacant manner, with dull, toneless words.
Then, like a charged machine, as if his body rather than his
mind were speaking, he began at once to pour forth the atrocious narrative.

"They took her," he said, simply. "Maybe you didn't know
it, or weren't sure of it; but I've been doing all my new sculptures from life — even that last group. Marta was posing for
me this forenoon — only an hour ago — or less. I had hoped
to finish her part of the modeling today; and she wouldn't have
had to come gain for this particular piece. I hadn't called the
Things this time, since I knew she was beginning to fear them
more and more. I think she feared them on my account more
than her own — and they were making me a little uneasy too,

by the boldness with which they sometimes lingered when I had ordered them to leave, and the way they would sometimes appear when I didn't want them.

"I was busy with some of the final touches on the girl-figure, and wasn't even look at Marta, when suddenly I knew that the Things were there. The smell told me, if nothing else — I guess you know what the smell is like. I looked up and found that the studio was full of them — they had never before appeared in such numbers. They were surrounding Marta, were crowding and jostling each other, were all reaching toward her with their filthy talons; but even then, I didn't think that they could harm her. They aren't material beings, in the sense that we are, and they really have no physical power outside their own plane. All they do have is a sort of snaky mesmerism, and they'll always try to drag you down to their own dimension by means of it. God help anyone who yields to them; but you don't have to go, unless you are weak, or willing. I've never had any doubt of my power to resist them, and I didn't really dream they could do anything to Marta.

"It startled me, though, when I saw the whole crowding hell-pack, and I ordered them to go pretty sharply. I was angry — and somewhat alarmed, too. But they merely grimaced and slavered, with that slow, twisting movement of their lips that is like a voiceless gibbering, and then they closed in on Marta, just as I represented them doing in that accursed group of sculpture. Only there were scores of them now, instead of merely seven.

"I can't describe how it happened, but all at once their foul talons had reached the girl; they were pawing her, were pulling at her hands, her arms, her body. She screamed — and I hope I'll never hear another scream so full of black agony and soul-unhinging fright. Then I knew that she had yielded to them — either from choice, or from excess of terror — and knew that they were taking her away.

"For a moment, the studio wasn't there at all — only a long, gray, oozing plain, beneath skies where the fumes of hell were writing like a million ghostly and distorted dragons. Marta was sinking into that ooze, and the Things were all about her, gathering in fresh hundred from every side, fighting each other for place, sinking with her like bloated, misshapen fen-creatures into their native slime. Then everything vanished — and I was standing here in the studio all along with these damned sculptures."

He paused for a little, and stared with dreary, desolate eyes at the floor. Then:

"It was awful, Philip, and I'll never forgive myself for having anything to do with those monsters. I must have been a little mad, but I've always had a strong ambition to create some real stuff in the field of the grotesque and visionary and macabre. I don't suppose you ever suspected, back in my stodgy phase, that I had a veritable appetence for such things. I wanted to do in sculpture what Poe and Lovecraft and Baudelaire have done in literature, what Rops and Goya did in pictorial art.

"That was what led me into the occult, when I realized my limitations. I knew that I had to see the dwellers of the invisible worlds before I could depict them. I wanted to do it. I longed for this power of vision and representation more than anything else. And then, all at once, I found that I had the power of summoning the unseen. . . .

"There was no magic involved, in the usual sense of the word — no spells and circles, no pentacles and burning gums from old sorcery books. At bottom, it was just will power, I guess — a will to divine the satanic, to summon the innumerable malignities and grotesqueries that people planes other than ours, or mingle unperceived with humanity.

"You've no idea what I have beheld, Philip. These statues of mine — these devils, vampires, lamias, satyrs — were all done from life, or, at least from recent memory. The originals are

what the occultists would call elementals, I suppose there are
endless worlds, contiguous to our own, or co-existing with it,
that such beings inhabit. All the creations of myth and fantasy,
all the familiar spirits that sorcerers have evoked, are resident
in these worlds.

"I made myself their master, I levied upon them at will.
Then, from a dimension that must be a little lower than all others, a little nearer the ultimate nadir of hell, I called the innom-
inate beings who posed for this new figure-piece.

"I don't know what they are, but I have surmised a good
deal. They are hateful as the worms of the Pit, they are malevolent as harpies, they drool with a poisonous hunger not to be
named or imagined. But I believed that they were powerless to
do anything outside their own sphere, and I've always laughed
at them when they tried to entice me — even though that
snakish mental pull of theirs was rather creepy at times. It was
as if soft, invisible, gelatinous arms were trying to drag you
down from the firm shore into a bottomless bog.

"They are hunters — I am sure of that — the Hunters from
Beyond. God knows what they will do to Marta now that they
have her at their mercy. That vast, viscid, miasma-haunted
place to which they took her is awful beyond the imagining of
Satan. Perhaps — even there — they couldn't harm her body.
But bodies aren't what they want — it isn't for human flesh
that they grope with those ghoulish claws, and gape and slaver
with those gangrenous mouths. The brain itself — and the
soul, too — is their food: they are the creatures who prey on
the minds of madmen and madwomen, who devour the disem-
bodied spirits that have fallen from the cycles of incarnation,
have gone down beyond the possibility of rebirth.

"To think of Marta in their power — it is worse than hell
or madness. Marta loved me, and I loved her, too, though I did-
n't have the sense to realize it, wrapped as I was in my dark,
baleful ambition and impious egotism. She was afraid for me,
and I believe she surrendered voluntarily to the Things. She

must have thought they would leave me alone if they secured another victim in my place."

He ceased, and began to pace idly and feverishly about. I saw that his hollow eyes were alight with torment, as if the mechanical telling of his horrible story had in some manner served to requicken his crushed mind. Utterly and starkly appalled by his hideous revelations, I could say nothing, but could only stand and watch his torture-twisted face.

Incredibly, his expression changed, with a wild, startled look that was instantly transfigured into joy. Turning to follow his gaze, I saw that Marta was standing in the center of the room. She was nude, except for a Spanish shawl that she must have worn while posing. Her face was bloodless as the marble of a tomb, and her eyes were wide and blank, as if she had been drained of all life, of all thought or emotion or memory, as if even the knowledge of horror had been taken away from her. It was the face of the living dead, and the soulless mask of ultimate idiocy; and the joy faded from Cyprian's eyes as he stepped toward her.

He took her in his arms, he spoke to her with a desperate, loving tenderness, with cajoling and caressing words. She made no answer, however, no movement of recognition or awareness, but stared beyond him with her blank eyes, to which the daylight and the darkness, the void air and her lover's face, would henceforward be the same. He and I both knew, in that instant, that she would never again respond to any human voice, or to human love or terror; that she was like an empty cerement, retaining the outward form of that which the worms have eaten in their mausolean darkness. Of the noisome pits wherein she had been, of that bournless realm and its pullulating phantoms, she could tell us nothing: her agony had ended with the terrible mercy of complete forgetfulness.

Like one who confronts the Gorgon, I was frozen by her wide and sightless gaze. Then, behind her, where stood an array of carven Satans and lamias, the room seemed to recede, the walls and floors dissolved in a seething, unfathomable gulf, amid whose pestilential vapors the statutes were mingled in momentary and loathsome ambiguity with the ravening faces, the hunger-contorted forms that swirled toward us from their ultra-dimensional limbo like a devil-laden hurricane from Malebolge. Outlined against that boiling measureless cauldron of malignant storm, Marta stood like an image of glacial death and silence in the arms of Cyprian. Then, once more, after a little, the abhorrent vision faded, leaving only the diabolic statuary.

I think that I alone had beheld it; that Cyprian had seen nothing but the dead face of Marta. He drew her close, he repeated his hopeless words of tenderness and cajolery. Then, suddenly, he released here with a vehement sob of despair. Turning away, while she stood and still looked on with unseeing eyes, he snatched a heavy sculptor's mallet from the table on which it was lying, and proceeded to smash with furious blows the newly-modeled group of gargoyles, till nothing was left but the figure of the terror maddened girl, crouching above a mass of cloddish fragments and formless, half-dried clay.

The Vaults of Abomi

As an interne in the terrestrial hospital at Ignarth, I had charge of the singular case of Rodney Severn, the one surviving member of the Octave Expedition to Abomi, and took down the following story from his dictation. Severn had been brought to the hospital by the Martian guides of the Expedition. He was suffering from a horribly lacerated and inflamed condition of the scalp and brow, and was wildly delirious part of the time and had to be held down in his bed during recurrent seizures of a mania whose violence was doubly inexplicable in view of his extreme debility.

The lacerations, as will be learned from the story, were mainly self-inflicted. They were mingled with numerous small round wounds, easily distinguished from the knife-slashes, and arranged in regular circles, through which an unknown poison had been injected into Severn's scalp. The causation of these wounds was difficult to explain: unless one were to believe that Severn's story was true, and was no mere figment of his illness. Speaking for myself, in the light of what afterwards occurred, I feel that I have no other recourse than to believe it. There are strange things on the red planet; and I can only second the wish that was expressed by the doomed archaeologist in regard to future explorations.

The night after he finished telling me his story, while another doctor than myself was supposedly on duty, Severn managed to escape from the hospital, doubtless in one of the strange seizures at which I have hinted: a most astonishing thing, for he had seemed weaker than ever after the long strain of his terrible narrative, and his demise had been hourly expected. More astonishing still, his bare footsteps were found in the desert, going toward Abomi, till they vanished in the path of a light sand-storm; but no trace of Severn himself has yet been discovered.

The Narrative of Rodney Severn

If the doctors are correct in their prognostication, I have only a few Martian hours of life remaining to me. In those hours I shall endeavor to relate, as a warning to others who might follow in our footsteps, the singular and frightful happenings that terminated our researches among the ruins of Abomi. Somehow, even in my extremity, I shall contrive to tell the story; since there is no one else to do it. But the telling will be toilsome and broken; and after I am done, the madness will recur, and several men will restrain me, lest I should leave the hospital and return across many desert leagues to those abominable vaults beneath the compulsion of the malignant and malevolent virus which is permeating my brain. Perhaps death will release me from that abhorrent control, which would urge me down to bottomless underworld warrens of terror for which the saner planets of the solar system can have no analogue. I say *perhaps* . . . for, remembering what I have seen, I am not sure that even death will end my bondage. . . .

There were eight of us, professional archaeologists with more or less terrene and interplanetary experience, who set forth with native guides from Ignarh, the commercial metropolis of Mars, to inspect that ancient, aeon-deserted city. Allan Octave, our official leader, held his primacy by virtue of knowing more about Martian archaeology than any other Terrestrial on the planet; and others of the party, such as William Harper and Jonas Halgren, had been associated with him in many of his previous researches. I, Rodney Severn, was more or a new-comer, having spent but a few months on Mars; and the greater part of my own ultra-terrene delvings had been confined to Venus.

I had often heard of Abomi, in a vague and legendary sort of manner, and never at first hand. Even the ubiquitous Octave had never seen it. Builded by an extinct people whose history has been lost in the latter, decadent eras of the planet, it remains a dim and fascinating riddle whose solution has never been approached . . . and which, I trust, may endure forever-more unsolved by man. Certainly I hope that no one will ever follow in our steps. . . .

Contrary to the impression we had received from Martian stories, we found that the semi-fabulous ruins lay at no great distance from Ignarh with its terrestrial colony and consulates. The nude, spongy-chested natives had spoken deterringly of vast deserts filled with ever-swirling sand-storms, through which we must pass to reach Abomi; and in spite of our munif-icent offers of payment, it had been difficult to secure guides for the journey. We had provisioned ourselves amply and had pre-pared for all emergencies that might eventuate during a long trip. Therefore, we were pleased as well as surprised when we came to the ruins after seven hours of plodding across the flat, treeless, orange-yellow desolation to the south-west of Ignarh. On account of the lesser gravity, the journey was far less tiring than one who is unfamiliar with Martian conditions might expect. But because of the thin, Himalaya-like air, and the pos-sible strain on our hearts, we had been careful not to hasten.

Our coming to Abomi was sudden and spectacular. Climbing the low slope of a league-long elevation of bare and deeply eroded stone, we saw before us the shattered walls of our destination, whose highest tower was notching the small, remote sun that glared in stifled crimson through the floating haze of fine sand. For a little, we thought that the domelesss, three-angled towers and broken-down monoliths were those of some unlegended city, other than the one we sought. But the disposition of the ruins, which lay in a sort of arc for almost the entire extent of the low and gneissic elevation, together with the type of architecture, soon convinced us that we had found our goal. No other ancient city on Mars had been laid out in that manner; and the strange, many-terraced buttresses of the thick walls, like the stairways of forgotten Anakim, were peculiar to the prehistoric race that had built Abomi. Moreover, Abomi was the one remaining example of this architecture, aside from a few fragments in the neighborhood of Ignarh, which we had previously examined.

I have seen the hoary, sky-confronting walls of Macchu Pichu amide the desolate Andes, and the teocallis that are buried in the Mexican jungles. And I have seen the frozen, giant-builded battlements of Uogam on the glacial tundras of the nightward hemisphere of Venus. But these were as things of yesteryear, bearing at least the memory or the intimation of life, compared with the awesome and lethiferous antiquity, the cycle-enduring doom of a petrified sterility, that seemed to invest Abomi. The whole region was far from the life-giving canals beyond whose environs even the more noxious flora and fauna are seldom found; and we had seen no living thing since our departure from Ignarh. But here, in this place of eternal bareness and solitude, it seemed that life could never have been. The stark, eroded stones were things that might have been reared by the toil of the dead, to house the monstrous ghouls and demons of primal desolation.

I think we all received the same impression as we stood staring in silence while the pale, sanies-like sunset fell on the dark and megalithic ruins. I remember gasping a little, in an air that seemed to have been touched by the irrespirable chill of death; and I heard the same sharp, laborious intake of breath from others of our party.

"That place is deader than an Egyptian morgue," observed Harper.

"Certainly it is far more ancient," Octave assented. "According to the most reliable legends, the Yorhis, who built Abomi, were wiped out by the present ruling race at least forty thousand years ago."

"There's a story, isn't there," said Harper, "that the last remnant of the Yorhis was destroyed by some unknown agency — something too horrible and outré to be mentioned even in a myth?"

"Of course, I've heard that legend," agreed Octave. "Maybe we'll find evidence among the ruins, to prove or disprove it. The Yorhis may have been cleaned out by some terrible epidemic, such as the Yashta pestilence, which was a kind of green mold that ate all the bones of the body, starting with the teeth and nails. But we needn't be afraid of getting it, if there are any mummies in Abomi — the bacteria will all be dead as their victims, after so many cycles of planetary desiccation. Anyway, there ought to be a lot for us to learn. The Aihais have always been more or less shy of the place. Few have ever visited it; and none, as far as I can find, have made a thorough examination of the ruins."

The sun had gone down with uncanny swiftness, as if it had disappeared through some sort of prestigitation rather than the normal process of setting. We felt the instant chill of the blue-green twilight; and the ether above us was like a huge, transparent dome of sunless ice, shot with a million bleak sparklings that were the stars. We donned the coats and helmets of Martian fur, which must always be worn at night; and going on to westward of the walls, we established our camp in their lee, so that we might be sheltered a little from the *jaar*, that cruel desert wind that always blows from the east before dawn. Then, lighting the alcohol lamps that had been brought along for cooking purposes, we huddled around them while the evening meal was prepared and eaten.

Afterwards, for comfort rather than because of weariness, we retired early to our sleeping-bags; and the two Aihais, our guides, wrapped themselves in the cerement-like folds of grey *bassa*-cloth which are all the protection their leathery skins appear to require even in sub-zero temperatures.

Even in my thick, double-lined bag, I still felt the rigor of the night air; and I am sure it was this, rather than anything else, which kept me awake for a long while and rendered my eventual slumber somewhat restless and broken. Of course, the strangeness of our situation, and the weird proximity of those aeonian walls and towers may in some measure have contributed to my unrest. But at any rate, I was not troubled by even the least presentiment of alarm or danger; and I should have laughed at the idea that anything of peril could lurk in Abomi, amid whose undreamable and stupefying antiquities the very phantoms of its dead must long since have faded into nothingness.

I remember little, however, except the feeling of interminable duration that often marks a shallow, and interrupted sleep. I recall the marrow-piercing wind that moaned above us toward midnight, and the sand that stung my face like a fine hail as it passed, blowing from desert to immemorial desert; and I recall the still, inflexible stars that grew dim for awhile with that fleeing ancient dust. Then the wind went by; and I drowsed again, with starts of semi-wakefulness. At last, in one of these, I knew vaguely that the small twin moons, Phobos and Deimos, had risen and were making huge and spectral shadows with the ruins and were casting an ashen glimmer on the shrouded forms of my companions.

I must have been half-asleep; for the memory of that which I saw is doubtful as any dream. I watched beneath drooping lids the tiny moons that had topped the domeless triangular towers; and I saw the far-flung shadows that almost touched the bodies of my fellow archaeologists.

The whole scene was locked in a petrific stillness; and none of the sleepers stirred. Then, as my lids were about to close, I received an impression of movement in the frozen gloom; and it seemed to me that a portion of the foremost shadow had detached itself and was crawling toward Octave, who lay nearer to the ruins than we others.

Even though my heavy lethargy, I was disturbed by a warning of something unnatural and perhaps ominous. I started to sit up; and even as I moved, the shadowy object, whatever it was, drew back and became merged once more in the greater shadow. Its vanishment startled me into full wakefulness; and yet I could not be sure that I had actually seen the thing. In that brief, final glimpse, it had seemed like a roughly circular piece of cloth or leather, dark and crumpled, and twelve or fourteen inches in diameter, that ran along the ground with the doubling movement of an inch-worm, causing it to fold and unfold in a startling manner as it went.

I did not go to sleep again for nearly an hour; and if it had not been for the extreme cold, I should doubtless have gotten up to investigate and make sure whether I had really beheld an object of such bizarre nature or had merely dreamt it. I lay staring at the deep ebon shadow in which it had disappeared, while a series of fanciful wonderings followed each other in antic procession though my mind. Even then, though somewhat perturbed, I was not aware of any actual fear or intuition of possible menace. And more and more I began to convince myself that the thing was too unlikely and fantastical to have been anything by the figment of a dream. And at last I nodded off into light slumber.

The chill, demoniac sighing of the *jaar* across the jagged walls awoke me, and I saw that the faint moonlight had received the hueless accession of early dawn. We all arose, and prepared our breakfast with fingers that grew numb in spite of the spirit-lamps. Then, shivering, we ate, while the sun leapt over the horizon like a juggler's ball. Enormous, gaunt, without gradations of shadow or luminosity, the ruins beetled before us in the thin light, like the mausolea of primordial giants, that abide from darkness-eaten aeons to confront the last dawn of an expiring orb.

My queer visual experience during the night had taken on more than ever a fantasmagoric unreality; and I gave it no more than a passing thought and did not speak of it to the others. But, even as the faint, distorted shadows of slumber often tinge one's waking hours, it have contributed to the nameless mood in which I found myself: a mood in which I felt the unhuman alienage of our surroundings and the black fathomless antiquity of the ruins like an almost unbearable oppression. The feeling seemed to be made of a million spectral adumbrations that oozed unseen but palpable from the great, unearthly architecture; that weighed upon me like tomb-born incubi, but were void of form and meaning such as could be comprehended by human thought. I appeared to move, not in the open air, but in the smothering gloom of sealed sepulchral vaults; to choke with a death-fraught atmosphere, with the miasmata of aeon-old corruption.

My companions were all eager to explore the ruins; and of course it was impossible for me to even mention the apparently absurd and baseless shadows of my mood. Human beings on other worlds than their own are often subject to nervous and psychic symptoms of this sort, engendered by the unfamiliar forces, the novel radiations of their environment. But, as we approached the buildings in our preliminary tour of examination, I lagged behind the others, seized by a paralyzing panic that left me unable to move or breathe for a few moments. A dark, freezing clamminess seemed to pervade my brain and muscles and suspend their inmost working. Then it lifted; and I was free to go on and follow the others.

Strangely, as it seemed, the two Martians refused to accompany us. Stolid and taciturn, they gave no explicit reason; but evidently nothing would induce them to enter Abomi. Whether or not they were afraid of the ruins, we were unable to determine; their enigmatic faces, with the small oblique eyes and huge, flaring nostrils, betrayed neither fear nor any other emotion intelligible to man. In reply to our questions, they merely said that no Aihai had set foot among the ruins for ages. Apparently there was some mysterious tabu in connection with the place.

For equipment in that preliminary tour, we took along only a crowbar and two picks. Our other tools, and some cartridges of high explosives, we left at out camp, to be used later if necessary, after we had surveyed the ground. One or two of us owned automatics; but these also were left behind; for it seemed absurd to imagine that any form of life would be encountered among the ruins.

Octave was visibly excited as we began our inspection. and maintained a running fire of exclamatory comment. The rest of us were subdued and silent; and I think that my own feeling, in a measure, was shared by many of the others. It was impossible to shake the somber awe and wonder that fell upon us from those megalithic stones.

I have no time to describe the ruins minutely, but must hasten on with my story. There is much that I could not describe anyway; for the main area of the city was destined to remain unexplored.

We went on for some distance among the triangular, terraced buildings, following the zig-zag streets that conformed to this peculiar architecture. Most of the towers were more or less dilapidated; and everywhere we saw the deep erosion wrought by cycles of flowing wind and sand, which, in many cases, had worn into roundness the sharp angles of the mighty walls. We entered some of the towers through high, narrow doorways, but found utter emptiness within. Whatever they had contained in the way of furnishings must long ago have crumbled into dust; and the dust had been blown away by the searching desert gales. On some of the outer walls, there was evidence of carving or lettering; but all of it was so worn down and obliterated by time that we could trace only a few fragmentary outlines, of which we could make nothing.

At length we came to a wide thoroughfare, which ended in the wall of a vast terrace, several hundred yards long by perhaps forty in height, on which the central buildings were grouped like a sort of citadel or acropolis. A flight of broken steps, designed for longer limbs than those of men or even the gangling modern Martians, afforded access to the terrace, which had seemingly been hewn from the plateau itself.

Pausing, we decided to defer our investigation of the higher buildings, which, being more exposed than the others, were doubly ruinous and dilapidated, and in all likelihood would offer little for our trouble. Octave had begun to voice his disappointment over our failure to find anything in the nature of artifacts or carvings that would throw light on the history of Abomi.

Then, a little to the right of the stairway, we perceived an entrance in the main wall, half-choked with ancient débris. Behind the heap of detritus, we found the beginning of a downward flight of steps. Darkness poured from the opening like a visible flood, noisome and musty with primordial stagnancies of decay; and we could see nothing below the first steps, which gave the appearance of being suspended over a black gulf.

Octave and myself and several others had brought along electric torches, in case we should need them in our explorations. It had occurred to us that there might be subterranean vaults or catacombs in Abomi, even as in the latter-day cities of Mars, which are often more extensive underground than above; and such vaults would be the likeliest place in which to look for vestiges of the Yorhi civilization.

Throwing his torch beam into the abyss, Octave began to descend the stairs. His eager voice called us to follow.

Again, for an instant, the unknown, irrational panic froze my faculties, and I hesitated while the others pressed forward behind me. Then, as before, the terror passed; and I wondered at myself for being overcome by anything too absurd and unfounded. I followed Octave down the steps, and the others came trooping after me.

At the bottom of the high, awkward steps, we found ourselves in a long and roomy vault, like a subterranean hallway. Its floor was deep with siftings of immemorial dust; and in places there were heaps of a coarse grey powder, such as might be left by the decomposition of certain fungi that grow in the Martian catacombs, under the canals. Such fungi, at one time, might conceivably have existed in Abomi; but, owing to the prolonged and excessive dehydration, they must have died out long ago. Nothing, surely, not even a fungus, could have lived in those arid vaults for many aeons past.

The air was singularly heavy, as if the lees of an ancient atmosphere, less tenuous than that of Mars today, had settled down and remained in that stagnant darkness. It was harder to breathe than the outer air: it was filled with unknown effluvia; and the light dust arose before us at every step, diffusing a faintness of bygone corruption, like the dust of powdered mummies.

At the end of the vault, before a strait and lofty doorway, our torches revealed an immense shallow urn or pan, supported on short cube-shaped legs, and wrought from a dull blackish-green material which suggested some bizarre alloy of metal and porcelain. The thing was about four feet across, with a thick rim adorned by writhing indecipherable figures, deeply etched as if by acid. In the bottom of the bowel perceived a deposit of dark and cinder-like fragments, which gave off a slight but disagreeable pungence, like the phantom of some more powerful odor. Octave, bending over the rim began to cough and sneeze as he inhaled it.

"That stuff, whatever it was, must have been a pretty strong fumigant," he observed. "The people of Abomi may have used it to disinfect the vaults."

The doorway beyond the shallow urn admitted us to a larger chamber, whose floor was comparatively free of dust. We found that the dark stone beneath our feet was marked off in multiform geometric patterns, traced with ochreous ore, amid which, as in Egyptian cartouches, hieroglyphics and highly formalized drawings were enclosed. We could make little from most of them; but the figures in many were doubtless designed to represent the Yorhis themselves. Like the Aihais, they were tall and angular, with great, bellows-like chests; and they were depicted as possessing a supplementary third arm, which, in vestigial form, sometimes occurs among the Aihais. The ears and nostrils, as far as we could judge, were not so huge and flaring as those of the modern Martians. All of these Yorhis were represented as being nude; but in one of the cartouches, done in a far hastier style than the others, we perceived two figures whose high, conical craniums were wrapped in what seemed to be a sort of turban, which they were about to remove or adjust. The artist seemed to have laid a peculiar emphasis on the odd gesture with which the sinuous, four-jointed fingers were plucking at these head-dresses; and the whole posture was unexplainably contorted.

From the second vault, passages ramified in all directions, leading to a veritable warren of catacombs. Here, enormous pot-bellied urns of the same material as the fumigating-pan, but taller than a man's head and fitted with angular-handled stoppers, were ranged in solemn rows along the walls, leaving scant room for two of us to walk abreast. When we succeeded in removing one of the huge stoppers, we saw that the jar was filled to the rim with ashes and charred fragments of bone. Doubtless (as is still the Martian custom) the Yorhis had stored the cremated remains of whole families in single urns.

Even Octave became silent as we went on; and a sort of meditative awe seemed to replace his former excitement. We others, I think, were utterly weighed down to a man by the solid gloom of a concept-defying antiquity, into which it seemed that we were going further and further at every step.

The shadows fluttered before use like the monstrous and misshapen wings of phantom bats. There was nothing anywhere but the atom-like dust of ages, and the jars that held the ashes of a long-extinct people. But, clinging to the high roof in one of the further vaults, I saw a dark and corrugated patch of circular form, like a withered fungus. It was impossible to reach the thing; and we went on after peering at it with many futile conjectures. Oddly enough, I failed to remember at that moment the crumpled, shadowy object I had seen or dreamt the night before.

I have no idea how far we had gone, when we came to the last vault; but it seemed that we had been wandering for ages in that forgotten underworld. The air was growing fouler and more irrespirable, with a thick, sodden quality, as if from a sediment of material rottenness; and we had about decided to turn back. Then, without warning, at the end of a long-urn-lined catacomb, we found ourselves confronted by a blank wall.

Here, we came upon one of the strangest and most mystifying of our discoveries — a mummified and incredibly desiccated figure, standing erect against the wall. It was more than seven feet in height, of a brown, bituminous color, and was wholly nude except for a sort of black cowl that covered the upper head and drooped down at the sides in wrinkled folds. From the three arms, and general contour, it was plainly one of the ancient Yorhis — perhaps the sole member of this race whose body had remained intact.

We all felt an inexpressible thrill at the sheer age of this shrivelled thing, which, in the dry air of the vault, had endured through all the historic and geologic vicissitudes of the planet, to provide a visible link with lost cycles.

Then, as we peered closer with our torches, we saw *why* the mummy had maintained an upright position. At ankles, knees, waist, shoulders and neck it was shackled to the wall by heavy metal bands, so deeply eaten and embrowned with a sort of rust that we had failed to distinguish them at first sight in the shadow. The strange cowl on the head, when studied closer, continued to baffle us. It was covered with a fine, mold-like pile, unclean and dusty as ancient cobwebs. Something about it, I know not what, was abhorrent and revolting.

"By Jove! this is a real find!" ejaculated Octave, as he thrust his torch into the mummified face, where shadows moved like living things in the pit-deep hollows of the eyes and the huge triple nostrils and wide ears that flared upward beneath the cowl.

Still lifting the torch, he put out his free hand and touched the body very lightly. Tentative as the touch had been, the lower part of the barrel-like torso, the legs, the hands and fore-arms all seemed to dissolve into powder, leaving the head and upper body and arms still hanging in their metal fetters. The progress of decay had been queerly unequal, for the remnant portions gave no sign of disintegration.

Octave cried out in dismay, and then began to cough and sneeze, as the cloud of brown powder, floating with airy light-ness, enveloped him. We others also stepped back to avoid the powder. Then, above the spreading cloud, I saw an unbeliev-able thing. The black cowl on the mummy's head began to curl and twitch upward at the corners, it writhed with a verminous motion, it fell from the withered cranium, seeming to fold and unfold convulsively in mid-air as it fell. Then it dropped on the bare head of Octave who, in his disconcertment at the crum-bling of the mummy, had remained standing close to the wall. At that instant, in a start of profound terror, I remembered the thing that had inched itself from the shadows of Abomi in the light of the twin moons, and had drawn back like a figment of slumber at my first waking movement.

Cleaving closely as a tightened cloth, the thing enfolded Octave's hair and brow and eyes, and he shrieked wildly, with incoherent pleas for help, and tore with frantic fingers at the

cowl, but failed to loosen it. Then his cries began to mount in
a mad crescendo of agony, as if beneath some instrument of
infernal torture; and he danced and capered blindly about the
fault, eluding us with strange celerity as we all sprang forward
in an effort to reach him and release him from his weird encum-
brance; but the thing that had fallen on his head was plainly
some unclassified form of Martian life, which, contrary to all
the known laws of science, had survived in those primordial
catacombs. We must rescue him from its clutches if we could.

We tried to close in on the frenzied figure of our chief —
which, in the far from roomy space between the last urns and
the wall, should have been an easy matter. But, darting away,
in a manner doubly incomprehensible because of his blind-
folded condition, he circled about us and ran past, to disappear
among the urns toward the outer labyrinth of intersecting catacombs.

"My God! What has happened to him?" cried Harper. "The
man acts as if he were possessed."

There was obviously no time for a discussion of the enigma,
and we all followed Octave as speedily as our astonishment
would permit. We had lost sight of him in the darkness, and
when we came to the first division of the vaults, we were doubtful as to which passage he had taken, till we heard a shrill
scream, several times repeated, in a catacomb on the extreme
left. There was a weird, unearthly quality in those screams,
which may have been due to the long-stagnant air or the peculiar acoustics of the ramifying caverns. But somehow I could
not imagine them as issuing from human lips — at least not
from those of a living man. They seemed to contain a soulless,
mechanical agony, as if they had been wrung from a devil-dri-
ven corpse.

Thrusting our torches before us into the lurching, fleeing
shadows, we raced along between rows of mighty urns. The
screaming had died away in sepulchral silence; but far off we
heard the light and muffled thud of running feet. We followed

in headlong pursuit; but, gasping painfully in the vitiated, miasmal air, we were soon compelled to slacken our pace without coming in sight of Octave. Very faintly, and further away than ever, like the tomb-swallowed steps of a phantom, we heard his vanishing footfalls. Then they ceased, and we heard nothing, except our own convulsive breathing, and the blood that throbbed in our temple-veins like steadily beaten drums of alarm.

We went on, dividing our party into three contingents when we came to a triple branching of the caverns. Harper and Halgren and myself took the middle passage; and after we had gone on for an endless interval without finding any trace of Octave, and had threaded our way through recesses piled to the roof with colossal urns that must have held the ashes of a hundred generations, we came out in the huge chamber with the geometric floor designs. Here, very shortly, we were joined by the others, who had likewise failed to locate our missing leader.

It would be useless to detail our renewed and hour-long search of the myriad vaults, many of which we had not hitherto explored. All were empty, as far as any sign of life was concerned. I remember passing once more through the vault in which I had seen the dark, rounded patch on the ceiling, and noting with a shudder that the patch was gone. It was a miracle that we did not lose ourselves in that underworld maze; but at last we came back to the final catacomb in which we had found the shackled mummy.

We heard a measured and recurrent clangor as we neared the place — a most alarming and mystifying sound under the circumstances. It was like the hammering of ghouls on some forgotten mausoleum. When we drew nearer, the beams of our torches revealed a sight that was no less unexplainable than unexpected. A human figure, with its back toward us and the head concealed by a swollen black object that had the size and form of a sofa cushion, was standing near the remains of the mummy and was striking at the wall with a pointed metal bar.

How long Octave had been there, and where he had found the bar, we could not know. But the blank wall had crumbled away beneath his furious blows, leaving on the floor a pile of cement-like fragments; and a small, narrow door, of the same ambiguous material as the cinerary urns and the fumigating-pan, had been laid bare.

Amazed, uncertain, inexpressibly bewildered, we were all incapable of action or volition at that moment. The whole business was too fantastic and too horrifying, and it was plain that Octave had been overcome by some sort of madness. I, for one, felt the violent upsurge of sudden nausea when I had identified the loathsomely bloated thing that clung to Octave's head and drooped in obscene tumescence on his neck. I did not dare to surmise the causation of its bloating.

Before any of us could recover our faculties. Octave flung aside the metal bar and began to fumble for something in the wall. It must have been a hidden spring; though how he could have known its location or existence is beyond all legitimated conjecture. With a dull, hideous grating, the uncovered door swung inward, thick and ponderous as a mausolean slab, leaving an aperture from which the nether midnight seemed to well like a flood of aeon-buried foulness. Somehow, at that instant, our electric torches to flicker and grow dim; and we all breathed a suffocating fetor, like a draft from inner worlds of immemorial putrescence.

Octave had turned toward us now, and he stood in an idle posture before the open door, like one who has finished some ordained task. I was the first of our party to throw off the paralyzing spell; and pulling out a clasp-knife — the only semblance of a weapon which I carried — I ran over to him. He moved back, but not quickly enough to evade me, when I stabbed with the four-inch blade at the black, turgescent mass that enveloped his whole upper head and hung down upon his eyes.

What the thing was, I should prefer not to imagine — if it were possible to imagine. It was formless as a great slug, with neither head nor tail nor apparent organs — an unclean, puffy, leathery thing, covered with that fine, mold-like fur of which I have spoken. The knife tore into it as if through rotten parchment, making a long gash, and the horror appeared to collapse like a broken bladder. Out of it there gushed a sickening torrent of human blood, mingled with dark, filiated masses that may have been half-dissolved hair, and floating gelatinous lumps like molten bone, and shreds of a curdy white substance. At the same time, Octave began to stagger, and went down at full length on the floor. Disturbed by his fall, the mummy-dust arose about him in a curling cloud, beneath which he lay mortally still.

Conquering my revulsion, and choking with the dust, I bent over him and tore the flaccid, oozing horror from his head. I came with unexpected ease, as if I had removed a limp rag: but I wish to God that I had let it remain. Beneath, there was no longer a human cranium, for all had been eaten away, even to the eyebrows, and the half-devoured brain was laid bare as I lifted the cowl-like object. I dropped the unnamable thing from fingers that had grown suddenly nerveless, and it turn over as it fell, revealing on the nether side many rose of pinkish suckers, arranged in circles about a pallid disk that was covered with nerve-like filaments, suggesting a sort of plexus.

My companions had pressed forward behind me; but, for an appreciable interval, no one spoke.

"How long do you suppose he has been dead?" It was Halgren who whispered the awful question, which we had all been asking ourselves. Apparently no one felt able or willing to answer it; and we could only stare in horrible, timeless fascination at Octave.

At length I made an effort to avert my gaze; and turning at random, I saw the remnants of the shackled mummy, and noted for the fist time, with mechanical, unreal horror, the half-eaten

condition of the withered head. From this, my gaze was diverted
to the newly opened door at one side, without perceiving for a
moment what had drawn my attention. Then, startled, I beheld
beneath my torch, far down beyond the door, as if in some
nether pit, a seething, multitudinous, worm-like movement of
crawling shadows. They seemed to boil up in the darkness; and
then, over the broad threshold of the vault, there poured the
verminous vanguard of a countless army: things that were kindred to the monstrous, diabolic leech I had torn from Octave's
eaten head. Some were thin and flat, like writhing, doubling
disks of cloth or leather, and others were more or less poddy, and
crawled with glutted slowness. What they had found to feed on
in the sealed, eternal midnight I do not know; and I pray that I
never shall know.

I sprang back and away from them, electrified with terror,
sick with loathing, and the black army inched itself unendingly
with nightmare swiftness from the unsealed abyss, like the nau-
seous vomit of horror-sated hells. As it poured toward us, bury-
ing Octave's body from sight in a writhing wave, I saw a stir of
life from the seemingly dead thing I had cast aside, and saw the
loathly struggle which it mad to right itself and join the others.

But neither I nor my companions could endure to look
longer. We turned and ran between the mighty rows of urns,
with the slithering mass of demon leeches close upon us, and
scattered in blind panic when we came to the first division of
the vaults. Heedless of each other or of anything but the
urgency of flight, we plunged into the ramifying passages at
random. Behind me, I heard someone stumble and go down,
with a curse that mounted to an insane shrieking; but I knew
that if I halted and went back, it would be only to invite the
same baleful doom that had overtaken the hindmost of our
party.

Still clutching the electric torch and my open clasp-knife, I
ran along a minor passage which, I seemed to remember, would
conduct with more or less directness upon the large outer vault

with the painted floor. Here I found myself alone. The others had kept to the main catacombs; and I heard far off a muffled babel of mad cries, as if several of them had been seized by their pursuers.

It seemed that I must have been mistaken about the direction of the passage; for it turned and twisted in an unfamiliar manner, with many intersections, and I soon found that I was lost in the black labyrinth, where the dust had lain unstirred by living feet for inestimable generations. The cinerary warren had grown still once more; and I heard my own frenzied panting, loud and stertorous as that of a Titan in the dead silence.

Suddenly, as I went on, my torch disclosed a human figure coming toward me in the gloom. Before I could master my startlement, the figure had passed me with long, machine-like strides, as if returning to the inner vaults. I think it was Harper, since the height and build were about right for him; but I am not altogether sure, for the eyes and upper head were muffled by a dark, inflated cowl, and the pale lips were locked as if in a silence of tetanic torture — or death. Whoever he was, he had dropped his torch; and he was running blindfold, in utter darkness, beneath the impulsion of that unearthly vampirism, to seek the very fountain-head of the unloosed horror. I knew that he was beyond human help; and I did not even dream of trying to stop him.

Trembling violently, I resumed my flight, and was passed by two more of our party, stalking by with mechanical swiftness and sureness, and cowled with those Satanic leeches. The others must have returned by way of the main passages; for I did not meet them; and I was never to see them again.

The remainder of my flight is a blur of pandemonian terror. Once more, after thinking that I was near the outer cavern, I found myself astray, and fled through a ranged eternity of monstrous urns, in vaults that must have extended for an unknown distance beyond our explorations. It seemed that I had gone on for years; and my lungs were choking with the aeon-dead air, and my legs were reading to crumble beneath me, when I saw far off a tiny point of blessed daylight. I ran toward it, with all the terrors of the alien darkness crowding behind me, and accursed shadows flittering before, and saw that the vault ended in a low, ruinous entrance littered by rubble on which there fell an arc of thin sunshine.

It was another entrance than the one by which we had penetrated this lethal underworld. I was within a dozen feet of the opening when, without sound or other intimation, something dropped upon my head from the roof above, blinding me instantly and closing upon me like a tautened net. My brow and scalp, at the same time, were shot through with a million needle-like pangs — a manifold, ever-growing agony that seemed to pierce the very bone and converge from all sides upon my inmost brain.

The terror and suffering of that moment were worse than aught which the hells of earthly madness or delirium could ever contain. I felt the foul, vampiric clutch of an atrocious death — and of more than death.

I believe that I dropped the torch; but the fingers of my right hand had still retained the open knife. Instinctively — since I was hardly capable of conscious volition — I raised the knife and slashed blindly, again and again, many times, at the thing that had fastened its deadly folds upon me. The blade must have gone through the clinging monstrosity, to gash my own flesh in a score of places; but I did not feel the pain of those wounds in the million-throbbing torment that possessed me.

At last I saw light, and saw that a black strip, loosed from above my eyes and dripping with my own blood, was hanging down my cheek. It writhed a little, even as it hung, and I ripped it away, and ripped the other remnants of the thing, tatter by oozing, bloody tatter, from off my brow and head. Then I staggered toward the entrance; and the wan light turned to a far, receding, dancing flame before me as I lurched and fell outside the cavern — a flame that fled like the last star of creation above the yawning, sliding chaos and oblivion into which I descended. . . .

I am told that my unconsciousness was of brief duration. I came to myself, with the cryptic faces of the two Martian guides bending over me. My head was full of lancinating pains, and half-remembered terrors closed upon my mind like the shadows of mustering harpies. I rolled over, and looked back toward the cavern-mouth, from which the Martians, after finding me, had seemingly dragged me for some little distance. The mouth was under the terraced angle of an outer building, and within sight of our camp.

I stared at the black opening with hideous fascination, and descried a shadowy stirring in the gloom — the writhing, verminous movement of things that pressed forward from the darkness but did not emerge into the light. Doubtless they could not endure the sun, those creatures of ultramundane night and cycle-sealed corruption.

It was then that the ultimate horror, the beginning madness, came upon me. Amid my crawling revulsion, my nausea prompted desire to flee from that seething cavern-mouth, there rose an abhorrently conflicting impulse to return: to thread my backward way through all the catacombs, as the others had done; to go down where never men save they, the inconceivably doomed and accursed, had ever gone: to seek beneath that damnable compulsion a nether world that human thought can never picture. There was a black light, a soundless calling, in the vaults of my brain; the implanted summons of the Thing, like a permeating and sorcerous poison. It lured me to the subterranean door that was walled up by the dying people of Abomi, to immure those hellish and immortal leeches, those dark parasites that engraft their own abominable life on the half-eaten brains of the dead. It called me to the depths beyond, where dwell the noisome, necromantic Ones, of whom the leeches, with all their powers of vampirism and diabolism, are but the merest minions. . . .

It was only the two Aihais who prevented me from going back. I struggled, I fought them insanely as they strove to retard me with their spongy arms; but I must have been pretty thoroughly exhausted from all the superhuman adventures of the day; and I went down once more, after a little, into fathomless nothingness, from which I floated out at long intervals, to realize that I was being carried across the desert toward Ignarh.

Well, that is all my story. I have tried to tell it fully and coherently, at a cost that would be unimaginable to the sane . . . to tell it before the madness falls upon me again, as it will very soon — as it is doing now . . . . Yes, I have told my story . . . and you have written it all out, haven't you? Now I must go back to Abomi — back across the desert and down through all the catacombs to the vaster vaults beneath. Something is in my brain, that commands me and will direct me . . . I tell you, I must go . . . .

The Nameless Offspring

*Many and multiform are the dim horrors of Earth, infesting
her ways from the prime. They sleep beneath the unturned
stone; they rise with the tree from its roots; they move beneath
the sea and in subterranean places; they dwell in the inmost
adyta; they emerge betimes from the shutten sepulcher of
haughty bronze and the low grave that is sealed with clay.
There be some that are long known to man, and others as yet
unknown that abide the terrible latter days of their revealing.
Those which are the most dreadful and the loathliest of all are
haply still to be declared. But among those that have revealed
themselves aforetime and have made manifest their veritable
presence, there is one which may not openly be named for its
exceeding foulness. It is that spawn which the hidden dweller
in the vaults has begotten upon mortality.*

— From the *Necronomicon* of Abdul Alhazred.

In a sense, it is fortunate that the story I must now relate
should be so largely a thing of undetermined shadows, of
half-shaped hints and forbidden inferences. Otherwise, it
could never be written by human hand or read by human eye.
My own slight part in the hideous drama was limited to its
last act; and to me its earlier scenes were merely a remote and
ghastly legend. Yet, even so, the broken reflex of its unnatural
horrors has crowded out in perspective the main events of
normal life; has made them seem no more than frail gossamers, woven on the dark, windy verge of some unsealed

abyss, some deep half-open charnel, wherein Earth's nethermost corruptions lurk and fester.

The legend of which I speak was familiar to me from childhood, as a theme of family whispers and head shakings, for Sir John Tremoth had been a schoolmate of my father. But I had never met Sir John, had never visited Tremoth Hall, till the time of those happenings which formed the final tragedy. My father had taken me from England to Canada when I was a small infant; he had prospered in Manitoba as an apiarist; and after his death the bee ranch had kept me too busy for years to execute a long-cherished dream of visiting my natal land and exploring its rural by-ways.

When, finally, I set sail, the story was pretty dim in my memory; and Tremoth Hall was no conscious part of my itinerary when I began a motorcycle tour of the English counties. In any case, I should never have been drawn to the neighborhood out of morbid curiosity, such as the frightful tale might possibly have evoked in others. My visit, as it happened, was purely accidental. I had forgotten the exact location of the place, and did not even dream that I was in its vicinity. If I had know, it seems to me that I should have turned aside, in spite of the circumstances that impelled me to seek shelter, rather than intrude upon the almost demoniacal misery of its owner.

When I came to Tremoth Hall, I had ridden all day, in early autumn, through a rolling countryside with leisurely, winding thoroughfares and lanes. The day had been fair, with skies of pale azure above noble parks that were tinged with the first amber and crimson of the fallowing year. But toward the middle of the afternoon, a mist had come in from the hidden ocean across low hills and had closed me about with its moving phantom circle. Somehow, in that deceptive fog, I managed to lose my way, to miss the mile-post that would have given me my direction to the town where I had planned to spend the ensuing night.

I went on for a while, at random, thinking that I should soon reach another crossroad. The way that I followed was little more than a rough lane and was singularly deserted. The fog had darkened and drawn closer, obliterating all horizons; but from what I could see of it, the country was one of heath and boulders, with no sign of cultivation. I topped a level ridge and went down a long, monotonous slope as the mist continued to thicken with twilight. I thought that I was riding toward the west; but before me, in the wan dusk, there was no faintest gleaming or flare of color to betoken the drowned sunset. A dank odor that was touched with salt like the smell of sea marshes, came to meet me.

The road turned at a sharp angle, and I seemed to be riding between downs and marshland. The night gathered with an almost unnatural quickness, as if in hast to overtake me; and I began to feel a sort of dim concern and alarm, as if I had gone astray in regions that were more dubious than an English county. The fog and twilight seemed to withhold a silent landscape of chill and deathly, disquieting mystery.

Then, to the left of my road and a little before me, I saw a light that somehow suggested a mournful and tear-dimmed eye. It shone among blurred, uncertain masses that were like trees from a ghostland wood. A nearer mass, as I approached it, was resolved into a small lodge-building, such as would guard the entrance of some estate. It was dark and apparently unoccupied. Pausing and peering, I saw the outlines of a wrought-iron gate in a hedge of untrimmed yew.

It all had a desolate and forbidding air; and I felt in my very narrow the brooding chillness that had come in from the unseen marsh in that dismal, ever-coiling fog. But the light was promise of human nearness on the lonely downs; and I might obtain shelter for the night, or at least find someone who could direct me to a town or inn.

Somewhat to my surprise, the gate was unlocked. It swung inward with a rusty grating sound, as if it had not been opened for a long time; and pushing my motorcycle before me, I followed a weed-grown drive toward the light. The rambling mass of a large manor-house disclosed itself, among trees and shrubs whose artificial forms, like the hedge of ragged yew, were assuming a wilder grotesquery than the had received from the hand of the topiary.

The fog had turned into a bleak drizzle. Almost groping in the gloom, I found a dark door, at some distance from the window that gave forth the solitary light. In response to my thrice-repeated knock, I heard at length the muffled sound of slow, dragging footfalls. The door was opened with a gradualness that seemed to indicate caution or reluctance, and I saw before me an old man, bearing a lighted taper in his hand. His fingers trembled with palsy or decrepitude, and monstrous shadows flickered behind him in a dim hallway, and touched his wrinkled features as with the flitting of ominous, batlike wings.

"What do you wish, sir?" he asked. The voice, though quavering and hesitant, was far from churlish and did not suggest the attitude of suspicion and downright inhospitality which I had begun to apprehend. However, I sensed a sort of irresolution or dubiety; and as the old man listened to my account of the circumstances that had led me to knock at that lonely door, I saw that he was scrutinizing me with a keenness that belied my first impression of extreme senility.

"I knew you were a stranger in these parts," he commented, when I had finished. "But might I inquire your name, sir?"

"I am Henry Chaldane."

"Are you not the son of Mr. Arthur Chaldane?"

Somewhat mystified, I admitted the ascribed paternity.

"You resemble your father, Sir. Mr. Chaldane and Sir John Tremoth were great friends, in the days before your father went to Canada. Will you not come in, Sir? This is Tremoth Hall. Sir John has not been in the habit of receiving guests for a long time; but I shall tell him that you are here; and it may be that he will wish to see you."

Startled, and not altogether agreeably surprised at the discovery of my whereabouts, I followed the old man to a book-lined study whose furnishings bore evidence of luxury and neglect. Here he lit an oil lamp of antique fashion, with a dusty, painted shade, and left me along with the dustier volumes and furniture.

I felt a queer embarrassment, a sense of actual intrusion, as I waited in the wan yellow lamplight. There came back to me the details of the strange, horrific, half-forgotten story I had overheard from my father in childhood years.

Lady Agatha Tremoth, in the first year of their marriage, had become the victim of cataleptic seizures. The third seizure had apparently terminated in death, for she did not revive after the usual interval, and displayed all the familiar marks of the rigor mortis. Lady Agatha's body was place in the family vaults, which were of almost fabulous age and extent, and had been excavated in the hill behind the manor-house. On the day following the interment, Sir John, troubled by a queer, insistent doubt as to the finality of the medical verdict, had reentered the vaults in time to hear a wild cry, and had found Lady Agatha sitting up in her coffin. The nailed lid was lying on the stone floor, and it seemed impossible that it could have been removed by the struggles of the frail woman. However, there was no other plausible explanation, though Lady Agatha herself could throw little light on the circumstances of her strange resurrection.

Half-dazed, and almost delirious, in a state of dire terror that was easily understandable, she told an incoherent tale of her experience. She did not seem to remember struggling to free herself from the coffin, but was troubled mainly by recollections of a pale, hideous, unhuman face which she had seen in the gloom on awakening from her prolonged and deathlike sleep. It was the sight of this face, stooping over her as she lay in the *open* coffin, that had caused her to cry out so wildly. The thing had vanished before Sir John's approach, fleeing swiftly to the inner vaults; and she had formed only a vague idea of its bodily appearance. She thought, however, that it was large and white, and ran like an animal on all fours, though its limbs were semihuman.

Of course, her tale was regarded as a sort of dream, or a figment of delirium induced by the awful shock of her experience, which had blotted out all recollection of its true terror. But the memory of the horrible face and figure had seemed to obsess her permanently, and was plainly fraught with associations of mind-numbing fear. She did not recover from her illness, but lived on in a shattered condition of brain and body; and nine months later she died, after giving birth to her first child.

Her death was a merciful thing; for the child, it seemed, was one of those appalling monsters that sometimes appear in human families. The exact nature of its abnormality was not known, though frightful and divergent rumors had purported to emanate from the doctor, nurses and servants who had seen it. Some of the latter had left Tremoth Hall and had refused to return, after a single glimpse of the monstrosity.

After Lady Agatha's death, Sir John had withdrawn from society: and little or nothing was divulged in regard to his doings or the fate of the horrible infant. People said, however, that the child was kept in a locked room with iron-barred windows, which no one but Sir John himself had ever entered. The tragedy had blighted his whole life, and he had become a recluse, living alone with one or two faithful servants, and allowing his estate to decline grievously through neglect.

Doubtless, I thought, the old man who had admitted me was one of the remaining servitors. I was still reviewing the dreadful legend, still striving to recollect certain particulars that had almost passed from memory, when I heard the sound of footsteps which, from their slowness and feebleness, I took to be those of the returning manservant.

However, I was mistaken; for the person who entered was plainly Sir John Tremoth himself. The tall, slightly bent figure, the face that was lined as if by the trickling of some corrosive acid, where marked with a dignity that seemed to triumph over the double ravages of mortal sorrow and illness. Somehow — though I could have calculated his real age — I had expected an old man; but he was scarcely beyond middle life. His cadaverous pallor and feeble tottering walk were those of a man who is stricken with some fatal malady.

His manner, as he addressed me, was impeccably courteous and even gracious. But the voice was that of one to whom the ordinary relations and actions of life had long since become meaningless and perfunctory.

"Harper tells me that you are the son of my old school friend, Arthur Chaldane," he said. "I bid you welcome to such poor hospitality as I am able to offer. I have not received guests for many years, and I fear you will find the Hall pretty dull and dismal and will think me an indifferent host. Nevertheless, you must remain, at least for the night. Harper has gone to prepare dinner for us."

"You are very kind," I replied. "I fear, however that I am intruding. If —"

"Not at all," he countered firmly. "You must be my guest. It is miles to the nearest inn, and the fog is changing into a heavy rain. Indeed, I am glad to have you. You must tell me all about your father and yourself at dinner. In the meanwhile I'll try to find a room for you, if you'll come with me."

He led me to the second floor of the manor-house and down a long hall with beams and panels of ancient oak. We passed several doors which were doubtless those of bed-chambers. All were closed, and one of the doors was re-enforced with iron bars, heavy and sinister as those of a dungeon cell. Inevitably I surmised that this was the chamber in which the monstrous child had been confined, and also I wondered if the abnormality still lived, after a lapse of time that must have been nearly thirty years. How abysmal, how abhorrent, must have been its departure from the human type, to necessitate an

immediate removal from the sight of others! And what charac-
teristics of its further development could have rendered necessary the massive bars on an oaken door which, by itself, was
strong enough to have resisted the assaults of any common
man or beast?

Without even glancing at the door, my host went on, carrying a taper that scarcely shook in his feeble fingers. My curious reflections, as I followed him were interrupted with nerve-
shattering suddenness by a loud cry that seemed to issue from
the barred room. The sound was a long, ever-mounting ululation, infra-bass at first like the tomb-muffled voice of a demon,
and rising through abominable degrees to a shrill, ravenous
fury, as if the demon had emerged by a series of underground
steps to the open air. It was neither human not bestial, it was
wholly preternatural, hellish, macabre; and I shuddered with
an insupportable eeriness, that still persisted when the demon
voice, after reaching its culmination, had returned by reverse
degrees to a profound sepulchral silence.

Sir John had given no apparent heed to the awful sound,
but had gone on with no more than his usual faltering. He had
reached the end of the hall, and was pausing before the second
chamber from the one with the sealed door.

"I'll let you have this room," he said. "It's just beyond the
one that I occupy." He did not turn his face toward me as he
spoke; and his voice was unnaturally toneless and restrained. I
realized with another shudder that the chamber he had indicated as his own was adjacent to the room from which the
frightful ululation had appeared to issue.

The chamber to which he now admitted me had manifestly
not been used for years. The air was chill, stagnant, unwhole-
some, with an all-pervading mustiness; and the antique furniture had gathered the inevitably increment of dust and cobwebs. Sir John began to apologize.

"I didn't realize the condition of the room," he said. I'll send Harper after dinner, to do a little dusting and clearing, and put fresh linen on the bed."

I protested, rather vaguely, that there was no need for him to apologize. The unhuman loneliness and decay of the old manor-house, its lustrums and decades of neglect, and the corresponding desolation of its owner, had impressed me more painfully than ever. And I dared not speculate overmuch concerning the ghastly secret of the barred chamber, and the hellish howling that still echoed in my shaken nerves. Already I regretted the singular fortuity that had drawn me to that place of evil and festering shadows. I felt an urgent desire to leave, to continue my journey even in the face of the bleak autumnal rain and wind-blown darkness. But I could think of no excuse that would be sufficiently tangible and valid. Manifestly, there was nothing to do but remain.

Our dinner was served in a dismal but stately room, by the old man whom Sir John had referred to as Harper. The meal was plain but substantial and well-cooked; and the service was impeccable. I had begun to infer that Harper was the only servant — a combination of valet, butler, housekeeper and chef.

In spite of my hunger, and the pains taken by my host to make me feel at ease, the meal was a solemn and almost funereal ceremony. I could not forget my father's story; and still less could I forget the sealed door and the baleful ululation. Whatever it was, the monstrosity still lived; and I felt a complex mingling of admiration, pity and horror as I looked at the gaunt and gallant face of Sir John Tremoth, and reflected upon the lifelong hell to which he had been condemned, and the apparent fortitude with which he had borne its unthinkable ordeals. A bottle of excellent sherry was brought in. Over this, we sat for an hour or more. Sir John spoke at some length concerning my father, of whose death he had not heard; and he drew me out in regard to my own affairs with the subtle adroitness of a polished man of the world. He said little about himself, and not even by hint or implication did he refer to the tragic history which I have outlined.

Since I am rather abstemious, and did not empty my glass with much frequency, the major part of the heavy wine was consumed by my host. Toward the end, it seemed to bring out in him a curious vein of confidentiality; and he spoke for the first time of the ill health that was all too patent in his appearance. I learned that he was subject to that most painful form of heart disease, angina pectoris, and had recently recovered from an attack of unusual severity.

"The next one will finish me," he said. "And it may come at any time — perhaps tonight." He made the announcement very simply, as if he were voicing a commonplace or venturing a prediction about the weather. Then, after a slight pause, he went on, with more emphasis and weightiness of tone:

"Maybe you'll think me queer, but I have a fixed prejudice against burial or vault interment. I want my remains to be thoroughly cremated, and have left careful directions to that end. Harper will see to it that they are fulfilled. Fire is the cleanest and purest of the elements, and it cuts short all the damnable processes between death and ultimate disintegration. I can't bear the idea of some moldy, worm-infested tomb."

He continue to discourse on the subject for some time, with a singular elaboration and tenseness of manner that showed it to be a familiar theme of thought, if not an actual obsession. It seemed to possess a morbid fascination for him; and there was a painful light in his hollow, haunted eyes, and a touch of rigidly subdued hysteria in his voice, as he spoke. I remembered the interment of Lady Agatha, and her tragic resurrection, and the dime, delirious horror of the vaults that had formed an inexplicable and vaguely disturbing part of her story. It was not hard to understand Sir John's aversion to burial; but I was far from suspecting the full terror and ghastliness on which his repugnance had been founded.

Harper had disappeared after bringing the sherry; and I surmised that he had been given orders for the renovation of my room. We had now drained our last glasses; and my host had ended his peroration. The wind, which had animated him briefly, seemed to die out, and he looked more ill and haggard than ever. Pleading my own fatigue, I expressed a wish to retire, and he, with his invariable courtliness, insisted on seeing me to my chamber and making sure of my comfort, before seeking his own bed.

In the hall above, we met Harper, who was just descending from a flight of stairs that must have led to an attic or third floor. He was carrying a heavy iron pan, in which a few scraps of meat remained; and I caught an odor of pronounced gaminess, almost virtual putrescence, from the pan as he went by. I wondered if he had been feeding the unknown monstrosity, and if perhaps its food were supplied to it through a trap in the ceiling of the barred room. The surmise was reasonable enough, but the odor of the scraps, by a train of remote, half-literary association, had begun to suggest other surmises which, it would seem, were beyond the realm of possibility and reason. Certain evasive, incoherent hints appeared to point themselves suddenly to an atrocious and abhorrent whole. With imperfect success, I assured myself that the thing I had fancied was incredible to science; was a mere creation of superstitious diablerie. No, it could not be . . . here in England, of all places . . . that corpse-devouring demon of Oriental tales and legends . . . the *ghoul*.

Contrary to my fears, there was no repetition of the fiendish howling as we passed the secret room. But I thought that I heard a measured crunching, such as a large animal would make in devouring its food.

My room, though still drear and dismal enough, had been cleared of its accumulated dust and matted gossamers. After a personal inspection, Sir John left me and retired to his own chamber. I was struck by his deathly pallor and weakness, as he said good night to me, and felt guiltily apprehensive that the strain of receiving and entertaining a guest might have aggravated the dire disease from which he suffered. I seemed to detect actual pain and torment beneath his careful armor of urbanity, and wondered if the urbanity had not been maintained at an excessive cost.

The fatigue of my day-long journey, together with the heavy wine I had drunk, should have conduced to early slumber. But though I lay with tightly closed lids in the darkness, I could not dismiss those evil shadows, those black and charnel larvae, that swarmed upon me from the ancient house. Insufferable and forbidden things besieged me with filthy talons, brushed me with noisome coils, as I tossed through eternal hours and lay staring at the gray square of the storm-darkened window. The dripping of the rain, the sough and moan of the wind, resolved themselves to a dread mutter of half-articulate voices that plotted against my peace and whispered loathfully of nameless secrets in demonian language.

At length, after the seeming lapse of nocturnal centuries, the tempest died away, and I no longer heard the equivocal voices. The window lightened a little in the black wall; and the terrors of my night-long insomnia seemed to withdraw partially, but without bringing the surcease of slumber. I became aware of utter silence; and then, in the silence, of a queer, faint, disquieting sound whose cause and location baffled me for many minutes.

The sound was muffled and far off at times; then it seemed to draw near, as if it were in the next room. I began to identify it as a sort of scratching, such as would be made by the claws of an animal on solid woodwork. Sitting up in bed, and listening attentively, I realized with a fresh start of horror that it came from the direction of the barred chamber. It took on a strange resonance; then it became almost inaudible; and suddenly, for awhile, it ceased. In the interim, I heard a single groan, like that of a man in great agony or terror. I could not mistake the source of the groan, which had issued from Sir John Tremoth's room; not was I doubtful any longer as the causation of the scratching.

The groan was not repeated; but the damnable clawing sound began again and was continued till day-break. then, as if the creature that had cause the noise were wholly nocturnal in its habits, the faint, vibrant rasping ceased and was not resumed. In a state of dull, nightmarish apprehension, drugged with weariness and want of sleep, I had listened to it with intolerably straining ears. With its cessation, in the hueless livid dawn, I slid into a deep slumber, from which the muffled and amorphous specters of the old Hall were unable to detain me any longer.

I was awakened by a loud knocking on my door — a knocking in which even my sleep-confused senses could recognize the imperative and urgent. It must have been close upon midday; and feeling guilty at having overslept so egregiously, I ran to the door and opened it. The old manservant, Harper, was standing without, and his tremulous, grief-broken manner told me before he spoke that something of dire import had occurred.

"I regret to tell you, Mr. Chaldane," he quavered, "that Sir John is dead. He did not answer my knock as usual; so I made bold to enter his room. He must have died early this morning."

Inexpressibly shocked by his announcement, I recalled the single groan I had heard in the gray beginning of dawn. My host, perhaps, had been dying at that very moment. I recalled, too, the detestable nightmare scratching. Unavoidably, I wondered if the groan had been occasioned by fear as well as by physical pain. Had the strain and suspense of listening to that hideous sound brought on the final paroxysm of Sir John's malady? I could not be sure of the truth; but my brain seethed with awful and ghastly conjectures.

With the futile formalities that one employs on such occasions, I tried to condole with the aged servant, and offered him such assistance as I could in making the necessary arrangements for the disposition of his master's remains. since there was no telephone in the house, I volunteered to find a doctor who would examine the body and sign the death certificate. The old man seemed to feel a singular relief and gratitude.

"Thank you, sir," he said fervently. Then, as if in explanation: "I don't want to leave Sir John — I promised him that I'd keep a close watch over his body." He went on to speak of Sir John's desire for cremation. It seemed that the baronet had left explicit directions for the building of a pyre of driftwood on the hill behind the Hall, the burning of his remains on this pyre, and the sowing of his ashes on the fields of the estate. These directions he had enjoined and empowered the servant to carry out as soon after death as possible. No one was to be present at the ceremony, except Harper and the hired pall bearers; and Sir John's nearer relatives — none of whom lived in the vicinity — were not to be informed of his demise till all was over.

I refused Harper's offer to prepare my breakfast, telling him that I could obtain a meal in the neighboring village. There was a strange uneasiness in his manner; and I realized, with thoughts and emotions not to be specified in this narrative, that he was anxious to begin his promised vigil beside Sir John's corpse.

It would be tedious and unnecessary to detail the funereal afternoon that followed. The heavy sea fog had returned; and I seemed to grope my way through a sodden but unreal world as I sought the nearby town. I succeeded in locating a doctor and also in securing several men to build the pyre and act as pall bearers. I was met everywhere with an odd taciturnity, and no one seemed willing to comment on Sir John's death or to speak of the dark legendry that was attached to Tremoth Hall.

Harper, to my amazement, had proposed that the cremation should take place at once. This, however, proved to be impracticable. When all the formalities and arrangements had been completed, the fog turned into a steady, everlasting downpour which rendered impossible the lighting of the pyre; and we were compelled to defer the ceremony. I had promised Harper that I should remain at the Hall till all was done; and so it was that I spent a second night beneath that roof of accurst and abominable secrets.

The darkness came on betimes. After a last visit to the village, in which I procured some sandwiches for Harper and myself in lieu of dinner, I returned to the lonely Hall. I was met by Harper on the stairs, as I ascended to the death-chamber. There was an increased agitation in his manner, as if something had happened to frighten him.

"I wonder if you'd keep me company tonight, Mr. Chaldane," he said. "It's a gruesome watch that I'm asking you to share, and it may be a dangerous one. But Sir John would thank you, I am sure. If you have a weapon of any sort, it will be well to bring it with you."

It was impossible to refuse his request, and I assented at once. I was unarmed; so Harper insisted on equipping me with an antique revolver, of which he himself carried the mate.

"Look here, Harper," I said bluntly, as we followed the hall to Sir John's chamber, "what are you afraid of?"

He flinched visibly at the question and seemed unwilling to answer. Then, after a moment, he appeared to realize that frankness was necessary.

"It's the thing in the barred room," he explained. "You must have heard it, sir. We've had the care of it, Sir John and I, these eight and twenty years; and we've always feared that it might break out. It never gave us much trouble — as long as we kept it well-fed. But for the last three nights, it has been scratching at the thick oaken wall of Sir John's chamber, which is something it never did before. Sir John thought it knew that he was going to die, and that it wanted to reach his body — being hungry for other food than we had given it. That's why we must guard him closely tonight, Mr. Chaldane. I pray to God that the wall will hold; but the thing keeps on clawing and clawing, like a demon; and I don't like the hollowness of the sound — as if the wall were getting pretty thin."

Appalled by this confirmation of my own most repugnant surmise, I could offer no rejoinder, since all comment would have been futile. With Harper' open avowal, the abnormality took on a darker and more encroaching shadow, a more potent and tyrannic menace. Willingly would I have foregone the promised vigil — but this, of course, it was impossible to do.

The bestial, diabolic scratching, louder and more frantic than before, assailed my ears as we passed the barred room. All too readily, I understood the nameless fear that had impelled the old man to request my company. The sound was inexpressibly alarming and nerve-sapping, with its grim, macabre, with a hideous, tearing vibrancing, when we entered the room of death.

During the whole course of that funeral day, I had refrained from visiting this chamber, since I am lacking in the morbid curiosity which impels many to gaze upon the dead. So it was that I beheld my host for the second and last time. Fully dressed and prepared for the pyre, he lay on the chill white bed whose heavily figured, arras-like curtains had been drawn back. The room was lit by several tall tapers, arranged on a little table in curious brazen candelabras that were greened with antiquity; but the light seemed to afford only a doubtful, dolorous glimmering in the drear spaciousness and mortuary shadows.

Somewhat against my will, I gazed on the dead features, and averted my eyes very hastily. I was prepared for the stony pallor and rigor, but not for the full betrayal of that hideous revulsion, that inhuman terror and horror, which must have corroded the man's heart through infernal years; and which, with almost superhuman control, he had masked from the casual beholder in life. The revelation was too painful, and I could not look at him again. In a sense, it seemed that he was not dead; that he was still listening with agonized attention to the dreadful sounds that might well have served to precipitate the final attack of his malady.

There were several chairs, dating, I think, like the bed itself, from the seventeenth century. Harper and I seated ourselves near the small table and between the deathbed and the paneled wall of blackish wood from which the ceaseless clawing sound appeared to issue. In tacit silence, with drawn and cocked revolvers, we began our ghastly vigil.

As we sat and waited, I was driven to picture the unnamed monstrosity; and formless or half-formed images of charnel nightmare pursued each other in chaotic succession through my mind. An atrocious curiosity, to which I should normally have been a stranger, prompted me to question Harper; but I was restrained by an even more powerful inhibition. On his part, the old man volunteered no information or comment whatever, but watched the wall with fear-bright eyes that did not seem to waver in his palsy-nodding head.

It would be impossible to convey the unnatural tension, the macabre suspense and baleful expectation of the hours that followed. The woodwork must have been of great thickness and hardness, such as would have defied the assaults of any normal creature equipped only with talons or teeth; but in spite of such obvious arguments as these, I thought momentarily to see it crumble inward. The scratching noise went on every instant. At recurrent intervals, I seemed to hear a low, eager, doglike whining, such as a ravenous animal would make when it neared the goal of its burrowing.

Neither of us had spoken of what we should do, in case the monster should attain its objective; but there seemed to be an unvoiced agreement. However, with a superstitiousness of which I should not have believed myself capable, I began to wonder if the monster possessed enough of humanity in its composition to be vulnerable to mere revolver bullets. To what extent would it display the traits of its unknown and fabulous paternity? I tried to convince myself that such questions and

wonderings were patently absurd; but was drawn to them
again and again, as if by the allurement of some forbidden gulf.

The night wore on, like the flowing of a dark, sluggish
stream; and the tall, funeral tapers had burned to within an
inch of their verdigris-eaten sockets. It was this circumstance
alone that gave me an idea of the passage of time; for I seemed
to be drowning in a black eternity, motionless beneath the
crawling and seething of blind horrors. I had grown so accus-
tomed to the clawing noise in the woodwork, and the sound
had gone on so long, that I deemed its evergrowing sharpness
and hollowness a mere hallucination; and so it was that the end
of our vigil came without apparent warning.

Suddenly, as I stared at the wall and listened with frozen
fixity, I heard a harsh, splintering sound, and saw that a narrow
strip had broken loose and was hanging from the panel. Then,
before I could collect myself or credit the awful witness of my
senses, a large semicircular portion of the wall collapsed in
many splinters beneath the impact of some ponderous body.

Mercifully, perhaps, I have never been able to recall with
any degree of distinctness the hellish thing that issued from the
panel. The visual shock, by its own excess of horror, has almost
blotted the details from memory. I have, however, the blurred
impression of a huge, whitish, hairless and semi-quadruped
body, of canine teeth in a half-human face, and long hyena
mails at the end of forelimbs that were both arms and legs. A
charnel stench precede the apparition, like a breath from the
den of some carrion-eating animal; and then, with a single
nightmare leap, the thing was upon us.

I heard the staccato crack of Harper's revolver, sharp and
vengeful in the closed room; but there was only a rusty click
from my own weapon. Perhaps the cartridge was too old; at any
rate, it had misfired. Before I could press the trigger again, I
was hurled to the floor with terrific violence, striking my head
against the heavy base of the little table. A black curtain, span-
gled with countless fires, appeared to fall upon me and to blot

the room from sight. Then all the fires went out, and there was
only darkness.

Again, slowly, I became conscious of flame and shadow; but
the flame was bright and flickering, and seemed to grow ever
more brilliant. Then my dull, doubtful senses were sharply
revived and clarified by the acrid odor of burning cloth. The
features of the room returned to vision, and I found that I was
lying huddled against the overthrown table, gazing toward the
death-bed. The guttering candles had been hurled to the floor.
One of them was eating a slow circle of fire in the carpet beside
me; and another, spreading, had ignited the bed curtains,
which were flaring swiftly upward to the great canopy. Even as
I lay staring, huge, ruddy tatters of the burning fabric fell upon
the bed in a dozen places, and the body of Sir John Tremoth
was ringed about with starting flames.

I staggered heavily to my feet and giddy with the fall that
hurled me into oblivion. The room was empty, except for the
old manservant, who lay near the door, moaning indistinctly.
The door itself stood open, as if someone — or something had
gone out during my period of unconsciousness.

I turned again to the bed, with some instinctive, half-
formed intention of trying to extinguish the blaze. The flames
were spreading rapidly, were leaping higher, but they were not
swift enough to veil from my sickened eyes the hands and features — if one could any longer call them such — of that which
had been Sir John Tremoth. Of the last horror that had overtaken him, I must forbear explicit mention; and I would that I
could likewise avoid the remembrance. All too tardily had the
monster been frightened away by the fire. . . .

There is little more to tell. Looking back once more, as I
reeled from the smoke-laden room with Harper in my arms,
I saw that the bed and its canopy had become a mass of
mounting flames. The unhappy baronet had found in his own
death-chamber the funeral pyre for which he had longed.

It was nearly dawn when we emerged from the doomed manor-house. The rain had ceased, leaving a heaven lined with high and dead-gray clouds. The chill air appeared to revive the aged manservant, and he stood feebly beside me, uttering not a word, as we watched an ever-climbing spire of flame that broke from the somber roof of Tremoth Hall and began to cast a sullen glare on the unkempt hedges.

In the combined light of the fireless dawn and the lurid conflagration, we both saw at our feet the semihuman, monstrous footprints, with their make of long and canine nails, that had been trodden freshly and deeply in the rain-wet soil. They came from the direction of the manor-house, and ran toward the heath-clad hill that rose behind it.

Still without speaking, we followed the steps. Almost without interruption, they led to the entrance of the ancient family vaults, to the heavy iron door in the hillside that had been closed for a full generation by Sir John Tremoth's order. The door itself swung open, and we saw that its rusty chain and lock had been shattered by a strength that was more than the strength of man or beast. Then, peering within, we saw the clay-touched outline of the unreturning footprints that went downward into mausolean darkness on the stairs.

We were both weaponless, having left our revolvers behind us in the death-chamber; but we did not hesitate long. Harper possessed a liberal supply of matches; and looking about I found a heavy billet of water-soaked wood, which might serve in lieu of a cudgel. In grim silence, with tacit determination, and forgetful of any danger, we conducted a thorough search of the well-nigh interminable vaults, striking match after match as we went on in the must shadows.

The traces of ghoulish footsteps grew fainter as we followed them into those black recesses; and we found nothing anywhere but noisome dampness and undisturbed cobwebs and the countless coffins of the dead. The thing that we sought had vanished utterly, as if swallowed up by the subterranean walls.

At last we returned to the entrance. There, as we stood blinking in the full daylight, with gray and haggard faces, Harper spoke for the first time, saying in his slow, tremulous voice:

"Many years ago — soon after Lady Agatha's death — Sir John and I searched the vaults from end to end; but we could find no trace of the thing we suspected. Now, as then, it is useless to seek. There are mysteries which, God helping, will never be fathomed. We know only that the offspring of the vaults has gone back to the vaults. There may it remain."

Silently, in my shaken heart, I echoes his last words and his wish.

Ubbo-Sathla

". . . For Ubbo-Sathla is the source and the end. Before the
coming of Zhothaqquah or Yok-Zothoth or Kthulhut from the
stars, Ubbo-Sathla dwelt in the steaming fens of the new-
made Earth: a mass without head or members, spawning the
grey, formless efts of the prime and the grisly prototypes of ter-
rene life. . . . And all earthly life, it is told, shall go back at
last through the great circle of time to Ubbo-Sathla."

— The Book of Eibon.

Paul Tregardis found the milky crystal in a litter of odd-
ments from many lands and eras. He had entered the
shop of the curio dealer through an aimless impulse,
with no particular object in mind, other than the idle distraction of eyeing and fingering a miscellany of far-gathered things.
Looking desultorily about, his attention had been drawn by a
dull glimmering on one of the tables; and he had extricated the
queer orb-like stone from its shadowy, crowded position
between an ugly little Aztec idol, the fossil egg of a dinornis,
and an obscene fetich of black wood from the Niger.

The thing was about the size of a small orange and was
slightly flattened at the ends, like a planet at its poles. It puzzled Tregardis, for it was not like an ordinary crystal, being
cloudy and changeable, with an intermittent glowing in its
heart, as if it were alternately illumed and darkened from
within. Holding it to the wintry window, he studied it for
awhile without being able to determine the secret of this sin-

gular and regular alternation. His puzzlement was soon com-
plicated by a dawning sense of vague and unrecognizable
familiarity, as if he had seen the thing before under circumstances that were now wholly forgotten.

He appealed to the curio-dealer, a dwarfish Hebrew with
an air of dusty antiquity, who gave the impression of being
lost to commercial considerations in some web of cabbalistic
revery.

"Can you tell me anything about this?"

The dealer gave an indescribable, simultaneous shrug of
his shoulders and his eye-brows.

"It is very old — palaeogean, one might say. I cannot tell
you much, for little is known. A geologist found it in
Greenland, beneath glacial ice, in the Miocene strata. Who
knows? It may have belonged to some sorcerer of primeval
Thule. Greenland was a warm, fertile region, beneath the sun
of Miocene times. No doubt it is a magic crystal; and a man
might behold strange visions in its heart, if he looked long
enough."

Tregardis was quite startled; for the dealer's apparently
fantastic suggestion had brought to mind his own delvings in
a branch of obscure lore; and, in particular, had recalled *The
Book of Eibon*, that strangest and rarest of occult forgotten volumes, which is said to have come down through a series of
manifold translations from a prehistoric original written in
the lost language of Hyperborea. Tregardis, with much difficulty, had obtained the medieval French version — a copy
that had been owned by many generations of sorcerers and
Satanists — but had never been able to find the Greek manuscript from which the version was derived.

The remote, fabulous original was supposed to have
been the work of a great Hyperborean wizard, from whom
it had taken its name. It was a collection of dark and baleful myths, of liturgies, rituals and incantations both evil and
esoteric. Not without shudders, in the course of studies that

the average person would have considered more than singular, Tregardis had collated the French volume with the frightful *Necronomicon* of the mad Arab, Abdul Alhazred. He had found many correspondences of the blackest and most appalling significance, together with much forbidden data that was either unknown to the Arab or omitted by him . . . or by his translators.

Was this what he had been trying to recall, Tregardis wondered? — the brief, casual reference, in *The Book of Eibon*, to a cloudy crystal that had been owned by the wizard Zon Mezzarnalech, in Mhu Thulan? Of course, it was all too fantastic, too hypothetic, too incredible — but Mhu Thulan, that northern portion of ancient Hyperborea, was supposed to have corresponded roughly with Modern Greenland, which had formerly been joined as a peninsula to the main continent. Could the stone in his hand, by some fabulous fortuity, be the crystal of Zon Mezzamalech?

Tregardis smiled at himself with inward irony for even conceiving the absurd notion. Such things did not occur — at least, not in present-day London; and in all likelihood, *The Book of Eibon* was sheer superstitious fantasy, anyway. Nevertheless, there was something about the crystal that continued to tease and inveigle him.

He ended by purchasing it, at a fairly moderate price. The sum was named by the seller and paid by the buyer without bargaining.

With the crystal in his pocket, Paul Tregardis hastened back to his lodgings instead of resuming his leisurely saunter. He installed the milky globe on his writing table, where it stood firmly enough on one of its oblate ends. Then, still smiling at his own absurdity, he took down the yellow parchment manuscript of *The Book of Eibon* from its place in a somewhat inclusive collection of recherché literature. He opened the vermiculated leather cover with hasps of tarnished steel, and read over to himself, translating from the archaic French as he read, the paragraph that referred to Zon Mezzamalech:

"This wizard, who was mighty among sorcerers, had found a cloudy stone, orb-like and somewhat flattened at the ends, in which he could behold many visions of the terrene past, even to the Earth's beginning, when Ubbo-Sathla, the unbegotten source, lay vast and swollen and yeasty amid the vaporing slime . . . But of that which he beheld, Zon Mezzamalech left little record; and people say that he vanished presently, in a way that is not known; and after him the cloudy crystal was lost."

Paul Tregardis laid the manuscript aside. Again there was something that tantalized and beguiled him, like a lost dream or a memory forfeit to oblivion. Impelled by a feeling which he did not scrutinize or question, he sat down before the table and began to stare intently into the cold, nebulous orb. He felt an expectation which, somehow, was so familiar, so permeative a part of his consciousness, that he did not even name it to himself.

Minute by minute he sat, and watched the alternate glimmering and fading of the mysterious light in the heart of the crystal. By imperceptible degrees, there stole upon him a sense of dreamlike duality, both in respect to his person and his surroundings. He was still Paul Tregardis — and yet he was someone else; the room was his London apartment — and a chamber in some foreign but well-known place. *And in both milieus he peered steadfastly into the same crystal.*

After an interim, without surprise on the part of Tregardis, the process of re-identification became complete. He knew that he was Zon Mezzamalech, a sorcerer of Mhu Thulan, and a student of all lore anterior to his own epoch. Wise with dreadful secrets that were not known to Paul Tregardis, amateur of anthropology and the occult sciences in latter-day London, he sought by means of the milky crystal to attain an even older and more fearful knowledge.

He had acquired the stone in dubitable ways, from a more than sinister source. It was unique and without fellow in any land or time. In its depths, all former years, all things that have ever been, were supposedly mirrored, and would reveal themselves to the patient visionary. And through the crystal, Zon Mezzamalech had dreamt to recover the wisdom of the gods who died before the Earth was born. They had passed to the lightless void, leaving their lore inscribed upon tablets of ultra-stellar stone; and the tablets were guarded in the primal mire by the formless, idiotic demiurge, Ubbo-Sathla. Only by means of the crystal could he hope to find and read the tablets.

For the first time, he was making trial of the globe's reputed virtues. About him an ivory-panelled chamber, filled with his magic books and paraphernalia, was fading slowly from his consciousness. Before him, on a table of some dark Hyperborean wood that had been graven with grotesque ciphers, the crystal appeared to swell and deepen, and in its filmy depth he beheld a swift and broken swirling of dim scenes, fleeting like the bubbles of a millrace. As if he looked upon an actual world, cities, forests, mountains, seas and meadows flowed beneath him, lightening and darkening as with the passage of days and nights in some weirdly accelerated stream of time.

Zon Mezzamalech had forgotten Paul Tregardis — had lost the remembrance of his own entity and his own surroundings in Mhu Thulan. Moment by moment, the flowing vision in the crystal became more definite and distinct, and the orb itself deepened till he grew giddy, as if he were peering from an insecure height into some never-fathomed abyss. He knew that time was racing backward in the crystal, was unrolling for him the pageant of all past days; but a strange alarm had seized him, and he feared to gaze longer. Like one who has nearly fallen from a precipice, he caught himself with a violent start and drew back from the mystic orb.

Again, to his gaze, the enormous whirling world into which he had peered was a small and cloudy crystal on his rune-wrought table in Mhu Thulan. Then, by degrees, it seemed that the great room with sculptured panels of mammoth ivory was narrowing to another and dingier place; and Zon Mezzamalech, losing his preternatural wisdom and sorcerous power, went back by a weird regression into Paul Tregardis.

And yet not wholly, it seemed, was he able to return. Tregardis, dazed and wondering, found himself before the writing table on which he had set the oblate sphere. He felt the confusion of one who has dreamt and has not yet fully awakened from the dream. The room puzzled him vaguely, as if something were wrong with its size and furnishings; and his remembrance of purchasing the crystal from a curio dealer was oddly and discrepantly mingled with an impression that he had acquired it in a very different manner.

He felt that something very strange had happened to him when he peered into the crystal; but just what it was he could not seem to recollect. It had left him in the sort of psychic muddlement that follows a debauch of hashish. He assured himself that he was Paul Tregardis, that he lived on a certain street in London, that the year was 1932; but such commonplace verities had somehow lost their meaning and their validity; and everything about him was shadow-like and insubstantial. The very walls seemed to waver like smoke; the people in the streets were phantoms of phantoms; and he himself was a lost shadow, a wandering echo of something long forgot.

He resolved that he would not repeat his experiment of crystal-gazing. The effects were too unpleasant and equivocal. But the very next day, by an unreasoning impulse to which he yielded almost mechanically, without reluctation, he found himself seated before the misty orb. Again he became the sorcerer Zon Mezzamalech in Mhu Thulan; again he dreamt to retrieve the wisdom of the antemundane gods; again he drew back from the deepening crystal with the terror of one who fears to fall; and once more — but doubtfully and dimly, like a failing wraith — he was Paul Tregardis.

Three times did Tregardis repeat the experience on successive days; and each time his own person and the world about him became more tenuous and confused than before. His sensations were those of a dreamer who is on the verge of waking; and London itself was unreal as the lands that slip from the dreamer's ken, receding in filmy mist and cloudy light. Beyond it all, he felt the looming and crowding of vast imageries, alien but half-familiar. It was as if the phantasmagoria of time and space were dissolving about him, to reveal some veritable reality — or another dream of space and time.

There came, at last, the day when he sat down before the crystal — and did not return as Paul Tregardis. It was the day when Zon Mezzamalech, boldly disregarding certain evil and portentous warnings, resolved to overcome his curious fear of failing bodily into the visionary world that he beheld — a fear that had hitherto prevented him from following the backward stream of time for any distance. He must, he assured himself, conquer this fear if he were ever to see and read the lost tablets of the gods. He had beheld nothing more than a few fragments of the years of Mhu Thulan immediately posterior to the present — the years of his own life-time; and there were inestimable cycles between these years and the Beginning.

Again, to his gaze, the crystal deepened immeasurably, with scenes and happenings that flowed in a retrograde stream. Again the magic ciphers of the dark table faded from his ken, and the sorcerously carven walls of his chamber melted into less than dream. Once more he grew giddy with an awful vertigo as he bent above the swirling and milling of the terrible gulfs of time in the worldlike orb. Fearfully, in spite of his resolution, he would have drawn away; but he had looked and leaned too long. There was a sense of abysmal failing, a suction as of ineluctable winds, of maelstroms that bore him down through fleet unstable visions of his own past life into antenatal years and dimensions. He seemed to endure the pangs of an inverse dissolution; and then he was no longer Zon Mezzamalech, the wise and learned watcher of the crystal, but an actual part of the weirdly racing stream that ran back to re-attain the Beginning.

He seemed to live unnumbered lives, to die myriad deaths, forgetting each time the death and life that had gone before. He fought as a warrior in half-legendary battles; he was a child playing in the ruins of some olden city of Mhu Thulan; he was the king who had reigned when the city was in its prime, the prophet who had foretold its building and its doom. A woman, he wept for the bygone dead in *necropoli* long-crumbled; an antique wizard, he muttered the rude spells of earlier sorcery; a priest of some pre-human god, he wielded the sacrificial knife in cave-temples of pillared basalt. Life by life, era by era, he re-traced the long and groping cycles through which Hyperborea had risen from savagery to a high civilization.

He became a barbarian of some troglodytic tribe, fleeing from the slow, turreted ice of a former glacial age into lands illumed by the ruddy flare of perpetual volcanoes. Then, after incomputable years, he was no longer man, but a man-like beast, roving in forests of giant fern and calamite, or building an uncouth nest in the boughs of mighty cycads.

Through aeons of anterior sensation, of crude lust and hunger, of aborignal terror and madness, there was someone — or something that went ever backward in time. Death became birth, and birth was death. In a slow vision of reverse change, the earth appeared to melt away, and sloughed off the hills and mountains of its latter strata. Always the sun grew larger and hotter above the fuming swamps that teemed with a crasser life, with a more fulsome vegetation. And the thing that had been Paul Tregardis, that had been Zon Mezzamalech, was a part of all the monstrous devolution. It flew with the claw-tipped wings of a pterodactyl, it swam in tepid seas with the vast, winding bulk of an ichthyosaurus, it bellowed uncouthly with the armored throat of some forgotten behemoth to the huge moon that burned through primordial mists.

At length, after aeons of immemorial brutehood, it became one of the lost serpent-men who reared their cites of black gneiss and fought their venomous wars in the world's first continent. It walked undulously in ante-human streets, In strange crooked vaults; it peered at primeval stars from high, Babelian towers; it bowed with hissing litanies to great serpent-idols. Through years and ages of the ophidian era it returned, and was a thing that crawled in the ooze, that had not yet learned to think and dream and build. And the time came when there was no longer a continent, but only a vast, chaotic marsh, a sea of slime, without limit or horizon, without shore or elevation, that seethed with a blind writhing of amorphous vapors.

There, in the grey beginning of Earth, the formless mass that was Ubbo-Sathla reposed amid the slime and the vapors. Headless, without organs or members, it sloughed from its oozy sides, in a slow, ceaseless wave, the amoebic forms that were the archetypes of earthly life. Horrible it was, if there had been aught to apprehend the horror; and loathsome, if there had been any to feel loathing. About it, prone or tilted in the mire, there lay the mighty tablets of star-quarried stone that were writ with the inconceivable wisdom of the premundane gods.

And there, to the goal of a forgotten search, was drawn the thing that had been — or would sometime be — Paul Tregardis and Zon Mezzamalech. Becoming a shapeless eft of the prime, it crawled sluggishly and obliviously across the fallen tablets of the gods, and fought and ravened blindly with the other spawn of Ubbo-Sathla.

Of Zon Mezzamalech and his vanishing, there is no mention anywhere, save the brief passage in *The Book of Eibon*. Concerning Paul Tregardis, who also disappeared, there was a curt notice in several of the London papers. No one seems to have known anything about him: he is gone as if he had never been; and the crystal, presumably, is gone too. At least, no one has found it.

The Werewolf of Averoigne

1. The Deposition of Brother Gerome

I a poor scrivener and the humblest monk of the Benedictine Abbey of Perigon, have been asked by our abbot Theophile to write down this record of a strange evil that is still rampant, still unquelled. And, ere I have done writing, it may be that the evil shall come forth again from its lurking-place, and again be manifest.

We, the friars of Perignon, and all others who have knowledge of this thing, agree that its advent was coeval with the first rising of the red comet which still burns nightly, a flying balefire, above the moonless hills. Like Satan's rutilant hair, trailing on the wind of Gehenna as he hastens worldward, it rose below the Dragon in early summer; and now it follows the Scorpion toward the western woods. Some say that the horror came from the comet, flying without wings to earth across the stars. And truly, before this summer of 1369, and the lifting of that red, disastrous scourge upon the heavens, there was no rumor or legend of such a thing in all Averoigne.

As for me, I must deem that the beast is a spawn of the seventh hell, a foulness born of the bubbling, flame-blent ooze; for it has no likeness to the beasts of earth, to the creatures of air and water. And the comet may well have been the fiery vehicle of its coming.

To me, for my sins and unworthiness, was it first given to behold the beast. Surely the sight thereof was a warning of those ways which lead to perdition: for on that occasion I had broken the rule of St. Benedict which forbids eating during a one-day's errand away from the monastery. I had tarried late, after bearing a letter from Theophile to the good priest of Ste. Zenobie, though I should have been back well before evensong. And also, apart from eating, I had drunk the mellow white wine of Ste. Zenobie with its kindly people. Doubtless because I had done these things, I met the nameless, night-born terror in the woods behind the abbey when I returned.

The day had vanished, fading unaware; and the long summer even, without moon, had thickened to a still and eldritch darkness ere I approached the abbey postern. And hurrying along the forest path, I felt an eerie fear of the gnarled, hunchback oaks and their pit-deep shadows. And when I saw between their antic boughs the vengefully streaming fire of the new comet, which seemed to pursue me as I went, the goodly warmth of the wine died out and I began to regret my truancy. For I knew that the comet was a harbinger of ill, an omen of death and Satanry to come.

Now, as I passed among the ancient trees that tower thickly, growing toward the postern, I thought that I beheld a light from one of the abbey windows and was much cheered thereby. But, going on, I saw that the light was near at hand, beneath a lowering bough beside my path; and moreover, it moved as with the flitting of a restless fenfire, and was wholly dissimilar to the honest glow of a lamp, lantern or taper. And the light was of changeable color, being pale as a corposant, or ruddy as new-spilled blood, or green as the poisonous distillation that surrounds the moon.

Then, with ineffable terror, I beheld the thing to which the light clung like a hellish nimbus, moving as it moved, and revealing dimly the black abomination of head and limbs that were not those of any creature wrought by God. The horror stood erect, rising to the height of a tall man, and it moved with the swaying of a great serpent, and its members undulated as if they were boneless. The round black head, having no visible ears or hair, was thrust foreward on a neck of snakish length. Two eyes, small and lidless, glowing hotly as coals from a wizard's brazier, were set low and near together in the formless face above the serrate gleaming of bat-like teeth.

This much I saw, and no more, ere the thing went past me with the strange nimbus flaring from venomous green to a wrathful red. Of its actual shape, and the number of its limbs, I could form no just notion. It uttered no sound, and its motion was altogether silent. Running and slithering rapidly, it disappeared in the bough-black night, among the antique oaks; and I saw the hellish light no more.

I was nigh dead with fear when I reached the abbey and sought admittance at the postern. And the porter who came at last to admit me, after I had knocked many times, forbore to chide me for my tardiness when I told him of that which I had seen in the moonless wood.

On the morrow, I was called before Theophile, who rebuked me sternly for my breach of discipline, and imposed a penance of daylong solitude. Being forbidden to hold speech with the others, I did not hear till the second morn of the thing that was found before nones in the wood behind Perigon, where I had met the nameless beast.

The thing was a great stag which had been slain in some ungodly fashion, not by wolf or hunter or poacher. It was unmarked by any wound, other than a wide gash that had laid bare the spine from neck to tail; and the spine itself had been shattered and the white marrow sucked therefrom; but no other portion of the stag had been devoured. None could surmise the nature of the beast that slew and ravened in such a manner; but many, for the first time, began to credit my tale, which the abbot and the brothers had hitherto looked upon as a sort of drunken dream. Verily, they said, a creature from the Pit was abroad, and this creature had killed the stag and had sucked the marrow from its broken spine. And I, aghast with the recollection of that loathly vision, marvelled at the mercy of God, which had permitted me to escape the doom of the stag.

None other, it seemed, had beheld the monster on that occasion; for all the monks, save me, had been asleep in the dormitory; and Theophile had retired early to his cell. But, during the nights that followed the slaying of the stag, the presence of this baleful thing was made manifest to all.

Now, night by night, the comet greatened, burning like an evil mist of blood and fire, while the stars bleached before it and terror shadowed the thoughts of men. And in our prayers, from prime to evensong, we sought to deprecate the unknown ills which the comet would bring in its train. And day by day, from peasants, priests, woodcutters and others who came to visit the abbey, we heard the tale of fearsome and mysterious depredations, similar in all ways to the killing of the stag.

Dead wolves were found with their chines laid open and the spinal marrow gone; and an ox and a horse were treated in like fashion. Then, it would seem, the beast grew bolder — or else it wearied of such humble prey as deer and wolves, horses and oxen.

At first, it did not strike at living men, but assailed the helpless dead like some foul eater of carrion. Two freshly buried corpses were found lying in the cemetery at Ste. Zenobie, where the thing had dug them from their graves and had laid open their vertebrae. In each case, only a little of the marrow had been eaten; but as if in rage or disappointment, the cadavers had been torn into shreds from crown to heel, and the tatters of their flesh were mixed inextricably with the rags of their cerements. From this, it would seem that only the spinal marrow of creatures newly killed was pleasing to the monster.

Thereafter the dead were not molested; but a grievous toll was taken from the living. On the night following the desecration of the graves, two charcoal-burners, who plied their trade in the forest at a distance of no more than a mile from Perigon, were slain foully in their hut. Other charcoal-burners, dwelling nearby, heard the shrill screams that fell to sudden silence; and peering fearfully through the chinks of their bolted doors, they saw anon in the grey starlight the departure of a black, obscenely glowing shape that issued from the hut. Not till dawn did they dare to verify the fate of their hapless fellows, who, they then discovered, had been served in the same manner as the wolves and other victims of the beast.

When the tale of this happening was brought to the abbey, Theophile called me before him and questioned me closely anent the apparition which I had encountered. He, like the others, had doubted me first, deeming that I was frightened by a shadow or by some furtive creature of the wood. But, after the series of atrocious maraudings, it was plain to all that a fiendish thing such as had never been fabled in Averoigne, was abroad and ravening through the summer woods. And moreover it was plain that this thing was the same which I had beheld on the eve of my return from Ste. Zenobie.

Our good abbot was greatly exercised over this evil, which had chosen to manifest itself in the neighborhood of the abbey, and whose depredations were all committed within a five-hours' journey of Perigon. Pale from his over-strict austerities and vigils, with hollow cheeks and burning eyes, Theophile called me before him and made me tell my story over and over, listening as one who flagellates himself for a fancied sin. And though I, like all others, was deeply sensible of this hellish horror and the scandal of its presence, I marvelled somewhat at the godly wrath and indignation of our abbot, in whom blazed a martial ardor against the minions of Asmodai.

"Truly," he said, "there is a great devil among us, that has risen with the comet from Malebolge. We, the monks of Perigon, must go forth with cross and holy water to hunt the devil in its hidden lair, which lies haply at our very portals."

So, on the afternoon of that same day, Theophile, together with myself and six others chosen for their hardihood, sallied forth from the abbey and made search of the mighty forest for miles around, entering with lifted crosses, by torchlight, the deep caves to which we came, but finding no fiercer thing than wolf or badger. Also, we searched the vaults of the ruined castle of Faussesflammes, which is said to be haunted by vampires. But nowhere could we trace the sable monster, or find any sign of its lairing.

Since then, the middle summer has gone by with nightly deeds of terror, beneath the blasting of the comet. Beasts, men, children, women, have been done to death by the monster, which, though seeming to haunt mainly the environs of the abbey, has ranged afield even to the shores of the river Isoil and the gates of La Frênaie and Ximes. And some have beheld the monster at night, a black and slithering foulness clad in changeable luminescence; but no man has ever beheld it by day.

Thrice has the horror been seen in the woods behind the abbey; and once, by full moonlight, a brother peering from his window descried it in the abbey garden, as it glided between the rows of peas and turnips, going toward the forest. And all agree that the thing is silent, uttering no sound, and is swifter in its motion than the weaving viper.

Much have these occurrences preyed on our abbot, who keeps his cell in unremitting prayer and vigil, and comes forth no longer, as was his wont, to dine and hold converse with the guests of the abbey. Pale and meager as a dying saint he grows, and a strange illness devours him as with perpetual fever; and he mortifies the flesh till he totters with weakness. And we others, living in the fear of God, and abhorring the deeds of Satan, can only pray that the unknown scourge be lifted from the land, and pass with the passing of the comet.

[*Soon after the above deposition, Brother Gerome was found dead in his cell. His body was in the same condition, had been served in the same manner, as the other victims of the Beast.*]

2. The Letter of Theophile to Sister Thérèse

. . . To you, my sister in God as well as by consanguinity, I must ease my mind (if this be possible) by writing again of the dread thing that harbors close to Perigon: for this thing has struck once more within the abbey walls, coming in darkness and without sound or other ostent than the Phlegethonian luster that surrounds its body and members.

I have told you of the death of Brother Gerome, slain at evening, in his cell, while he was copying an Alexandrian manuscript. Now the fiend has become even bolder; for last night it entered the dormitory, where the brothers sleep in their robes, girded and ready to rise instantly. And without waking the others, on whom it must have cast a Lethean spell, it took Brother Augustin, slumbering on his pallet at the end of the row. And the fell deed was not discovered till daybreak, when the monk who slept nearest to Augustin awakened and saw his body, which lay face downward with the back of the robe and the flesh beneath a mass of bloody tatters.

On this occasion, the Beast was not beheld by anyone; but at other times, full often, it has been seen around the abbey; and its craftiness and hardihood are beyond belief, except as those of an archdevil. And I know not where the horror will end; for exorcisms and the sprinkling of holy water at all doors and windows have failed to prevent the intrusion of the Beast; and God and Christ and all the holy Saints are deaf to our prayers.

Of the terror laid upon Averoigne by this thing, and the bale and mischief it has wrought outside the abbey, I need not tell, since all this will have come to you as a matter of common report. But here, at Perigon, there is much that I would not have rumored publicly, lest the good fame of the abbey should suffer. I deem it a humiliating thing, and a derogation and pollution of our sanctity, that a foul fiend should have ingress to our halls unhindered and at will.

There are strange whispers among the brothers, who believe that Satan himself has risen to haunt us. Several have met the Beast even in the chapel, where it has left an unspeakably blasphemous sign of its presence. Bolts and locks are vain against it; and vain is the lifted cross to drive it away. It comes and goes at its own choosing; and they who behold it flee in irrestrainable terror. None knows where it will strike next; and there are those among the brothers who believe it menaces me, the elected abbot of Perigon; since many have seen it gliding along the hall outside my cell. And Brother Constantin, the cellarer, who returned late from a visit to Vyones not long ago, swears that he saw it by moonlight as it climbed the wall toward that window of my cell which faces the great forest. And seeing Constantin, the thing dropped to the ground like a huge ape and vanished among the trees.

All, it would seem, save me, have beheld the monster. And now, my sister, I must confess a strange thing, which above all else would attest the influential power of Hell in this matter, and the hovering of the wings of Asmodai about Perigon.

Each night, since the coming of the comet and the Beast, I have retired early to my cell, with the intention of spending the nocturnal hours in vigil and prayer, as I am universally believed to do. And each night a stupor falls upon me as I kneel before Christ on the silver crucifix; and oblivion steeps my senses in its poppy; and I lie without dreams on the cold floor till dawn. Of that which goes on in the abbey I known nothing; and all the brothers might be done to death by the Beast, and their spines broken and such as is its invariable fashion, without my knowledge.

Haircloth have I worn, and thorns and thistle-burrs have I strewn on the floor, to awake me from this evil and ineluctable slumber that is like the working of some Orient drug. But the thorns and thistles are as a couch of paradisical ease, and I feel them not till dawn. And dim and confused are my senses when I awaken; and deep languor thralls my limbs. And day by day a lethal weakness grows upon me, which all ascribe to saintly pernoctations of prayer and austerity.

Surely I have become the victim of a spell, and am holden by a baleful enchantment while the Beast is abroad with its hellish doings. Heaven, in its inscrutable wisdom, punishing me for what sin I know not, has delivered me utterly to this bondage and has thrust me down the sloughs of a Stygian despair.

Ever I am haunted by an eerie notion, that the Beast comes nightly to earth from the red comet which passes like a fiery wain above Averoigne; and by day it returns to the comet, having eaten its fill of that provender for which it seeks. And only with the comet's fading will the horror cease to harry the land and infest Perigon. But I know not if this thought is madness, or a whisper from the Pit.

Pray for me, Thérèse, in my bewitchment and my despair: for God has abandoned me, and the yoke of hell has somehow fallen upon me; and naught can I do to defend the abbey from this evil. And I, in turn, pray that such things may touch you not nor approach you in the quiet cloisters of the convent at Ximes. . . .

3. The Story of Luc le Chaudronnier

Old age, like a moth in some fading arras, will gnaw my memories oversoon, as it gnaws the memories of all me. Therefore I write this record of the true origin and slaying of that creature known as the Beast of Averoigne. And when I have ended the writing, the record shall be sealed in a brazen box, and that box be set in a secret chamber of my house at Ximes, so that no man shall learn the dreadful verity of this matter till many years and decades have gone by. Indeed, it were not well for such evil prodigies to be divulged while any who took part in the happening are still on the earthward side of Purgatory. And at present the truth is known only to me and to certain others who are sworn to maintain secrecy.

The ravages of the Beast, however, are common knowledge, and have become a tale with which to frighten. Men say that it slew fifty people, night by night, in the summer of 1369, devouring in each case the spinal marrow. It ranged mostly about the abbey of Perigon and to Ximes and Ste. Zenobie and La Frênaie. Its nativity and lairing-place were mysteries that none could unravel; and church and state were alike powerless to curb its maraudings, so that a dire terror fell upon the land and people went to and fro as in the shadow of death.

From the very beginning, because of my own commerce with occult things and with the spirits of darkness, the baleful Beast was the subject of my concern. I knew that it was no creature of earth or of the terrene hells, but had come with the flaming comet from ulterior space; but regarding its character and attributes and genesis, I could learn no more at first than any other. Vainly I consulted the stars and made use of geomancy and necromancy; and the familiars whom I interrogated professed themselves ignorant, saying that the Beast was altogether alien and beyond the ken of sublunar devils.

Then I bethought me of the ring of Eibon, which I had inherited from my fathers, who were also wizards. The ring had come down, it was said, from ancient Hyperborea; and it was made of a redder gold than any that the earth yields in latter cycles, and was set with a great purple gem, somber and smouldering, whose like is no longer to be found. And in the gem an antique demon was held captive, a spirit from prehuman worlds and ages, which would answer the interrogation of sorcerers.

So, from a rarely opened casket, I brought out the ring of Eibon and made such preparations as were needful for the questioning of the demon. And when the purple stone was held inverted above a small brazier filled with hotly burning amber, the demon made answer, speaking in a voice that was like the shrill singing of fire. It told me the origin of the Beast, which belonged to a race of stellar devils that had not visited the earth since the foundering of Atlantis; and it told me the attributes of the Beast, which, in its own proper from, was invisible and intangible to men, and could manifest itself only in a fashion supremely abominable. Moreover, it informed me of a method by which the Beast could be banished, if overtaken in a tangible shape. And even to me, the student of darkness and evil, the revelations were a source of horror and surprise.

Musing on these dark matters, I waited among my books and braziers and alembics, for the stars had warned me that my intervention would be required in good time.

Toward the end of August, when the great comet was beginning to decline a little, there occurred the lamentable death of Sister Thérèse, killed by the Beast in her cell at the Benedictine convent of Ximes. On this occasion, the Beast was plainly seen by late passers as it ran down the convent wall by moonlight from a window; and others met it in the shadowy streets or watched it climb the city ramparts, running like a monstrous beetle or spider on the sheer stone as it fled from Ximes to regain its hidden lair.

To me, following the death of Thérèse, there came privily the town marshal, together with a priest from the household of the Bishop of Ximes. And the two, albeit with palpable hesitation, begged my advice and assistance in the laying of the Beast.

"You, Messire le Chaudronnier," they said, "are reputed to know the arcanic arts of sorcery, and the spells that summon or dismiss evil demons and other spirits. Therefore, in dealing with this devil, it may be that you shall succeed where all others have failed. Not willingly do we employ you in the matter, since it is not seemly for the church and the law to ally themselves with wizardry. But the need is desperate, lest the demon should take other victims; and in return for your aid, we can promise you a goodly reward of gold and a guarantee of lifelong immunity from all inquisition and prosecution which your doings might otherwise invite. The Bishop of Ximes, and the

Archbishop of Vyones, are privy to this offer, which must remain secret."

"I ask no reward," I replied, "if it be in my power to rid Averoigne of this scourge. But you have set me a difficult task, and I must prepare myself for the undertaking, in which I shall require certain aid."

"All assistance that we can give you shall be yours to command," they said. "Men-at-arms shall attend you, if need be; and all doors shall be opened at your request. We have consulted Theophile, the abbot of Perigon, and the grief-smitten brother of the lately slain Thérèse, who is most zealous for the laying of the fiend, and will admit you to the abbey. The horror seems to center thereabout, and two of the monks have been done to death, and the abbot himself, it is rumored, has been haunted by the Beast. Therefore, it may be that you will wish to visit Perigon."

I reflected briefly, and said:

"Go now, but send to me, an hour before sunset, two men-at-arms with horses, and a third steed; and let the men be chosen for their valor and discretion: for this very night I shall visit the abbey."

Now, when the priest and the marshal had gone, I spent several hours in making reading for my journey. It was necessary, above all other things, to compound a certain rare powder that had been recommended by the demon in the purple gem; for only by the casting of this powder could the Beast be driven away before its time. The ingredients of the powder were named in the *Book of Eibon*, that manual written by an old Hyperborean wizard, who in his day had dealt with ultra-mundane spirits akin to the demon of the comet; and had also been the owner of the ring.

Having compounded the powder, I stored it in a bag of viper-skin. And soon after I had finished my preparations, the two men-at-arms and the horses came to my house, as had been stipulated.

The men were stout and tested warriors, clad in chain-mail, and carrying spears and swords. I mounted the third horse, a black and spirited mare, and we rode forth from Ximes toward Perigon, taking a direct and little-used way which ran for many miles through the werewolf-haunted forest.

My companions were taciturn, speaking only in brief answer to some question; and this pleased me, for I knew that they would maintain a discreet silence regarding that which might occur before dawn. Swiftly we rode, while the sun sank in a redness as of welling blood among the tall trees; and the darkness wove its thickening webs from bough to bough, closing upon us like some inextricable net of death and evil. Deeper we went, into the brooding woods; and even I, the master of sorceries, trembled a little at the knowledge of all that was abroad in the darkness.

Undelayed and unmolested, however, we came to the abbey at late moonrise, when all the monks, except the aged porter, had retired to their dormitory. The porter, who had received word of our coming, would have admitted us; but this, as it happened, was no part of my plan. Saying I had reason to believe that the Beast would re-enter the abbey that very night, I told the porter my intention of waiting outside the walls to intercept it, and merely asked him to accompany us in a tour of the building's exterior, so that he could point out the various rooms. this he did, and during the course of the tour, he indicated a certain high window in the second story as being that of the abbot Theophile's chamber. The window faced the forest, and I remarked the abbot's rashness in leaving it open. This, the porter told me, was his invariable habit. Behind the window we could see the glimmering of a taper, as if the abbot were keeping late vigil.

We had committed our horses to the porter's care. After he had conducted us around the abbey and had left us, we returned to the space beneath Theophile's window and began our long watch in silence.

Pale and hollow as the face of a corpse, the moon rose higher, swimming above the somber oaks and pines, and pouring a spectral silver on the grey stone of the abbey walls. In the west the comet flared among the lusterless Signs, veiling the lifted sting of the Scorpion as it sank.

We waited hour by hour in the shortening shadow of a high pine, where none could see us from the abbey. When the moon had passed over, falling westward, the shadow began to lengthen toward the wall. All was mortally still, and we saw no movement, apart from the slow changing of the light and shade. Half-way between midnight and dawn, the taper went out in Theophile's cell, as if it had burned to the socket; and thereafter the room remained dark.

Unquestioning, with ready spears, the two men-at-arms campanioned me in that vigil. Well they knew the demonian terror which they might face before down; but there was no trace of trepidation in their bearing. And knowing much that they could not know, I held in my hands for instant use the bag of viper-skin that contained the Hyperborean powder.

The men stood nearer than I to the forest, facing it perpetually according to a strict order that I had given. But nothing stirred in the fretted gloom; and the skies grew paler, as if with morning twilight. Then, an hour before sunrise, when the shadow of the great pine had reached the wall and was climbing toward Theophile's window, there came the thing which I had anticipated. Very suddenly it came, and with no warning of its nearness, a horror of hellish red light, swift as a kindling, windblown flame, that leapt from the forest gloom and sprang upon us where we stood stiff and weary from our night-long vigil.

One of the men-at-arms was borne to the ground, and I saw above him, in a floating redness as of blood, the black and serpentine from of the Beast. A round and snakish head, without ears or nose, was tearing at the man's armor with sharp innumerable teeth, and I heard the teeth grate and clash on the linked iron as I stepped forward and flung the powder of Eibon at the Beast. The second man-at-arms, undaunted, would have assailed it with his spear, but this I forbade.

The floating powder, fine as a dust of mummia, seemed to dim the bloody light as it fell; and the thing seemed to change horribly beneath our gaze, undergoing an incredible metamorphosis. Moment by moment it took on the wavering similitude of man, like a werewolf that returns from his beasthood; and the red light grew dimmer, and the unclean blackness of its flesh appeared to flow and swirl, assuming the weft of cloth, and becoming the folds of a dark robe and coal such as are worn by the Benedictines. Then, from the cowl, a face began to peer, glimmering pale and thin in the shadow; and the thing covered its face with sooty claws that were turning into hands, and shrank away from me as I pressed upon it, sprinkling it with the remainder of the powder.

Now I had driven it against the abbey wall; and there, with a wild, despairing cry that was half-human, half-demonaic, the thing turned from me and clawed frantically at the grey stone as if it would climb toward the abbot's window in that monstrous fashion that had been its wont. Almost, for a breath, it seemed to run upward, hanging to the wall like a bat or a great beetle. But the change had progressed too far, and it dropped back in the shadow of a pine, and tottering strangely as if with sudden mortal weakness, fell to the ground and lay huddled in its monkish garments like a black night-bird with broken vans.

The rays of the gibbous moon, sifting thinly through the boughs, lay cold and cadaverous on the dead face; though the body was immersed in shadow. And the face, even as I had expected, was that of the abbot Theophile, who had once been pointed out to me in Ximes. Already the peace of death was upon him; and horror had left no sign on the shut eyelids and the sealed lips; and there was no mark on the worn and haggard cheeks, other than that which might come from the saintly rigor of prolonged austerities.

The man-at-arms who had been struck down by the Beast was unharmed, though sorely bruised beneath his mail. He and his fellow stood beside me, saying naught; and I knew that they had recognized the dead abbot. So, while the moon grew grey with the nearness of dawn, I made them swear an awful oath of secrecy, and enjoined them to bear faithful witness to the statement I must make before the monks of Perigon.

Then, having settle this matter, so that the good renown of the holy Theophile should rest unharmed, we aroused the porter and acquainted him with the abbot's lamentable death. And we told this story, averring that the Beast had come upon us unaware, and had gained the abbot's cell before we could prevent it, and had come forth again, carrying Theophile with its snakish members as if to bear him away to the sunken comet. Then, by means of a wizard powder, I had routed the unclean Beast, compelling it to relinquish its prey. And the thing had vanished in a cloud of sulphurous fire and vapor; but Theophile had died from the horror of his plight while the Beast was descending the wall. His death, I said, was a true martyrdom, and would not be in vain: the Beast would no longer plague the country or bedevil Perigon, since the use of Hyperborean powder was a sure exorcism.

This tale was accepted by the Brothers, who grieved mightily for their good abbot. Indeed, the tale was true enough in its fashion, for Theophile had been innocent and and was wholly ignorant of the foul change that had come upon him nightly in his cell, and the deeds that were done by the Beast through his loathfully transfigured body. Each night the thing had come from the comet to assuage its hellish hunger; and being otherwise impalpable and powerless, it had use the abbot for its energumen, molding his flesh in the image of some obscene monster from beyond the stars.

After Theophile's death, the Beast was seen no more in Averoigne; and the murderous deeds were not repeated. And in time the comet passed to other heavens, fading slowly; and the black terror it had wrought became a varying legend, even as all other bygone things. And they who read this record in future ages will believe it not, saying that no demon or malign spirit could ever have prevailed upon true holiness. Indeed, it were well that none should believe the story: for strange abominations pass evermore between earth and moon and athwart the galaxies; and the gulf is haunted by that which it were madness for man to know. Unnamable things have come to us in alien horror, and shall come again. And the evil of the stars is not as the evil of earth.

The Eidolon of the Blind

S welling and towering swiftly, like a genie loosed from one
of Solomon's bottles, the cloud rose on the planet's rim. A
rusting and colossal column, it strode above the dead
plain, through a sky that was dark as the brine of desert seas
that have ebbed down to desert pools.

"Looks like a blithering sandstorm," commented Maspic,
pointing with a lean and sun-swart hand.

"It can't very well be anything else," agreed Bellman rather
curtly. "Any other kind of storm is simply unheard-of in these
equatorial regions. It's the sort of hell-twister that the Aihais
call the *zoorth* — and I don't recommend a lungful of that fer-
ruginous dust."

"There's a cave in the old river-bank, to the right," said
Chivers, the third member of the party, whose restless, ever-
darting eyes were accipitrine in their range and keenness.

The trio of earthmen, hard-bitten adventurers who dis-
dained the somewhat undependable services of Martian guides,
had started five days before from the outpost of Ahoom, into
the uninhabited region called the Chaur. Here, in the beds of
great rivers that had not flowed for cycles, it was rumored that
the pale, platinum-like gold of Mars could be found lying in
heaps, like sand or salt. If fortune were propitious, their years
of unwilling alienage on the red planet would soon be at an
end. They had been warned against the Chaur, and had heard

some queer tales in Ahoom regarding the reasons why former prospectors had not returned. But danger, no matter how dire or exotic, was merely a part of their daily routine. With a fair chance of unlimited gold at the journey's end, they would have gone down through Gehenna.

Their food-supplies and water-barrels were carried on the backs of three of those curious mammals called *vortlups*, which, with elongated legs and necks and horny-plated bodies, might seemingly have been some fabulous combination of llama and saurian. These animals, though extravagantly ugly, were tame and obedient, and were well-adapted to desert travel, being able to go without water for months at a time.

For the past two days they had followed the mile-wide course of a nameless ancient river, winding among hills that had dwindled to mere hummocks through aeons of exfoliation. So far, they had found nothing but pebbles and sand, *and rust*. Heretofore the sky had been silent and stirless: the remote sun, the tenuous air, were such as might brood above domains of eternal death; and nothing moved on the river-bottom, whose boulders were bare even of dead lichen. The malignant column of the *zoorth*, twisting and swelling toward them, was the first sign of animation they had discerned in that lifeless land.

Prodding their *vortlups* with the iron-pointed goads which alone could elicit any increase of speed from these sluggish armored monsters, the earthmen started off toward the cavern-mouth descried by Chivers. It was perhaps a third of a mile distant, and was high up in the shelving shore.

The *zoorth*, travelling with dread rapidity, had blotted out the sun ere they reached the bottom of the ancient slope. They moved through a sinister twilight that was colored like dried blood. The *vortlups*, protesting with raucous bellows, began to climb the beach, which was marked off in a series of more or less regular steps, that indicated the slow recession of its olden waters. The whirling column of sand had reached the opposite bank when they came to the cavern.

This cavern was in the face of a low cliff of iron-veined rock that had once rimmed the mighty water-course for some distance. The entrance had crumbled down in heaps of ferric oxide, and was quite narrow, but was high enough to admit the earthmen and their laden beasts of burden. Darkness, heavy as if with an immemorial weaving of black webs, clogged the interior. They could form no idea of the cave's dimensions till Bellman got out an electric torch from his bale of belongings and turned its prying beam into the sooty shadows.

To their surprise, the torch merely served to reveal the threshold of an indeterminate chamber that ran backward into unfathomable night, widening gradually, with a floor that was worn smooth as if by vanished waters.

The cavern opening had grown dark with the onset of the *zoorth*, and particles of sand were blown in upon the explorers, stinging their hands and faces like powdered adamant.

"The storm will last for half an hour, at least," said Bellman. "Shall we go on into the cave? Probably we won't find anything of much interest or value; but the exploration will serve to kill time anyway. And we might happen on a few violet rubies or amber-yellow sapphires, such as are sometimes discovered in these desert caverns. You two had better bring along your torches also, and flash them on the walls and floors as we go."

His companions thought the suggestion worth following. The *vortlups*, wholly insensible to the blowing sand in their scaly mail, were left behind near the entrance. Chivers, Bellman and Maspic, with their torch-beams tearing a clotted gloom that had perhaps never known the intrusion of light in all its former cycles, went on into the widening cave.

The place was bare, with the death-like emptiness of some long-abandoned catacomb. Its rusted floor and walls returned no gleam or sparkle to the playing torches. It sloped downward at an easy gradient; and the sides were water-marked at a height of six or seven feet. No doubt it had been in earlier aeons the channel of an underground offshoot from the mighty river. It had been swept clean of sand, boulders and pebbles, and was like the interior of some cyclopean conduit that might give upon a sub-Martian Erebus.

None of the three adventurers was overly imaginative or prone to nervous fancies. But all were beset by certain unaccountable impressions, vague and persistent, as they went on. Behind the manifold arras of cryptic silence, time and again, they seemed to hear a faint sub-auditory whisper, like the sight of sunken seas far down at some hemispheric depth. The thin air was tinged with a slight and doubtful darkness, and they felt the stirring of an almost imperceptible draft upon their faces, drawing from the unknown gulfs. Oddest of all was the nameless odor, reminding them both of animal-dens and the peculiar smell of Martian dwellings.

"Do you suppose we'll encounter any kind of life?" said Maspic, sniffing the air dubiously.

"Not likely." Bellman dismissed the query with his usual curtness. "Even the wild *vortlups* avoid the Chaur."

"But if there is water somewhere at the bottom of this cave, there may be life," persisted Maspic. "I seem to be smelling all sorts of queer things; and certainly there's a hint of dampness."

"We've got our revolvers," said Bellman. "But I doubt if we'll need them — as long as we don't meet any rival gold-hunters from the earth," he added cynically.

"Listen." The semi-whisper came from Chivers. "Do you fellows hear anything?"

All three had paused. At an indelimitable distance in the gloom ahead, they heard a curious, prolonged, equivocal noise. It seemed to baffle the ear with incongruous elements. It was a sharp rustling as of metal dragged over rock — and also it was somehow like the smacking of myriad mouths. Anon it receded and died out at a level that was seemingly far below, as if it had gone down into a great abyss.

"That's queer." Bellman seemed to make a reluctant admission.

"What is it?" queried Chivers. "One of the millipedal underground monsters, half a mile long, that the Martians tell about? Maybe we'd better go back."

"You've been hearing too many native fairy tales," reproved Bellman. "No terrestrial has ever seen anything of that kind. Many deep-lying caverns on Mars have been thoroughly explore; but those in desert regions, such as the Chaur, were devoid of life. I can't imagine what could have made that noise; but, in the interests of science, I'd like to go on and find out."

"I'm beginning to feel a little creepy," said Maspic. "The Aihais have some wicked stories about the Chaur; and like many other myths, they may well possess a factual foundation. But I'll go on if you others are game."

Without further argument or comment, the three continued their advance into the cave. They had been walking at a fair gait for fifteen minutes, and were now at least half a mile from the entrance. The floor was steepening, as if it had been the bed of a rapid torrent. The conformation of the walls had changed: on either hand there were high shelves of sullen metallic stone and columnated recesses which the flashed rays of the torches could not always fathom.

Bellman was leading the way, with the others close behind. His torch revealed the verge of a precipice, where the olden channel ended shearly and the shelves and walls pitch away on either side into incalculable space. Going to the very edge, he dipped his pencil of light down the abyss, disclosing only the vertical cliff that fell at his feet into darkness with no apparent bottom. The beam also failed to reach the further shore of the gulf, which, for all that Bellman and his companions could tell, might have been many leagues in extent.

Chivers and Maspic also turned their torch-beams into the ebon Tartarus, to be engulfed by its awesome vastitude of shadow and mystery.

"Looks as if we had found the original jumping-off place," observed Chivers. Looking about, he secured a loose lump of stone, the size of a small boulder, but rendered strangely light by the lesser Martian gravity. This fragment he hurled far out into the abysm. The earthman listened attentively for the sound of its fall; but several minutes went by; and there was no echo from the black profound.

Bellman started to examine the broken-off ledges on either side of the channel's terminus. To the right he discerned a downward-sloping shelf that skirted the abyss, running for an uncertain distance. Its beginning was little higher than the channel-bottom, and was readily accessible by means of two stair-like ledges. The shelf was two yards wide; and its gentle inclination, its remarkable evenness and regularity of surface conveyed the idea of an ancient road hewn in the face of the underworld cliff. It was overhung by the wall, as if by the sharply sundered half of a high arcade.

"There's our road to Hades," said Bellman. "And the down-grade is easy enough at that."

"*Facilis descensus Averno*,'" agreed Maspic. "But what's the use of going further? I, for one, have had enough darkness already. And if we were to find anything by going on, it would be valueless — or unpleasant."

Bellman hesitated. "Probably you're right. But I'd like to follow that ledge far enough to get some idea of the magnitude of the gulf. You and Chivers can wait here, if you're afraid."

Chivers and Maspic, apparently, were unwilling to avow whatever trepidation they may have felt. They followed Bellman along the shelf, hugging the inner wall as closely as its curvature would permit. Bellman, however, strode carelessly on the verge of the unknown abyss, often flashing his torch into the impenetrable darkness below.

More and more, through its uniform breadth, inclination and smoothness, and the demi-arch of cliff above, the shelf impressed the earthman as being an artificial road. But who could have made and used it? In what forgotten ages and for what enigmatic purpose had it been designed? The imagination of the terrestrials failed before the stupendous gulfs of Martian antiquity that yawned in such tenebrous queries.

Bellman thought that the wall curved inward by almost imperceptible degrees. No doubt they would round the entire abyss in time by following the road. Perhaps it wound in a slow, tremendous spiral, ever downward, about and about, to the very bowels of Mars.

He and the others were awed into lengthening intervals of silence by the very vastitude of this Erebus walled and vaulted and floored with night. They were horribly startled when they heard in the depths beneath the same peculiar long-drawn sound or combination of sounds that they had heard in the outer cavern. It suggested other images now: the rustling at times was a file-like scraping; the soft, methodical, myriad smacking was vaguely similar to the sucking noise made by some enormous creature that with-draws its feet from a quagmire.

The sound was inexplicable, terrifying. Part of its terror lay in an implication of *remoteness*, which appeared to signalize the enormity of its cause and to emphasize the unthinkable pro-fundity of the abysm. Heard in that planetary pit beneath a lifeless desert, it astonished — and shocked. Even Bellman, intrepid heretofore, began to succumb to the formless horror that rose up from the infinite blackness.

The sound grew fainter and ceased at length, giving some-how the monstrous idea that its maker had gone directly down on the perpendicular wall into nether reaches of the gulf.

"Shall we go back?" inquired Chivers.

"We might as well," assented Bellman without demur. "It would take all eternity to explore this place, anyhow."

They started to retrace their way along the ledge. All three, with that extra-tactile sense which warns of the approach of hidden danger, were now troubled by insidious intuitions.

Though the gulf had grown silent with that withdrawal of the strange noise to lower depths, they somehow felt that they were not alone. Whence the peril would come, or in what shape, they could not surmise; but a black panic assailed them on the endless, narrow ledge.

Maspic was a little ahead of the others. They had covered fully half the distance to the old cavern-channel, when his torch, playing for a dozen feet on the smooth path, illumined an array of whitish figures, four abreast, that blocked the way. The torches of Bellman and Chivers, coming close behind, brought out with hideous clearness the vanward limbs and faces of the throng, but could not determine its number.

The creatures, who stood perfectly motionless as if awaiting the earthmen, were generically similar to the Aihais or Martian natives. They seemed, however, to represent a degraded and aberrant type; and the fungus-like pallor of their bodies denoted many ages of underground life. They were smaller, too, than the Aihais, being perhaps five feet in height. They possessed the enormous flat nostrils, the flaring ears, the barrel chests and lanky limbs of the Martians — but all of them were eyeless. In the faces of some, there were faint, rudimentary slits where the eyes should have been; in the faces of others, there were deep and empty orbits that suggested a removal of the eyeballs.

"Lord! What a ghastly crew!" cried Maspic. "Where do they come from? And what do they want?"

"Can't imagine," said Bellman. "But our situation is somewhat ticklish — unless they are friendly. They must have been hiding on the shelves in the cavern above, when we entered."

Stepping boldly forward beside Maspic, he began to address the creatures in the guttural Aihai tongue, many of whose vocables are virtually beyond the utterance of an earthman. Some of the people stirred uneasily, and emitted harsh, cheeping sounds that bore little likeness to the Martian language. It was plain that they could not understand Bellman.

Sign-language, by reason of their blindness, would have been equally useless.

Bellman drew his revolver, enjoining the others to follow suit. "We've got to get through them somehow," he said. "And if they won't let us pass without interference —" The click of a cocked hammer served to finish the sentence.

As if the sound had been an awaited signal, the press of blind white beings sprang into sudden motion and surged forward upon the terrestrials. It was like the onset of an army of automatons, an irresistible striding of live machines, concerted and methodical, beneath the direction of a hidden power.

Bellman pulled his trigger, once, twice, thrice, at a point-blank range. It was impossible to miss; but the heavy bullets were futile as pebbles flung at the spate of an onrushing torrent. With a diabolical sureness, the foremost of the eyeless beings caught Bellman's lifted arm with long, three-jointed fingers and took the revolver from his grasp before he could press the trigger again. The creature did not try to deprive him of his electric torch, which he now carried in his left hand; and he saw the steely flash of the Colt as it hurtled down into darkness and space. Then the fungus-white bodies were all about him; and Maspic and Chivers, without have fired a single shot, were also deprived of their weapons; but, strangely enough, as it seemed, were permitted to retain their flashlights.

There was almost no slackening of the onward motion of the throng. Its foremost ranks, opening deftly on the narrow road, had included the earthmen and had forced them to turn backward. Tightly caught in the surge of nightmare bodies, they were borne resistlessly along. Handicapped by the fear of dropping their torches, they could do nothing against the ghastly torrent. Rushing with dreadful strides on a path that led over downward into the nighted gulf, and able to see only the lit backs and members of the creatures close before them, they became a part of that eyeless and cryptic army. It seemed that they moved no longer with human steps, but with the swift and automatic stalking of the clammy *things* that pressed about them. Thought, volition — even terror, were numbed by the unearthly rhythm of those abyss-ward beating feet.

Except for their torches, the night was absolute, unchangeable. It was older than the sun, it had brooded there through all past aeons in horror sightless and inviolate. It accumulated above them like a monstrous burden; it yawned with frightful profundities beneath. From it, the strengthening stench of stagnant waters rose. But there was no sound, other than the soft and measured thud of marching feet that descended into a bottomless Abaddon.

Somewhere, as if after the lapse of nocturnal ages, the pit-ward rushing had ceased. Bellman, Maspic and Chivers felt the pressure of crowded bodies relax; felt that they were standing still, while their brains continued to beat the unhuman measure of that terrifical descent.

Reason — and horror — returned to them slowly.

"My God! where are we?" said Bellman. He lifted his flashlight, and the circling ray recovered the throng of eyeless Martians, many of whom were dispersing in a huge and columned cavern where the gulf-skirting road had terminated. Six or seven of the beings remained, however, as if to keep guard over the earthmen. Close at hand, on the right, the level floor ended abruptly; and stepping to the verge, Bellman saw that the cavern was an open chamber hewn in the perpendicular wall of the abyss. Far, far below in the blackness, a phosphorescent glimmer played to and fro, like *noctilucae* on an underworld ocean. A slow, fetid wind blew upon him from the depths, and he heard the weird sighing of waters about the sunken cliffs: waters that had ebbed through untold cycles, during the planet's desiccation.

Bellman turned giddily from the verge. His companions, impelled by a fearful curiosity, were inspecting the cavern. The torch-beams, darting here and there, brought out the enormous, irregular columniations lined with deeply graven bas-reliefs that shocked the eye like a violent blow, conveying an ultra-human evil, a bottomless cosmic malignity, in the passing moment of disclosure.

The cavern was of stupendous extent, running far back in the cliff. There were numerous exits, giving no doubt on a warren of ramifications: the dwellings of the eyeless troglodytes that had captured Bellman and his fellows. The flashlights plunged amid the flapping shadows of shelved recession; caught the obscenely carven salients of far walls that climbed and beetled into inaccessible gloom; played on the blind creatures that went back and forth like monstrous, living fungi; gave to a brief visual existence the pale and polyp-like plants that clung noisomely to the nighted stone.

The place was overpowering. Beyond its revealed horrors, the earthmen felt a malign Presence; a power that benumbed and stupefied; a baleful somnolence, diffused eternally from a source that light could never reach. It seemed to draw them on amide the obscene columns, into the cavern, like men who drift down into sleep.

Step by step, with their guards following closely, they obeyed the summons. The cave deepened before them with undreamt-of vistas; the people gathered about them on every hand, moving in a weird and leprous procession. The evil, somnific magnetism grew heavier upon them — and then they came to the core of the horror.

Between the thick and seemingly topless pillars, the floor ascended in an altar of seven oblique and pyramidal tiers. On the top, there squatted an image of pale metal: a thing no larger than a hare, but monstrous beyond all imagining.

The Martians crowded about the earthmen. One of them took Bellman by the arm, as if urging him to climb the altar. With the slow steps of a dreamer, he mounted the sloping tiers, and Chivers and Maspic followed.

The image resembled nothing they had ever seen on the red planet. It was carved of whitish gold, and seemed to represent a humped animal or giant insect with a smooth and overhanging carapace from beneath which its head and members issued in tortoise fashion. The head was venomously flat, triangular — and eyeless. From the drooping corners of the slitted mouth, two long proboscides curved upward, hollow and cup-like at the ends. The thing was furnished with a series of short legs, issuing at uniform intervals from the carapace; and a curious double tail was coiled and braided beneath its crouching body. The feet were round, and had the shape of small, inverted goblets.

Unclean and bestial as a figment of some atavistic madness, the eidolon seemed to drowse on the altar. It troubled the mind with a horror past conception; it assailed the senses with a stupor as of primal night.

Dimly the earthmen saw that the altar swarmed with the blind Martians, who were crowding past them about the image. As if in some fantastic ritual of touch, these creatures were fondling the eidolon with their lank fingers, were tracing its loathsome outlines. Upon their brutal faces a narcotic ecstasy was imprinted. Compelled like sleepers in some abhorrent dream, Bellman, Chivers and Maspic followed their example.

The thing was cold and clammy to the touch. But it seemed to live and throb and swell under their fingertips. From it, in heavy, ceaseless waves, a dark vibration surged: an opiate power that clouded the eyes; that poured its baleful slumber into the blood.

With senses that swam in a strange darkness, the earthmen felt the pressure of thronging bodies that displaced them at the altar-summit. Others, recoiling as if satiate with the drug-like emanation, bore them along the oblique tiers to the cavern-floor. Still retaining their torches in nerveless fingers, they saw through a blackening blur the people that seethed up and down on the pyramid like a leprous, living frieze.

Chivers and Maspic, yielding first to the influence, slid to the floor in utter sopor. But Bellman, more resistant, seemed to

fall and drift through a world of lightless dreams. His sensations were anomalous, unfamiliar, confused to the last degree.
Everywhere there was a brooding, somnolent, palpable Power
for which he could find no visual image. In those dreams, he
somehow identified himself with the eyeless people; he moved
and lived as they in profound caverns, on nighted roads. And
yet he was something else — an Entity without name that
ruled over the blind and was worshipped by them; a thing that
dwelt in the nether deep, in the ancient putrescent waters, and
came forth at whiles to recover unspeakably. In that duality of
being, he sated himself at blind feasts — and was also
devoured. With all this, like a third element of identity, the pale
eidolon was associated — but only in a tactile sense, and not as
an optic memory. There was no light anywhere — and not even
the recollection of light.

Whether he passed from these obscure nightmares into
dreamless slumber, he could not know. His awakening, dark
and lethargic, was like a continuation of the dreams at first.
Then, opening his weighted lids, he saw the shaft of light that
lay on the stone from his fallen torch. The light poured against
something that he could not recognize in his drugged awareness. Yet it troubled him — and a dawning horror touched his
faculties into life.

By degrees, it came to him that the thing he saw was the
half-eaten body of one of the eyeless troglodytes. Some of the
members were missing; and the remainder was gnawed even to
the curiously articulated bones.

Bellman rose unsteadily and looked about with eyes that
still held a nebulous blurring of shadow. Close beside him his
companions lay in sodden stupor; and along the cavern and
upon the seven-tiered altar the devotees of the somnific image
were sprawled in monstrous attitudes.

His other senses began to awake from their lethargy, and he
thought that he heard a sound that was somehow familiar: a
sharp slithering, together with a measured sucking. The noise

withdrew among the massy pillars, beyond the sleeping bodies. A smell as of rotten water ringed the air; and he saw that there were many curious rings of wetness on the stone, such as might be made by the rims of inverted cups. They led away from the half-devoured Martian, into the darkness of that outer cover with verged upon the abyss: the direction in which the queer noise had passed, sinking now to inaudibility.

In Bellman's mind a mad terror rose and struggled with the spell that still benumbed him. He stooped down above Maspic and Chivers and shook them roughly in turn, till they opened their eyes and began to protest with drowsy mutters.

"Get up," he admonished them. "If we're ever to escape from this hell-hole, now's the time."

By dint of many oaths and objurgations and much muscular effort, he succeeded in dragging his companions to their feet. Lurching drunkenly, they followed him among the sprawled Martians, away from the pyramid on which the eidolon of white gold still brooded in malign somnolence above its worshippers.

"I wouldn't touch that thing again," said Bellman, "not if it were the only gold in the universe."

A clouding heaviness hung upon his brain and sense; but he felt a revival of volition and a strong desire to escape from the gulf and from all that dwelt in its darkness. Maspic and Chivers, more deeply enslaved by the drowsy power, accepted his leadership and guidance in a numb, mechanical fashion.

Bellman felt sure that he could retrace the route by which they had approached the altar. This, it seemed, was also the course that had been taken by the maker of the ring-like marks of fetid wetness. Wandering on amid the repugnantly carven columns for what seemed an enormous distance, the earthmen came at last to the sheer verge: that portico of the black Tartarus, from which they could look down on its ultimate gulf. Far beneath, on those putrefying waters, the phosphorescence ran in widening circles. To the very edge, at their feet, the watery rings were imprinted on the rock.

They turned away. Bellman, shuddering with half-memories of his blind dreams, found at the cavern's outer corner the beginning of that upward road which skirted the abyss: the road that would take them back to the lost sun.

At his injunction, Maspic and Chivers turned off their flashlights to conserve the batteries. It was doubtful how much longer these would last — and light was their prime necessity. His own torch would serve for the three until it became exhausted.

There was no sound or stirring of life from that cavern of lightless sleep and sightless horror where the Martians lay about the narcotizing image. But a fear such as he had never felt in all his adventurings cause Bellman to sicken and turn faint as he listened at its threshold and flashed his light for the last time on the unclean columns and the fouler shadows beyond.

The gulf, too, was silent; and the ripples of phosphor had ceased to widen on the sable waters. Yet somehow the silence was a thing that clogged the senses, retarded the limbs. Laden with sleep and stupor, it rose up around Bellman like the clutching slime of some nethermost pit, in which he must drown. With dragging effort, he began the ascent of the black road, hauling, kicking and cursing his half-stupefied companions till they responded like drowsy animals.

It was a climb through Limbo, a nightmare ascent from nadir through darkness that seemed palpable — and viscid. On and up forever they toiled, along the slow, monotonous, imperceptibly winding grade where all human measure of distance was lost, and time was meted only by the repetition of eternal steps. The night lowered before Bellman's feeble shaft of light; it closed behind like an all-engulfing sea, relentless and patient; biding its time till the torch should go out.

Looking over the verge at long intervals as they climbed, Bellman saw the gradual fading of the phosphorescence in the depths. Fantastic images rose in his mind: it was like the drowning of nebulae in some void beneath the universe; and he felt the giddiness of one who looks down upon infinite space. Anon, there was only blackness; and his brain swam with awful vertigo.

The minor urges of hunger, thirst, fatigue, had been trod under by the fear that impelled him. From Maspic and Chivers, very slowly, the clogging stupor lifted; and they too were sensible of an adumbration of terror vast as the night itself. Bellman, at first, had played the role of a slave-driver in urging them on; but now his blows and kicks and objurations were no longer needed.

Evil, somnolent, ancient, soporous, the night hung about them. It was like the thick and fetid fur of innumerable bats: a material thing that seemed to choke the lungs, to deaden all the senses. It was silent as the slumber of dead worlds. . . . But out of that silence, after the lapse of apparent years, a peculiar sound, of twofold nature, arose and overtook the fugitives: the sound of something that slithered over stone far down in the abyss; the sucking noise of a creature that withdrew its feet as if from an oozy quagmire. Inexplicable, and arousing mad, incongruous ideas, like a sound heard in delirium, it quickened the earthmen's terror into sudden frenzy.

"God! what is it?" breathed Bellman. He seemed to remember sightless things, abhorrent, palpable shapes of primal night, that were no part of human recollection. His dreams, and his dream-like experience in the cave — the white eidolon — the half-eaten troglodyte of the nether cliffs — the rings of wetness on the stone, leading toward the gulf — all returned like a teeming madness to assail him on that terrible road midway between the putrescent underworld and the surface of Mars.

His question was answered only by a continuation of the twofold noise. It seemed to grow louder — to ascend the wall beneath. Maspic and Chivers, snapping on their lights, began to run with frantic leaps along the perilous path; and Bellman, losing his last semblance of control, followed suit.

It was a race with unknown horror, a flight from some anonymous fear that thickened the blood. Above the labored beating of their hearts, the thudding of their feet, the men still heard that sinister, unaccountable sound. They seemed to race on through leagues of blackness; and yet the noise drew steadily nearer, climbing below them, as if its maker were a thing that walked on the sheer cliff.

Now the sound was appallingly close — and a little ahead. It ceased abruptly. The running lights of Maspic and Chivers, who moved abreast, discovered the crouching horror that filled the two-yard shelf from side to side.

Hardened adventurers though they were, the man would have shrieked with hysteria, or would have hurled themselves headlong from the precipice, if the sight had not thrown them into a sort of catalepsy. It was as if the pale idol of the pyramid, swollen to mammoth proportions, and loathsomely *alive*, had come up from the abyss and was squatting before them!

In every detail, the monstrosity was identical. The humped, enormous carapace, vaguely resembling that of the glyptodon, shone with a luster as of white gold. The white, eyeless had, alert and yet somnolent, was thrust forward on an arching neck. A dozen or more short legs, with goblet-shapen feet, protruded slantwise beneath the overhanging shell. The two proboscides, yard-long, with cupped ends, arose from the corners of the cruelly slitted mouth and waved slowly in air toward the earthmen.

An evil stupor, such as they had felt before the eidolon, bedrugged their faculties. They stood with their flashlights playing full on the Terror; and they could not move nor cry out when it reared suddenly erect, looming above them, and revealing its ridged belly and the queer double tail that slithered and rustled metallically on the stone as it moved. Its numerous feet, beheld in this posture, were hollow and chalice-like; and they oozed with mephitic wetness. No doubt they served for suction cups, enabling it to walk on a perpendicular surface.

Inconceivably swift and sure in its motions, with short strides on its hindmost members, levered by the tail, the monster came forward upon the dazed and helpless men. Unerringly, the proboscides curved over, and their cupped ends came down on Chivers' eyes. They rested there, covering the entire sockets, for a moment only. Then there was a wild, agonizing scream, as the hollow tips were withdrawn with a sweeping movement lithe and powerful as the lashing of serpents.

Chivers swayed slowly, nodding his head, and twisting about in half-narcotized pain. Maspic, standing at his side, saw in a dull and dream-like manner the gaping orbits from which the eyes were gone. It was the last thing that he ever saw. At that instant the monster turned from Chivers, and the terrible cups, dripping with blood and fetor, descended on Maspic's own eyes. . . .

Bellman, who had paused close behind the others, comprehended what was occurring like one who witnesses the abominations of a nightmare, but is powerless to intervene or flee. He saw the movements of the cupped members, he heard the single atrocious cry that was wrung from Chivers, and the swiftly ensuing scream of Maspic. Then, above the heads of his fellows, who still held their useless torches in tautened fingers, the proboscides came toward him. . . .

With blood rilling heavily on their blinded faces, with the somnolent, vigilant, implacable and eyeless Shape at their heels, herding them on, restraining them when they staggered at the brink, the three began their second descent of the road that went down forever to a night-bound Avernus.

Vulthoom

T o a cursory observer, it might have seemed that Bob Haines and Paul Septimus Chanler had little enough in common, other than the predicament of being stranded without funds on an alien world.

Haines, the third assistant pilot of an ether-liner, had been charged with insubordination by his superiors, and had been left behind in Ignarh, the commercial metropolis of Mars, and the port of all space-traffic. The charge against him was wholly a matter of personal spite; but so far, Haines had not succeeded in finding a new berth; and the month's salary paid to him at parting had been devoured with appalling swiftness by the piratic rates of the Tellurian Hotel.

Chanler, a professional writer of interplanetary fiction, had made a voyage to Mars to fortify his imaginative talent by a solid groundwork of observation and experience. His money had given out after a few weeks; the fresh supplies, expected from his publisher, had not yet arrived.

The two men, apart from their misfortunes, shared an illimitable curiosity concerning all things Martian. Their thirst for the exotic, their proclivity for wandering into places usually avoided by terrestrials, had drawn them together in spite of obvious differences of temperament, and had made them fast friends.

Trying to forget their worries, they had spent the past day in the queerly piled and huddled maze of old Ignarh, called by the Martians Ignar-Vath, on the eastern side of the great Yahan Canal. Returning at the sunset hour, and following the estrade of purple marble beside the water, they had nearly reached the mile-long bridge that would take them back to the modern city, Ignar-Luth, in which were the terrestrial consulates and shipping-offices and hotels.

It was the Martian hour of worship, when the Aihais gather in their roofless temples to implore the return of the passing sun. Like the throbbing of feverish metal pulses, a sound of ceaseless and innumerable gongs punctured the thin air. The incredibly crooked streets were almost empty; and only a few barges, immense rhomboidal sails of mauve and scarlet, crawled to and fro on the somber green waters.

The light waned with visible swiftness behind the top-heavy towers and pagoda-angled pyramids of Ignar-Luth. The chin of the coming night began to pervade the shadows of the huge solar gnomons that lined the canal at frequent intervals. The querulous clangours of the gongs died suddenly in Ignar-Vath, and left a weirdly whispering silence. The buildings of the immemorial city bulked enormous upon a sky of blackish emerald that was already thronged with icy stars.

A medley of untraceable exotic odors was wafted through the twilight. The perfume was redolent of alien mystery, and it thrilled and troubled the Earthmen, who became silent as they approached the bridge, feeling the oppression of eerie strangeness that gathered from all sides in the thickening gloom. More deeply than in daylight, they apprehended the muffled breathings and hidden, tortuous movement of a life forever inscrutable to the children of other planets. The void between Earth and Mars had been traversed; but who could cross the evolutionary gulf between Earthman and Martian?

The people were friendly enough in their taciturn way: they had tolerated the intrusion of terrestrials, had permitted commerce between the worlds. Their languages had been mastered, their history studied, by terrene savants. But it seemed that there could be no real interchange of ideas. Their civilization had grown old in diverse complexity before the foundering of Lemuria; its sciences, arts, religions, were hoary with inconceivable age; and even the simplest customs were the fruit of alien forces and conditions.

At that moment, faced with the precariousness of their situation, Haines and Chanler felt an actual terror of the unknown world that surrounded them with its measureless antiquity.

They quickened their paces. The wide pavement that bordered the canal was seemingly deserted; and the light, railless bridge itself was guarded only by the ten colossal statues of Martian heroes that loomed in war-like attitudes before the beginning of the first aerial span.

The Earthmen were somewhat startled when a living figure, little less gigantic than the carven images, detached itself from their deepening shadows and came forward with mighty strides.

The figure, nearly ten feet in height, was taller by a full yard than the average Aihai, but presented the familiar conformation of massively bulging chest and bony, many-angled limbs. The head was featured with high-flaring ears and pit-like nostrils that narrowed and expanded visibly in the twilight. The eyes were sunken in profound orbits, and were wholly invisible, save for tiny reddish sparks that appeared to burn suspended in the sockets of a skull. According to native customs, this bizarre personage was altogether nude; but a kind of circlet around the neck — a flat wire of curiously beaten silver — indicated that he was the servant of some noble lord.

Haines and Chanler were astounded, for they had never before seen a Martian of such prodigious stature. The apparition, it was plain, desired to intercept them. He paused before them on the pavement of seamless marble. They were even more amazed by the weirdly booming voice, reverberant as that of some enormous frog, with which he began to address. In spite of the interminably gutteral tones, the heavy slurring of certain vowels and consonants, they realized that the words were those of human language.

"My master summons you," bellowed the colossus. "Your plight is known to him. He will help you liberally, in return for a certain assistance which you can render him. Come with me."

"This sounds peremptory," murmured Haines. "Shall we go? Probably it's some charitable Aihai prince, who has gotten wind of our reduced circumstances. Wonder what the game is?"

"I suggest that we follow the guide," said Chanler, eagerly. "His proposition sounds like the first chapter of a thriller."

"All right," said Haines, to the towering giant. "Lead us to your master."

With strides that were moderated to match those of the Earthmen, the colossus led them away from the hero-guarded and into the greenish-purple gloom that had inundated Ignar-Vath. Beyond the pavement, an alley yawned like a high-mouthed cavern between lightless mansions and warehouses whose broad balconies and jutting roofs were almost contermi-nous in midair. The alley was deserted; and the Aihai moved like an overgrown shadow through the dusk and paused shadow-like in a deep and lofty doorway. Halting at his heels, Chanler and Haines were aware of a shrill metallic stridor, made by the opening of the door, which, like all Martian doors, was drawn upwards in the manner of a medieval portcullis. Their guide was silhouetted on the saffron light that poured from bosses of radio-active mineral set in the walls and roof of a circular ante-chamber. He preceded them, according to cus-tom; and following, they saw that the room was unoccupied. The door descended behind them without apparent agency or manipulation.

To Chanler, gazing about the windowless chamber, there came the indefinable alarm that is sometimes felt in a closed space. Under the circumstances, there seemed to be no reason to apprehend danger or treachery; but all at once he was filled with a wild longing to escape.

Haines, on his part, was wondering rather perplexedly why the inner door was closed and why the master of the house had not already appeared to receive them. Somehow, the house impressed him as being uninhabited; there was something empty and desolated in the silence that surrounded them.

The Aihai, standing in the centre of the bare, unfurnished room, had faced about as if to address the Earthmen. His eyes glowered inscrutably from their deep orbits; his mouth opened showing double rows of snaggy teeth. But no sound appeared to issue from his moving lips; and the notes that he emitted must have belonged to that scale of overtones, beyond human audition, of which the Martian voice is capable. No doubt the mechanism of the door had been actuated by similar overtones; and now, as seamless metal, began to descend slowly, as if dropping into a great pit. Haines and Chanler, startled, saw the saffron lights receding above them. They, together with the giant, were going down into the shadow and darkness, in a broad circular shaft. There was a ceaseless grating and shrieking of metal, setting their teeth on edge with its insupportable pitch.

Like a narrowing cluster of yellow stars, the lights grew grim and small above them. Still their descent continued; and they could no longer discern each other's faces, or the face of the Aihai, in the ebon blackness through which they fell. Haines and Chanler were beset with a thousand doubts and suspicions, and they began to wonder if they had been somewhat rash in accepting the Aihai's invitation.

"Where are you taking us?" said Haines bluntly. "Does your master live underground?"

"We go to my master," replied the Martian with cryptic finality. "He awaits you."

The cluster of lights had become a single star, had dwindled and faded as if in the night of infinity. There was a sense of irredeemable depth, as if they had gone down to the very core of that alien world. The strangeness of their situation filled the Earthmen with increasing disquiet. They had committed themselves to a clueless mystery that began to savour of menace and peril. Nothing was to be learned from their conductor. No retreat was possible — and they were both weaponless.

The strident shrieking of metal slowed and sank to a sullen whine. The Earthmen were dazzled by the ruddy brilliance that broke upon them through a circle of slender pillars that had replaced the walls of the shaft. An instant more, while they went down through the flooding light, and then the floor beneath them became stationary. They saw that it was now part of the floor of a great cavern lit by crimson hemispheres embedded in the roof. The cavern was circular, with passages that ramified from it in every direction, like the spokes of a wheel from the hub. Many Martians, no less gigantic than the guide, were passing swiftly to and fro, as if intent on enigmatic errands. The strange, muted clangours and thunder-like rumblings of hidden machinery throbbed in the air, vibrated in the shaken floor.

"What do you suppose we've gotten into?" murmured Chanler. "We must be many miles below the surface. I've never heard of anything like this, except in some of the old Aihai myths. This place might be Ravormos, the Martian underworld, where Vulthoom, the evil god, is supposed to lie asleep for a thousand years amid his worshippers."

The guide overheard him. "You have come to Ravormos," he boomed portentously. "Vulthoom is awake, and will not sleep again for another thousand years. It is he that has summoned you; and I take you now to the chamber of audience."

Haines and Chanler, dumbfounded beyond measure, followed the Martian from the strange elevator towards one of the ramifying passages.

"There must be some sort of foolery on foot," muttered Haines. "I've heard of Vulthoom, too, but he's a mere superstition, like Satan. The up-to-date Martians don't believe in him nowadays; though I have heard that there is still a sort of devil-cult among the pariahs and low-castes. I'll wager that some noble is trying to stage a revolution against the reigning emperor, Cykor, and has established his quarters underground."

That sounds reasonable," Chanler agreed. "A revolutionist might call himself Vulthoom: the trick would be true to the Aihai psychology. They have a taste for high-sounding metaphors and fantastic titles."

Both became silent, feeling a sort of awe before the vastness of the cavern-world whose litten corridors reached away on every hand. The surmises they had voiced began to appear inadequate: the improbable was verified, the fabulous had become the factual, and was engulfing them more and more. The far, mysterious clangours, it seemed, were of preternormal origin; the hurrying giants who passed athwart the chamber with unknown burdens conveyed a sense of supernatural activity and enterprise. Haines and Chanler were both tall and stalwart, but the Martians about them were all nine or ten feet in height. Some were closer to eleven feet, and all were muscled in proportion. Their faces bore a look of immense, mummy-like age, incongruous with their agility and vigor.

Haines and Chanler were led along a corridor from whose arched roof the red hemispheres, doubtless formed of artificially radio-active metal, glared down at intervals like imprisoned suns. Leaping from step to step, they descended a flight of giant stairs, with the Martian striding easily before them. He paused at the open portals of a chamber hews in the dark and basic adamantine stone.

"Enter," he said, and withdrew his bulk to let them pass.

The chamber was small but lofty, its roof rising like the interior of a spire. Its floor and walls were stained by the bloody violet beams of a single hemisphere far up in the narrowing dome. The place was vacant, and furnished only with a curious tripod of black metal, fixed in the centre of the floor. The tripod bore an oval block of crystal, and from this block, as if from a frozen pool, a frozen flower lifted, opening petals of smooth, heavy ivory that received a rosy tinge from the strange light. Block, flower, tripod it seemed were the parts of a piece of sculpture.

Crossing the threshold, the Earthmen became instantly aware that the throbbing thunders and cave-reverberant clangours had ebbed away in profound silence. It was as if they had entered a sanctuary from which all sound was excluded by a mystic barrier. The portals remained open behind them. Their guide, apparently, had withdrawn. But, somehow, they felt that they were not alone, and it seemed that hidden eyes were peering upon them from the blank walls.

Perturbed and puzzled, they stared at the pale flower, noting the seven tongue-like petals that curled softly outwards from a perforated heart like a small censer. Chanler began to wonder if it were really a carving, or an actual flower that had been mineralized through Martian chemistry. Then, startlingly, a voice appeared to issue from the blossom; a voice incredibly sweet, clear and sonorous, whose tones, perfectly articulate, were neither those of Aihai nor Earthman.

"I, who speak, am the entity known as Vulthoom," said the voice. "Be not surprised, or frightened: it is my desire to befriend you in return for a consideration which, I hope, you will not find impossible. First of all, however, I must explain certain matters that perplex you.

"No doubt you have heard the popular legends concerning me, and have dismissed them as mere superstitious. Like all myths, they are partly true and partly false. I am neither god nor demon, but a being who came to Mars from another universe in former cycles. Though I am not immortal, my span of life is far longer than that of any creature evolved by the worlds of your solar system. I am governed by alien biological laws, with periods of alternate slumber and wakefulness that involve centuries. It is virtually true, as the Aihais believe, that I sleep for a thousand years and remain conscious continually for another thousand.

"At a time when your ancestors were still the blood-bothers of the ape, I fled from my own world to this intercosmic exile, banished by implacable foes. The Martians say that I fell from heaven like a fiery meteor; and the myth interprets the descent of my ether-ship. I found a matured civilization, immensely inferior, however, to that from which I came.

"The kings and hierarchs of the planet would have driven me away; but I gathered a few adherents, arming them with weapons superior to those of Martian science; and after a great war, I established myself firmly and gained my adherents. On these, for their faithfulness, I conferred a longevity that is almost equal to my own. To ensure this longevity, I have also given them the gift of a slumber corresponding to mine. They sleep and wake with me.

"We have maintained this order of existence for many ages. Seldom have I meddled in the doings of the surface-dwellers. They, however, have converted me into an evil god or spirit; though evil, to me, is a word without meaning.

"I am the possessor of many senses and faculties unknown to you or to the Martians. My perceptions, at will, can be extended over large areas of space, or even time. Thus I learned your predicament; and I have called you here with the hope of obtaining your consent to a certain plan. To be brief, I have grown weary of Mars, a senile world that draws near to death; and I wish to establish myself in a younger planet. The Earth would serve my purpose well. Even now, my followers are building the new ether-ship in which I propose to make the voyage.

"I do not wish to repeat the experience of my arrival in Mars by landing among a people ignorant of me and perhaps universally hostile. You, being Earthmen, could prepare many

of your fellows for my coming, could gather proselytes to serve
me. Your reward — and theirs — would be the elixir of
longevity. And I have many other gifts . . . The precious gems
and metals that you prize so highly. Also, there are the flowers,
whose perfume is more seductive and persuasive than all else.
Inhaling that perfume, you will deem that even gold is worth-
less in comparison . . . and having breathed it, you and all others of your kind, will serve me gladly."

The voice ended, leaving a vibration that thrilled the nerves
of the listeners for some moments. It was like the cessation of a
sweet, bewitching music with overtones of evil scarcely to be
detected above the subtle melody. It bemused the senses of
Haines and Chanler, lulling their astonishment into a sort of
dreamy acceptance of the voice and its declarations.

Chanler made an effort to throw off the enchantment.

"Where are you?" he said. "And how are we to know that
you have told us the truth?"

"I am near you," said the voice, "but I do not choose, at this
time, to reveal myself. The proof of all that I have stated, however, will be revealed to you in due course. Before you is one of
the flowers of which I have spoken. It is not, as you have perhaps surmised, a work of sculpture, but it is an antholite, or fossil blossom, brought, with others of the same kind, from the
world to which I am native. Though scentless at ordinary temperatures, it yields a perfume under the application of heat. As
to the perfume . . . you must judge for yourselves."

The air of the chamber had been neither warm not cold.
Now, the Earthmen were conscious of a change, as if hidden
fires had been ignited. The warmth seemed to issue from the
metal tripod and the block of crystal, beating upon Haines and
Chanler like the radiation of some invisible tropic sun. It
became ardent but not insupportable. At the same time, insid-
iously, the terrestrials began to perceive the perfume, which was
like nothing they had ever inhaled. An elusive thread of other-
world sweetness, it curled about their nostrils, deepening

slowly but acceleratively to a spicy flood, and seeming to mix a pleasant coolness as of foliage-shaded air with the fervent heat.

Chanler was more vividly affected than Haines by the curious hallucinations that followed; though, apart from this differing degree of verisimilitude, their impressions were oddly alike. It seemed to Chanler, all at once, that the perfume was no longer wholly alien to him, but was something that he had remembered from other times and places. He tried to recall the circumstances of this prior familiarity, and his recollections, drawn up as if from the sealed reservoirs of an old existence, took the form of an actual scene that replaced the cavern-chamber about him. Haines was no part of these scene, but had disappeared from his ken, and the roof and walls had vanished, giving place to an open forest of fern-like trees. Their slim, pearly boles and tender frondage swarm in a luminous glory, like an Eden filled with the primal daybreak. The trees were tall, but taller still than they were the flowers that poured down from waving censers of carnal white an overwhelming and voluptuous perfume.

Chanler felt an indescribable ecstasy. It seemed that he had gone back to the fountains of time in the first world, and had drawn into himself inexhaustible life, youth and vigor from the glorious light and fragrance that had steeped his senses to their last nerve.

The ecstasy heightened, and he heard a singing that appeared to emanate from the mouths of the blossoms: a singing as of houris, that turned his blood to a golden philtre-brew. In the delirium of his faculties, the sound was identified with the blossoms' odour. It rose in giddying rapture insuppressible; and he thought that the very flowers soared like flames, and the trees aspired towards them, and he himself was a blown fire that towered with the singing to attain some ultimate pinnacle of delight. The whole world swept upwards in a tide of exaltation, and it seemed that the singing turned to articulate sound, and Chanler heard the words, "I am

Vulthoom, and thou art mine from the beginning of worlds, and shalt be mine until the end. . . ."

He awoke under circumstances that might almost have been a continuation of the visionary imagery he had beheld under the influence of the perfume. He lay on a bed of short, curling grass the colour of verd-antique, with enormous tiger-hued blossoms leaning about him, and a soft brilliance as of amber sunset filling his eyes between the trailing boughs of strange, crimson-fruited trees. Tardily, as he grew cognizant of his surroundings, he realized that the voice of Haines had awakened him, and saw that Haines was sitting near at hand on the curious sward.

"Say, aren't you ever coming out of it?" Chanler heard the crisp query as if through a film of dreams. His thoughts were bewildered, and his memories were oddly mixed with the pseudo-recollections, drawn as if from other lives, that had risen before him in his delirium. It was hard to disentangle the false from the real; but sanity returned to him by degrees; and with it came a feeling of profound exhaustion and nerve-weariness, which warned him that he had sojourned in the spurious paradise of a potent drug.

"Where are we now? and how did we get here?" he asked.

"As far as I can tell," returned Haines, "we're in a sort of underground garden. Some of those big Aihais must have brought us here after we succumbed to the perfume. I resisted the influence longer than you did; and I remember hearing the voice of Vulthoom as I went under. The voice said that he would give us forty-eight hours, terrestrial time, in which to think over his proposition. If we accept, he'll send us back to Ignarh with a fabulous sum of money — and a supply of those narcotic flowers."

Chanler was now fully awake. He and Haines proceeded to discuss their situation, but were unable to arrive at any definite conclusion. The whole affair was no less baffling than extraordinary. An unknown entity, naming himself after the Martian

Devil, had invited them to become his terrestrial agents or emissaries. Apart from the spreading of a propaganda designed to facilitate his advent on Earth, they were to introduce an alien drug that was no less powerful than morphine, cocaine or marihuana — and, in all likelihood, no less pernicious.

"What if we refuse?" said Chanler.

Vulthoom said that it would be impossible to let us return, in that case. But he didn't specify our fate — merely hinted that it would be unpleasant."

"Well, Haines, we've got to think our way out of this, if we can."

"I'm afraid that thinking won't help us much. We must be many miles below the surface of Mars — and the mechanism of the elevators, in all probability, is something that no Earthman could ever learn."

Before Chanler could offer any comment, one of the giant Aihais appeared among the trees, carrying two of the curious Martian utensils known as *kulpai*. These were large platters of semi-metallic earthenware, fitted with removable cups and rotatory carafes, in which an entire meal of liquids and solids could be served. The Aihai set the platters on the ground before Haines and Chanler, and then waited, immobile and inscrutable. The Earthmen, conscious of a ravening hunger, addressed themselves to the foodstuffs, which had been moulded or cut into various geometric forms. Though possibly of synthetic origin, the foods were delicious, and the Earthmen consumed them to the last cone and lozenge, and washed them down with a vinous garnet-coloured liquor from the carafes.

When they had finished, their attendant spoke for the first time.

"It is the will of Vulthoom that you should wander throughout Ravormos and behold the wonders of the caverns. You are at liberty to roam alone and unattended; or, if you prefer, I shall serve you as a guide. My name is Ta-Vho-Shai, and I am ready to answer any questions that you ask. Also, you may dismiss me at will."

Haines and Chanler, after a brief discussion, decided to accept this offer of ciceronage. They followed the Aihai through the garden, whose extent was hard to determine because of the misty amber luminance that filled it as if with radiant atoms, giving the impression of unbounded space. The light, they learned from Ta-Vho-Shai, was emitted by the lofty roof and walls beneath the action of an electro-magnetic force of wave-length short even than the cosmic rays; and it possessed all the essential qualities of sunlight.

The garden was composed of weird plants and blossoms, many of which were exotic to Mars, and had perhaps been imported from the alien solar system to which Vulthoom was native. Some of the flowers were enormous mats of petals, like a hundred orchids joined into one. There were cruciform trees, hung with fantastically long and variegated leaves that resembled heraldic pennons or scrolls of cryptic writing; and others were branched and fruited in outlandish ways.

Beyond the garden, they entered a world of open passages and chambered caverns, some of which were filled with machinery or with storage vats and urns. In others, immense ingots of precious and semi-precious metals were piled, and gigantic coffers spilled their flashing gems as if to tempt the Earthmen.

Most of the machines were in action, though untended, and Haines and Chanler were told that they could run in this manner for centuries or millenaries. Their operation was inexplicable even to Haines with his expert knowledge of mechanics. Vulthoom and his people had gone beyond the spectrum, and beyond the audible vibrations of sound, and had compelled the hidden forces of the universe to appear and obey them.

Everywhere there was a loud beating as of metal pulses, a mutter as of prisoned Afrits and servile iron titans. Valves opened and shut with a harsh clangour. There were rooms pil-

lared with strident dynamos; and others where groups of mysteriously levitated spheres were spinning silently, like suns and
planets in the void of space.

They climbed a flight of stairs, colossal as the steps of the
pyramid of Cheops, to a higher level. Haines, in a dream-like
fashion, seemed to remember descending these stairs, and
thought they were now nearing the chamber in which he and
Chanler had been interviewed by the hidden entity, Vulthoom.
He was not sure, however; and Ta-Vho-Shai led them through
a series of vast rooms that appeared to serve the purpose of laboratories. In most of these, there were age-old colossi, bending
like alchemists over furnaces that burned with cold fire, and
retorts that fumed with queer threads and ropes of vapour. One
room was untenanted, and was furnished with no apparatus,
other than three great bottles of clear, uncoloured glass, taller
than a tall man, and having somewhat the form of Roman
amphoras. To all appearances the bottles were empty; but they
were closed with double-handed stoppers that a human being
could scarcely have lifted.

"What are these bottles?" Chanler asked the guide.

"They are the bottles of Sleep," said the Aihai, with the
solemn and sententious air of a lecturer. "Each of them is filled
with a rare, invisible gas. When the time comes for the thousand-year slumber of Vulthoom, the gases are released; and
mingling, they pervade the atmosphere of Ravormos, even to
the lowest cavern, inducing sleep for a similar period in us who
serve Vulthoom. Time no longer exists; and eons are no more
than instants for the sleepers; and they awaken only at the hour
of Vulthoom's awakening."

Haines and Chanler, filled with curiosity, were prompted
to ask many questions, but most of these were answered
vaguely and ambiguously by Ta-Vho-Shai, who seemed eager
to continue his ciceronage through other and ulterior parts of
Ravormos. He could tell them nothing about the chemical
nature of the gases; and Vulthoom himself, if the veracity of

Ta-Vho-Shai could be trusted, was a mystery even to his own followers, most of whom had never beheld him in person.

Ta-Vho-Shai conducted the Earthmen from the room of bottles, and down a long straight cavern, wholly deserted, where a rumbling and pounding as of innumerable engines came to meet them. The sound broke upon them like a Niagara of evil thunders when they emerged finally in a sort of pillared gallery that surrounded a mile-wide gulf illumined by the terrible flaring of tongued fires that rose incessantly from its depths.

It was as if they looked down into some infernal circle of angry light and tortured shadow. Far beneath, they saw a colossal structure of curved and glittering girders, like the strangely articulated bones of a metal behemoth outstretched along the bottom of the pit. Around it, furnaces belched like the flaming mouths of dragons; tremendous cranes went up and down perpetually with a motion as of long-necked plesiosaurs; and the figures of giants, red as labouring demons, moved through the sinister glare.

"They build the ether-ship in which Vulthoom will voyage to the Earth," said Ta-Vho-Shai. "When all is ready, the ship will blast its way to the surface by means of atomic disintegrators. The very stone will melt before it like vapour. Ignar-Luth, which lies directly above, will be consumed as if the central fires of the planet had broken loose."

Haines and Chanler, appalled, could offer no rejoinder. More and more they were stunned by the mystery and magnitude, the terror and menace, of this unsuspected cavern-world. Here, they felt, a malign power, armed with untold arcana of science, was plotting some baleful conquest; a doom that might involve the people worlds of the system was being incubated in secrecy and darkness. They, it seemed, were helpless to escape and give warning, and their own fate was shadowed by insoluble gloom.

A gust of hot, metallic vapour, mounting from the abyss, burned corrosively in their nostrils as they peered from the gallery's verge. Ill and giddy, they drew back.

What lies beyond this gulf?" Chanler inquired, when his sickness had passed.

"The gallery leads to outer caverns, little used, which conduct on the dry bed of an ancient underground river. This riverbed, running for many miles, emerges in a sunken desert far below sea-level, and lying to the west Ignarh."

The Earthmen started at this information, which seemed to offer them a possible avenue of escape. Both, however, thought it well to dissemble their interest. Pretending fatigue, they asked the Aihai to lead them to some chamber in which they could rest awhile and discuss Vulthoom's proposition at leisure.

Ta-Vho-Shai, professing himself at their service in all ways, took them to a small room beyond the laboratories. It was a sort of bedchamber, with two tiers of couches along the walls. These couches, from their length, were evidently designed to accommodate the giant Martians. Here Haines and Chanler were left alone by Ta-Vho-Shai, who had tacitly inferred that his presence was no longer needed.

"Well," said Chanler, "it looks as if there is a chance of escape if we can only reach that river-bed. I took careful note of the corridors we followed on our return from the gallery. It should be easy enough — unless we are being watched without our knowledge."

"The only trouble is, it's too easy. . . . But anyway, we can try. Anything would be better than waiting around like this. After what we've seen and heard, I'm beginning to believe that Vulthoom really is the Devil — even though he doesn't claim to be."

"Those ten-foot Aihais give me the creeps," said Chanler. "I can readily believe they are a million years old, or thereabouts. Enormous longevity would account for their size and stature. Most animals that survive beyond the normal term of years become gigantic; and it stands to reason that these Martian men would develop in a similar fashion."

It was a simple matter to retrace their route to the pillared gallery that encircled the great abyss. For most of the distance, they had only to follow a main corridor; and the sound of the rumbling engineries alone would have guided them. They met no one in the passages; and the Aihais that they saw through open portals in laboratory rooms were deeply intent on enigmatic chemistries.

"I don't like this," muttered Haines. "It's too good to be true."

"I'm not so sure of that. Perhaps it simply hasn't occurred to Vulthoom and his followers that we might try to escape. After all, we know nothing about their psychology."

Keeping close to the inner wall, behind the thick pillars, they followed the long, slowly winding gallery on the right hand. It was lit only by the shuddering reflection of the tall flames in the pit below. Moving thus, they were hidden from the view of the labouring giants, if any of these had happened to look upwards. Poisonous vapours were blown towards them at intervals, and they felt the hellish heat of the furnaces; and the clangours of welding, the thunder of obscure machineries, beat upon them as they went with reverberations that were like hammer-blows.

By degrees they rounded the gulf, and came at last to its farther side, where the gallery curved backwards in its return towards the entrance corridor. Here, in the shadows, they discerned the unlit mouth of a large cavern that radiated from the gallery.

This cavern, they surmised, would lead them towards the sunken river-bed of which Ta-Vho-Shai had spoken. Haines, luckily, carried a small pocket-flash, and he turned its ray into the cavern, revealing a straight corridor with numerous minor intersections. Night and silence seemed to swallow them at a gulp, and the clangours of the toiling Titans were quickly and mysteriously muted as they hurried along the empty hall.

The roof of the corridor was fitted with metal hemispheres, now dark and rayless, that had formerly served to illuminate it in the same fashion as the other halls of Ravormos. A fine dust was stirred by the feet of the Earthmen as they fled; and soon the air grew chill and thin, losing the mild and somewhat humid warmth of the central caverns. It was plain, as Ta-Vho-Shai had told them, that these outer passages were seldom used or visited.

It seemed that they went on for a mile or more in that Tartarean corridor. Then the walls began to straighten, the floor roughened and fell steeply. There were no more cross-passages, and hope quickened in the Earthmen as they saw plainly that they had gone beyond the artificial caverns into a natural tunnel. The tunnel soon widened, and its floor became a series of shelf-formations. By means of these, they descended into a profound abyss that was obviously the river-channel of which Ta-Vho-Shai had told them.

The small flashlight barely sufficed to reveal the full extent of this underground waterway, in which there was no longer even a trickle of its pre-historic flood. The bottom, deeply eroded, and riffled with sharp boulders, was more than a hundred yards wide; and the roof arched into gloom irresoluble. Exploring the bottom tentatively for a little distance, Haines and Chanler determined by its Gradual falling the direction in which the stream had flowed. Following this downward course, they set out resolutely, praying that they would find no impassable barriers, no precipices of former cataracts to impede or prevent their egress in the desert. Apart from the danger of pursuit, they apprehended no other difficulties than these.

The obscure windings of the bottom brought them first to one side and then to the other as they groped along. In places the cavern widened, and they came to far-recessive beaches, terraced, and marked by the ebbing waters. High up on some of the beaches, there were singular formations resembling a type of mammoth fungi grown in caverns beneath the modern canals. These formations, in the shape of Herculean clubs, arose often to a height of three feet or more. Haines, impressed by their metallic sparkling beneath the light as he flashed it upon them, conceived a curious idea. Though Chanler protested against the delay, he climbed the shelving to examine a group of them more closely, and found, as he had suspected, that they were not living growths, but were petrified and heavily impregnated with minerals. He tried to break one of them loose, but it resisted all his tuggings. However, by hammering it with a loose fragment of stone, he succeeded in fracturing the base of the club, and it toppled over with an iron tinkling. The thing was very heavy, with a mace-like swelling at the upper end, and would make a substantial weapon in case of need. He broke off a second club for Chanler; and thus armed, they resumed their flight.

It was impossible to calculate the distance that they covered. The channel turned and twisted, it pitched abruptly in places, and was often broken into ledges that glittered with alien ores or were stained with weirdly brilliant oxides of azure, vermilion and yellow. The men floundered ankle-deep in pits of sable sand, or climbed laboriously over damlike barricades of rusty boulders, huge as piled menhirs. Ever and anon, they found themselves listening feverishly for any sound that would betoken pursuit. But silence brimmed the Cimmerian channel, troubled only by the clatter and crunch of their own footstep.

At last, with incredulous eyes, they saw before them the dawning of a pale light in the farther depths. Arch by dismal arch, like the throat of Avernus lit by nether fires, the enormous cavern became visible. For one exultant moment, they thought that they were nearing the channel mouth; but the light grew with an eerie and startling brilliance, like the flaming of furnaces rather than sunshine falling into a cave. Implacable, it crept along the walls and bottom and dimmed the ineffectual beam of Haines' torch as it fell on the dazzled Earthmen.

Ominous, incomprehensible, the light seemed to watch and threaten. They stood amazed and hesitant, not knowing whether to go on or retreat. Then, from the flaming air, a voice spoke as if in gentle reproof: the sweet, sonorous voice of Vulthoom.

"Go back as you came, O Earthlings. None may leave Ravormos without my knowledge or against my will. Behold! I have sent my Guardians to escort you."

The lit air had been empty to all seeming, and the river-bed was peopled only by the grotesque masses and squat shadows of boulders. Now, with the ceasing of the voice, Haines and Chanler saw before them, at a distance of ten feet, the instant apparition of two creatures that were comparable to nothing in the whole known zoology of Mars or Earth.

They rose from the rocky bottom to the height of giraffes, with shortish legs that were vaguely similar to those of Chinese dragons, and elongated spiral necks like the middle coils of great anacondas. Their heads were triple-faced, and they might have been the trimurti of some infernal world. It seemed that each face was eyeless, with tongue-shaped flames issuing voluminously from deep orbits beneath the slanted brows. Flames also poured in a ceaseless vomit from the gaping gargoyle mouths. From the head of each monster a triple comb of vermilion flared aloft in sharp serrations, glowing terribly; and both of them were bearded with crimson scrolls. Their necks and arching spines were fringed with sword-long blades that diminished into rows of daggers on the tapering tails; and their whole bodies, as well as this fearsome armament, appeared to burn as if they had just issued from a fiery furnace.

A palpable heat emanated from these hellish chimeras, and the Earthmen retreated hastily before the flying splotches, like the blown tatters of a conflagration, that broke loose from their ever-jetting eye-flames and mouth-flames.

"My God! These monsters are supernatural!" cried Chanler, shaken and appalled.

Haines, though palpably startled, was inclined to a more orthodox explanation. "There must be some sort of television behind this," he maintained, "though I can't imagine how it's possible to project three-dimensional images, and also create the sensation of heat. . . . I had an idea, somehow, that our escape was being watched."

He picked up a heavy fragment of metallic stone and heaved it at one of the glowing chimeras. Aimed unerringly, the fragment struck the frontal brow of the monster, and seemed to explode in a shower of sparks at the moment of impact. The creature flared and swelled prodigiously, and a fiery hissing became audible. Haines and Chanler were driven back by a wave of scorching heat; and their wardens followed them pace by pace on the rough bottom. Abandoning all hope of escape, they returned towards Ravormos, dogged by the monsters as they toiled through yielding sand and over the ledges and riffles.

Reaching the point where they had descended into the river channel, they found its upper stretches guarded by two more of these terrific dragons. There was no other recourse than to climb the lofty shelves into the acclivitous tunnel. Weary with their long flight, and enervated by a dull despair, they found themselves again in the outer hall, with two of their guardians now preceding them like an escort of infernal honour. Both were stunned by a realization of the awful and mysterious powers of Vulthoom; and even Haines had become silent, though his brain was still busy with a futile and desperate probing. Chanler, more sensitive, suffered all the chills and terrors that his literary imagination could inflict upon him under the circumstances.

They came at length to the columned gallery that circled the vast abyss. Midway in this gallery, the chimeras who preceded the Earthmen turned upon them suddenly with a fearsome belching of flames; and, as they paused in their intimidation, the two behind continued to advance towards them with a hissing as of Satanic salamanders. In that narrowing space, the heat was like a furnace-blast, and the columns afforded no shelter. From the gulf below, where the Martian titans toiled perpetually, a stupefying thunder rose to assail them at the same time; and noxious fumes were blown towards them in writhing coils.

"Looks as if they are going to drive us into the gulf," Haines panted, as he sought to draw breath in the fiery air. He and Chanler reeled before the looming monsters, and even as he spoke, two more of these hellish apparitions flamed into being at the gallery's verge, as if they had risen from the gulf to render impossible that fatal plunge which alone could have offered an escape from the others.

Half swooning, the Earthmen were dimly aware of a change in the menacing chimeras. The flaming bodies dulled and shrank and darkened, the heat lessened, the fires died down in the mouths and eye-pits. At the same time, the creatures drew closer, fawn loathsomely, and revealing whitish tongues and eyeballs of jet.

The tongues seemed to divide . . . they grew paler. . . . They were like flower-petals that Haines and Chanler had seen somewhere. The breath of the chimeras, like a soft gale, was upon the faces of the Earthmen . . . and the breath was a cool and spicy perfume that they had known before . . . the narcotic perfume that had overcome them following their audience with the hidden master of Ravormos. . . . Moment by moment, the monsters turned to prodigious blossoms; the pillars of the gallery became gigantic trees in a glamour of primal dawn; the thunders of the pit were lulled to a far-off sighing as of gentle seas on Edenic shores. The teeming terrors of Ravormos, the threat of a shadowy doom, were as things that had never been Haines and Chanler, oblivious, were lost in the paradise of the unknown drug. . . .

Haines, awakening darkly, found that he lay on the stone floor in the circling colonnade. He was alone, and the fiery chimeras had vanished. The shadows of his opiate swoon were roughly dissipated by the clangours that still mounted from the neighbouring gulf. With growing consternation and horror, he recalled everything that had happened.

He arose giddily to his feet, peering about in the semi-twilight of the gallery for some trace of his companion. The petrified fungus-club that Chanler had carried, as well as his own weapon, were lying where they had fallen from the fingers of the overpowered men. But Chanler was gone; and Haines shouted aloud with no other response than the eerily prolonged echoes of the deep arcade.

Impelled by an urgent feeling that he must find Chanler without delay, he recovered his heavy mace and started along the gallery. It seemed that the weapon could be of little use against the preternatural servants of Vulthoom; but somehow, the metallic weight of the bludgeon reassured him.

Nearing the great corridor that ran to the core of Ravormos, Haines was overjoyed when he saw Chanler coming to meet him. Before he could call out of a cheery greeting, he heard Chanler's voice:

"Hello, Bob, this is my first televisual appearance in tri-dimensional form. Pretty good, isn't it? I'm in the private laboratory of Vulthoom, and Vulthoom has persuaded me to accept his proposition. As soon as you've made up your mind to do likewise, we'll return to Ignarh with full instructions regarding our terrestrial mission, and funds amounting to a million dollars each. Think it over, and you'll see that there's nothing else to do. When you've decided to join us, follow the main corridor through Ravormos, and Ta-Vho-Shai will meet you and bring you into the laboratory."

At the conclusion of this astounding speech, the figure of Chanler, without seeming to wait for any reply from Haines, stepped lightly to the gallery's verge and floated out among the wreathing vapours. There, smiling upon Haines, it vanished like a phantom.

To say that Haines was thunderstruck would be putting it feebly indeed. In all verisimilitude, the figure and voice had been those of the flesh-and-blood Chanler. He felt an eerie chill before the thaumaturgy of Vulthoom, which could bring about a projection so veridical as to deceive him in this manner. He was shocked and horrified beyond measure by Chanler's capitulation; but somehow, it did not occur to him that any imposture had been practised.

"That devil has got him," thought Haines. "But I'd never have believed it. I didn't think he was that kind of a fellow at all."

Sorrow, anger, bafflement and amazement filled him alternately as he strode along the gallery; nor, as he entered the inner hall, was he able to decide on any clearly effective course of action. To yield, as Chanler had avowedly done, was unthinkably repugnant to him. If he could see Chanler again, perhaps he could persuade him to change his mind and resume an unflinching opposition to the alien entity. It was a degradation, and a treason to humankind, for any Earthman to lend himself to the more than doubtful schemes of Vulthoom. Apart from the projected invasion of Earth, and the spread of the strange, subtle narcotic, there was the ruthless destruction of Ignar-Luth that would occur when Vulthoom's ether-vessel should blast its way to the planet's surface. It was his duty, and Chanler's, to prevent all this if prevention were humanly possible. Somehow, they — or he alone if necessary — must stem the cavern-incubated menace. Bluntly honest himself, there was no thought of temporizing even for an instant.

Still carrying the mineraloid club, he strode on for several minutes, his brain preoccupied with the dire problem but powerless to arrive at any solution. Through a habit of observation more or less automatic with the veteran space-pilot, he peered through the doorways of the various rooms that he passed,

where the cupels and retorts of a foreign chemistry were tended
by age-old colossi. Then, without premeditation, he came to
the deserted room in which were the three mighty receptacles
that Ta-Vho-Shai had called the Bottles of Sleep. He remembered what the Aihai had said concerning their contents.

In a flash of desperate inspiration, Haines boldly entered
the room, hoping that he was not under the surveillance of
Vulthoom at the moment. There was no time for reflection or
other delay, if he were to execute the audacious plan that had
occurred to him.

Taller than his head, with the swelling contours of great
amphoras, and seemingly empty, the Bottles glimmered in the
still light. Like the phantom of a bulbous giant, he saw his own
distorted image in the upward-curving glass as he neared the
foremost one.

There was but one thought, one resolution, in his mind.
Whatever the cost, he must smash the Bottles, whose released
gases would pervade Ravormos and plunge the followers of
Vulthoom — if not Vulthoom himself — into a thousand-year
term of slumber.

He and Chanler, no doubt, would be doomed to share the
slumber; and for them, unfortified by the secret elixir of
immortality, there would be in all likelihood no awakening. But
under the circumstances it was better so; and, by the sacrifice,
a thousand years of grace would be accorded to the two planets. Now was his opportunity, and it seemed improbable that
there would ever be another one.

He lifted the petrified fungus-mace, he swung it back in a
swift arc, and struck without all his strength at the bellying
glass. There was a gong-like clangour, sonorous and prolonged,
and radiating cracks appeared from top to bottom of the huge
receptacle. At the second glow, it broke inwards with a shrill,
appalling sound that was almost an articulate shriek, and
Haines' face was fanned for an instant by a cool breath, gentle
as a woman's sigh.

Holding his breath to avoid the inhalation of the gas, he turned to the next Bottle. It shattered at the first stroke, and again he felt a soft sighing, that followed upon the cleavage.

A voice of thunder seemed to fill the room as he raised his weapon to assail the third Bottle: "Fool! you have doomed yourself and your fellow Earthman by this deed." The last words mingled with the crash of Haines' final stroke. A tomb-like silence followed, and the far-off, muted rumble of enginer-ies seemed to ebb and recede before it. The Earthmen stared for a moment at the riven Bottles, and then, dropping the useless remnant of his face, which had been shattered into several frag-ments, he fled from the chamber.

Drawn by the noise of breakage, a number of Aihais had appeared in the hall. They were running about in an aimless, unconcerted manner, like mummies impelled by a failing gal-vanism. None of them tried to intercept the Earthman.

Whether the slumber induced by the gases would be slow or swift in its coming, Haines could not surmise. The air of the caverns was unchanged as far as he could tell: there was no odour, no perceptible effect on his breathing. But already, as he ran, he felt a slight drowsiness, and a thin veil appeared to weave itself on all his senses. It seemed that faint vapours were forming in the corridor, and there was a touch insubstantiality in the very walls.

His flight was without definite goal or purpose. Like a dreamer in a dream, he felt little surprise when he found him-self lifted from the floor and borne along through midair in an inexplicable levitation. It was as if he were caught in a rushing stream, or were carried on invisible clouds. The doors of a hun-dred secret rooms, the mouths of a hundred mysterious halls, flew swiftly past him, and he saw in brief glimpses the colossi that lurched and nodded with the ever-spreading slumber as they went to and fro on strange errands. Then, dimly, he saw that he had entered the high-vaulted room that enshrined the fossil flower on its tripod of crystal and black metal. A door opened in the seamless stone of the further wall as he hurtled towards it. An instant more, while he seemed to fall downwards through a nether chamber beyond, among prodigious masses of unnamable machines, upon a revolving disc towering before him. The disc had not ceased to revolve, but the air still throbbed with its hellish vibration. The place was like a mechanical nightmare, but amid its confusion of glittering coils and dynamos, Haines beheld the form of Chanler, lashed upright with metal cords to a rack-like frame. Near him, in a still and standing posture, was the giant Ta-Vho-Shai; and immediately in front of him, there reclined an incredible thing whose further portions and members wound away to an indefinite distance amid the machinery.

Somehow, the thing was like a gigantic plant, with innumerable roots, pale and swollen, that ramified from a bulbular bole. This bole, half hidden from view, was topped with a vermilion cup like a monstrous blossom; and from the cup there grew an elfin figure, pearly-hued, and formed with exquisite beauty and symmetry; a figure that turned its Lilliputian face towards Haines and spoke in the sounding voice of Vulthoom:

"You have conquered for the time, but I bear no rancour towards you. I blame my own carelessness."

To Haines, the voice was like a far-off thunder heard by one who is half asleep. With halting effort, lurching as if he were about to fall, he made his way towards Chanler. Wan and haggard, with a look that puzzled Haines dimly, Chanler gazed upon him from the metal frame without speaking.

"I . . . smashed the Bottles," Haines heard his own voice with a feeling of drowsy unreality. "It seemed the only thing to do . . . since you had gone over to Vulthoom."

"But I hadn't consented," Chanler replied slowly. "It was all a deception . . . to trick you into consenting. . . . And they were torturing me because I wouldn't give in." Chanler's voice trailed away, and it seemed that he could say no more. Subtly, the pain and haggardness began to fade from his features, as if erased by the gradual oncoming of slumber.

Haines, laboriously trying to comprehend through his own drowsiness, perceived an evil-looking instrument, like a many-pointed metal goad, which drooped from the fingers of Ta-Vho-Shai. From the arc of needle-like tips, there fell a ceaseless torrent of electric sparks. The bosom of Chanler's shirt had been torn open, and his skin was stippled with tiny blue-black marks from chin to diaphragm . . . marks that formed a diabolic pattern. Haines felt a vague, unreal horror.

Through the Lethe that closed upon his senses more and more, he became aware that Vulthoom had spoken; and after an interval, it seemed that he understood the meaning of the words. "All my methods of persuasion have failed; but it matters little. I shall yield myself to slumber, though I could remain awake if I wished, defying the bases through my superior science and vital power. We shall all sleep soundly. . . and a thousand years are no more than a single night to my followers and me. For you, whose life-term is so brief, they will become — eternity. Soon I shall awaken and resume my plans of conquest . . . and you, who dared to interfere, will lie beside me then as a little dust . . . and the dust will be swept away."

The voice ended, and it seemed the elfin being began to nod in the monstrous vermilion cup. Haines and Chanler saw each other with growing, wavering dimness, as if through a grey mist that had risen between them. There was silence everywhere, as if the Tartarean engineries had fallen still, and the titans had ceased their labour. Chanler relaxed on the torture-frame, and his eyelids drooped. Haines tottered, fell, and lay motionless. Ta-Vho-Shai, still clutching his sinister instrument, reposed like a mummified giant. Slumber, like a silent sea, had filled the caverns of Ravormos.

The Treader of the Dust

*". . . The olden wizards knew him, and named him Quachil
Uttaus. Seldom is he revealed: for he dwelleth beyond the outermost circle, in the dark limbo of unsphered time and space.
Dreadful is the word that calleth him, though the word be
unspoken save in though: For Quachil Uttaus is the ultimate
corruption; and the instant of his coming is like the passage of
many ages; and neither flesh not stone may abide his treading,
but all things crumble beneath it atom from atom. And for
this, some have called him The Treader of the Dust."*

— *The Testaments of Carnamagos.*

I t was after interminable debate and argument with himself,
after many attempts to exorcise the dim, bodiless legion of
his fears, that John Sebastian returned to the house he had
left so hurriedly. He had been absent only for three days; but
even this was an interruption without precedent in the life of
reclusion and study to which he had given himself completely
following his inheritance of the old mansion together with a
generous income. At no time would he have defined fully the
reason of his flight: nevertheless, flight had seemed imperative.
There was some horrible urgency that had driven him forth;
but now, since he had determined to go back, the urgency was
resolved into a matter of nerves overwrought by too close and
prolonged application to his books. He had fancied certain
things: but the fancies were patently absurd and baseless.

Even if the phenomena that had perturbed him were not all imaginery, there must be some natural solution that had not occurred to his overheated mind at the time. The sudden yellowing of a newly purchased notebook, the crumbling of the sheets at their edges, were no doubt due to a latent imperfection of the paper; and the queer fading of his entries, which, almost overnight, had become faint as age-old writings, was clearly the result of cheap, faulty chemicals in the ink. The aspect of sheer, brittle, worm-hollowed antiquity which had manifested itself in certain articles of furniture, certain portions of the mansion, was no more than the sudden revealing of a covert disintegration that had gone on unnoticed by him in his sedulous application to dark but absorbing researches. And it was this same application, with its unbroken years of toil and confinement, which had brought about his premature aging; so that, looking back into the mirror on the morn of his flight, he had been startled and shocked as if by the apparition of a withered mummy. As to the manservant, Timmers — well, Timmers had been old ever since he could remember. It was only the exaggeration of sick nerves that had lately found in Timmers a decrepitude so extreme that it might fall, without the intermediacy of death, at any moment, into the corruption of the grave.

Indeed, he could explain all that had troubled him without reference to the wild, remote lore, the forgotten demonologies and systems into which he had delved. Those passages in *The Testaments of Carnamagos*, over which he had pondered with weird dismay, were relevant only to the horrors evoked by mad sorcerers in bygone eons. . . .

Sebastian, firm in such convictions, came back at sunset to his house. He did not tremble or falter as he crossed the pine-darkened grounds and ran quickly up the front steps. He fancied, but could not be sure, that there were fresh sings of dilapidation in the steps; and the house itself, as he approached it, had seemed to lean a little aslant, as if from some ruinous settling of the foundations: but this, he told himself, was an illusion wrought by the gathering twilight.

No lamps had been lit, but Sebastian was not unduly surprised by this, for he knew that Timmers, left to his own devices, was prone to dodder about in the gloom like a senescent old, long after the proper time of lamp-lighting. Sebastian, on the other hand, had always been averse to darkness or even deep shadow; and of late the aversion had increased upon him. Invariably he turned on all the bulbs in the house as soon as the daylight began to fail. Now, muttering his irritation at Timmers' remissness, he pushed open the door and reached hurriedly for the hall switch.

Because, perhaps, of a nervous agitation which he would not own to himself, he fumbled for several moments without finding the knob. The hall was strangely dark, and a glimmering from the ashen sunset, sifted between tall pines into the doorway behind him, was seemingly powerless to penetrate beyond its threshold. He could see nothing; it was as if the night of dead ages had laired in that hallway; and his nostrils, while he stood groping, were assailed by a dry pungency as of ancient dust, an odor as of corpses and coffins long indistinguishable in powdery decay.

At last he found the switch; but the illumination that responded was somehow dim and insufficient, and he seemed to detect a shadowy flickering, as if the circuit were at fault. However, it reassured him to see that the house, to all appearance, was very much as he had left it. Perhaps, unconsciously, he had feared to find the oaken panels crumbling away in riddled rottenness, the carpet falling into moth-eaten tatters; had apprehended the breaking through of rotted boards beneath his tread.

Where, he wondered now, was Timmers? The aged factotum, in spite of his growing senility, had always been quick to appear; and even if he had not heard his master enter, the switching on of the lights would have signalized Sebastian's return to him. But, though Sebastian listened with painful intentness, there was no creaking of the familiar tottery foot-steps. Silence hung everywhere, like a funereal, unstirred arras.

No doubt, Sebastian thought, there was some common-place explanation. Timmers had gone to the nearby village, perhaps to restock the larder, or in hope of receiving a letter from his master; and Sebastian had missed him on the way home from the station. Or perhaps the old man had fallen ill and was now lying helpless in his room. Filled with this latter thought, he went straight to Timmers' bed-chamber, which was on the ground floor, at the back of the mansion. It was empty, and the bed was neatly made and had obviously not been occupied since the night before. With a suspiration of relief that seemed to lift a horrid incubus from his bosom, he decided that his first conjecture had been correct.

Now, pending the return of Timmers, he nerved himself to another act of inspection, and went forthwith into his study. He would not admit to himself precisely what it was that he had feared to see; but at first glance, the room was unchanged, and all things were as they had been at the time of his hurried departure. The confused and high-piled litter of manuscripts, volumes, notebooks on his writing-table had seemingly lain untouched by anything but his own hand; and his bookshelves, with their bizarre and terrific array of authorities on dia-bolism, necromancy, goety, on all the ridiculed or outlawed sci-ences, were undisturbed and intact. On the old lecturn or read-ing-stand which he used for his heavier tomes, *The Testaments of Carnamagos*, in its covers of shagreen with hasps of human bone, lay open at the very page which had frightened him so unrea-sonably with its eldritch intimations.

Then, as he stepped forward between the reading-stand and the table, he perceived for the first time the inexplicable *dustiness* of everything. Dust lay everywhere: a fine gray dust like a powder of dead atoms. It had covered his manuscripts with a deep film, it had settled thickly upon the chairs, the lamp-shades, the volumes; and the rich poppy-like reds and yellows of the oriental rugs were bedimmed by its accumulation. It was as if many desolate years had passed through the chamber since his own departure, and had shaken from their shroud-like garments the dust of all ruined things. The mystery of it chilled Sebastian: for he knew that the room had been clean-swept only three days previously; and Timmers would have dusted the place each morning with meticulous care during his absence.

Now the dust rose up in a light, swirling cloud about him, it filled his nostrils with the same dry odor, as of fantastically ancient dissolution, that had met him in the hall. At the same moment he grew aware of a cold, gusty draft that had somehow entered the room. He thought that one of the windows must have been left open, but a glance assured him that they were shut, with tightly drawn blinds; and the door was closed behind. The draft was light as the sighing of a phantom, but wherever it passed, the fine, weightless powder soared aloft, filling the air and settling again with utmost slowness. Sebastian felt a weird alarm, as if a wind had blown upon him from chartless dimensions, or through some hidden rift of ruin; and simultaneously he was seized by a paroxysm of prolonged and violent coughing.

He could not locate the source of the draft. But, as he moved restlessly about, his eye was caught by a low long mound of the gray dust, which had heretofore been hidden from view by the table. It lay beside the chair in which he usually sat while writing. Near the heap was the feather-duster used by Timmers in his daily round of house-cleaning.

It seemed to Sebastian that the rigor of a great, lethal coldness had invaded all his being. He could not stir for several minutes, but stood peering down at the inexplicable mound. In the center of that mound he saw a vague depression, which might have been the mark of a very small footprint half erased by the gusts of air that had evidently taken much of the dust and scattered it about the chamber.

At last the power of motion returned to Sebastian. Without conscious recognition of the impulse that prompted him, he bent forward to pick up the feather-duster. But, even as his fingers touched it, the handle and the feathers crumbled into fine powder which, settling in a low pile, preserved vaguely the outlines of the original object!

A weakness came upon Sebastian, as if the burden of utter age and mortality had gathered crushingly on his shoulders between one instant and the next. There was a whirling of vertiginous shadows before his eyes in the lamplight, and he felt that he should swoon unless he sat down immediately. He put out his hand to reach the chair beside him — and the chair, at his touch, fell instantly into light, downward-sifting clouds of dust.

Afterward — how long afterward he could not tell — he found himself sitting in the high chair before the lectern on which *The Testaments of Carnamagos* lay open. Dimly he was surprised that the seat had not crumbled beneath him. Upon him, as once before, there was the urgency of swift, sudden flight from that accursed house: but it seemed that he had grown too old, too weary and feeble; and that nothing mattered greatly — not even the grisly doom which he apprehended.

Now, as he sat there in a state half terror, half stupor, his eyes were drawn to the wizard volume before him: the writings of that evil sage and seer, Carnamagos, which had been recovered a thousand years agone from some Graeco-Bactrian tomb, and transcribed by an apostate monk in the original Greek, in the blood of an incubus-begotten monster. In that volume were the chronicles of great sorcerers of old, and the histories of demons earthly and ultra-cosmic, and the veritable spells by which the demons could be called up and controlled and dismissed. Sebastian, a profound student of such lore, had long believed that the book was a mere

medieval legend; and he had been startled as well as gratified
when he found this copy on the shelves of a dealer in old
manuscripts and incunabula. It was said that only two copies
had ever existed, and that the other had been destroyed by
the Spanish Inquisition early in the thirteenth century.

The light flickered as if ominous wings had flown across it;
and Sebastian's eyes blurred with a gathering rheum as he read
again that sinister, fatal passage which had served to provoke
shadowy fears:

> *"Though Quachil Uttaus cometh but rarely, it had been well
> attested that his advent is not always in response to the spoken
> rune and the drawn pentacle. . . . Few wizards, indeed,
> would call upon a spirit so baleful. . . . But let it be under-
> stood that he who readeth to himself, in the silence of his cham-
> ber, the formula given hereunder, must incur a grave risk if in
> his heart there abide openly or hidden the least desire of death
> and annihilation. For it may be that Quachil Uttaus will
> come to him, bringing that doom which toucheth the body to
> eternal dust, and maketh the soul as a vapor for evermore dis-
> solved. And the advent of Quachil Uttaus is foreknowable by
> certain tokens; for in the person of the evocator, and even per-
> chance in those about him, will appear the signs of sudden age;
> and his house, and those belongings which he hath touched,
> will assume the marks of untimely decay and antiquity. . . ."*

Sebastian did not know that he was mumbling the sentences
half aloud as he read them; that he was also mumbling the terrible incantation that followed. . . . His thought crawled as if
through a chill and freezing medium. With a dull, ghastly certainty, he knew Timmers had not gone to the village; he should
have warned Timmers before leaving; he should have closed
and locked *The Testaments of Carnamagos* . . . for Timmers, in his
way was something of a scholar and was not without curiosity
concerning the occult studies of his master. Timmers was well
able to read the Greek of Carnamagos . . . even that dire and

soul-blasting formula to which Quachil Uttaus, demon of ultimate corruption, would respond from the outer void. . . . Too
well Sebastian divined the origin of the gray dust, the reason of
those mysterious crumblings. . . .

Again he felt the impulse of flight: but his body was a dry
dead incubus that refused to obey his volition. Anyway, he
reflected, it was too late now, for the signs of doom had gathered about him and upon him. . . . Yet, surely there had never
been in his heart the least longing for death and destruction.
He had wished only to pursue his delvings into the blacker
mysteries that environed the mortal estate. And he had always
been cautious, had never cared to meddle with magic circles
and evocations of perilous presences. He had known that there
were spirits of evil, spirits of wrath, perdition, annihilation: but
never, of his own will, should he have summoned any of them
from their night-bound abysms. . . .

His lethargy and weakness seemed to increase: it was as if
whole lustrums, whole decades of senescence had fallen upon
him in the drawing of a breath. The thread of his thoughts was
broken at intervals, and he recovered it with difficulty. His
memories, even his fears, seemed to totter on the edge of some
final forgetfulness. With dulled ears he heard a sound as of tim-
bers breaking and falling somewhere in the house; with
dimmed eyes like those of an ancient he saw the lights waver
and go out beneath the swooping of a bat-black darkness.

It was as if the night of some crumbling catacomb had
closed upon him. He felt at whiles the chill faint breathing of
the draft that had troubled him before with its mystery; and
again the dust rose up in his nostrils. Then he realized that the
room was not wholly dark, for he could discern the dim outlines of the lectern before him. Surely no ray was admitted by
the drawn window-blinds: yet somehow there was light. His
eyes, lifting with enormous effort, saw for the first time that a
rough, irregular gap had appeared in the room's outer wall,
high up in the north corner. Through it a single star shone into

the chamber, cold and remote as the eye of a demon glaring across intercosmic gulfs.

Out of that star — or from the spaces beyond it — a beam of livid radiance, wan and deathly, was hurled like a spear upon Sebastian. Broad as a plank, unwavering, immovable, it seemed to transfix his very body and to form a bridge between himself and the worlds of unimagined darkness.

He was as one petrified by the gaze of the Gorgon. Then, through the aperture of ruin, there came something that glided stiffly and rapidly into the room toward him, along the beam. The wall seemed to crumble, the rift widened as it entered.

It was a figure no larger than a young child, but sere and shriveled as some millennial mummy. Its hairless head, its unfeatured face, borne on a neck of skeleton thinness, were lined with a thousand reticulated wrinkles. The body was like that of some monstrous, withered abortion that had never drawn breath. The pipy arms, ending in bony claws were out-thrust as if ankylosed in the posture of an eternal dreadful groping. The legs, with feet like those of a pygmy Death, were drawn rightly together as though confined by the swathings of the tomb; nor was there any movement of striding or pacing. Upright and rigid, the horror floated swiftly down the wan, earthly gray beam toward Sebastian.

Now it was close upon him, its head level with his brow and its feet opposite his bosom. For a fleeting moment he knew that the horror had touched him with its outflung hands, with its starkly floating feet. It seemed to merge within him, to become one with his being. He felt that his veins were choked with dust, that his brain was crumbling cell by cell. Then he was no longer John Sebastian, but a universe of dead stars and worlds that fell eddying into darkness before the tremendous blowing of some ultra-stellar wind. . . .

The thing that immemorial wizards had named Quachil Uttaus was gone; and night and starlight had returned to that ruinous chamber. But nowhere was there any shadow of John

Sebastian: only a low mound of dust on the floor beside the lectern, bearing a vague depression like the imprint of a small foot . . . or of two feet that were pressed closely together.

The Infernal Star

"Accursed forevermore is Yamil Zacra, star of perdition, who sitteth apart and weaveth the web of his rays like a spider spinning in a garden. Even as far as the light of Yamil Zacra falleth among the worlds, so goeth forth the bane and the bale thereof. And the seed of Yamil Zacra, like a fiery tare, is sown in planets that know him only as the least of the stars. . . ."

— Fragment of a Hyperborean tablet.

From a somewhat prolonged acquaintance with Oliver Woadley, I can avow my belief that the story he told me, in explanation of the dire embarrassment from which I had rescued him, was infinitely beyond his powers of invention.

Returning on the train at 2 a.m., after a month in Chicago, to the large Mid-western city of which we were both denizens of long standing, I had gone to bed immediately with the hope that no one would interrupt my slumber for many hours to come. However, I was awakened at earliest dawn by a telephone call from Woadley, who, in a voice rendered virtually unrecognizable by agitation and distress, implored me to come at once and identify him at the local police station. He also begged me to loan him whatever clothing I could spare.

Hastening to comply with the twofold request, I found a pitifully dazed and bewildered Woadley, garbed only in the blanket with which the police had decorously provided him. Piecing together his own vague and half-coherent account with the story of the officer who had arrested him, I learned that he had been trying to reach his suburban residence a little before daybreak, via one of the main avenues, in a state of what may be termed Adamic starkness. At the same time, he seemed unable to provide any clear explanation of his plight. Concealing my astonishment, I bore witness to the sanity and respectability of my friend, and succeeded in persuading the forces of the law that his singular promenade *in puris naturabilis* was merely a case of noctambulism. Though I had never known him to be thus afflicted, I believed sincerely that this was the only conceivable explanation; though, it was quite staggering that he should have appeared in public or anywhere else without pajamas or night-gown. His evident confusion of mind, I thought, was such as would be shown by a rudely awakened sleepwalker.

After he had dressed himself in the somewhat roomily fitting suit which I had brought along for that purpose, I took Woadley to my apartments and fortified him with cognac, hot coffee and a generous breakfast, all of which he manifestly needed. Afterwards he became vociferously grateful and explanatory. I learned that he had summoned me to his assistance because he deemed me the only one of his friends sufficiently broadminded and unconventional to make allowance for the plight into which he had fallen. Especially, he had feared to call upon his own valet and housekeeper; and he had hoped to reach his home and enter it unobserved. Also, for the first time, he began to hint at a strange series of happenings which had preceded his arrest; and finally, with some reluctance, he told me the entire tale.

This story I have re-shaped hereunder in my own words. Unfortunately, I made no notes at the time; and I fear that some of the details are more impressionistic than precise in my memory. It is now impossible for Woadley to clarify them, since he forgot the whole experience shortly after unburdening himself, and denied positively that he had ever told me anything of the sort. This forgetfulness, however, must be regarded as a tacit confirmation of his tale, since it merely fulfills the doom declared against him by Tisaina.

Chapter I

The Finding of the Amulet

Woadley, it would seem, was the last person likely to undergo a translation in which the familiar laws of time and place were abrogated. For one thing, his faith in these laws was so implicit. Least of all, in the beginning, was he aware of any nascent impulse or aspiration toward things beyond the natural scope of mundane effort. The strange and the far-away had always bored him. His interest in astronomy and other orthodox but abstract sciences was very mild indeed; and sorcery was a theme that he had never even considered, except with the random superciliousness of the well-entrenched materialist. Evil, for him, was not the profound reverse ascension of the mind and soul, but was wholly synonymous with crime and social wrong-doing; and his own life had been blameless. A middle-aged bibliophile, with the means and leisure to indulge his proclivities, he asked nothing of life, other than a plenitude of Elzevirs and fine editions.

The strange process, which was to melt the solid world about him into less than shadow, began with the irritating error made by a book-dealer on whom he had always relied for infallible service. He had ordered from this dealer the well-known Hampshire edition of the novels of Jane Austen; and, opening the box, found immediately that volume X of the set was missing. In its place was a book that resembled the other volumes only through the general form and black leather binding. The cover of this book was conspicuously worn and dull, and without lettering of any sort. Even before he had examined its contents, the substitution impressed Woadley as being an unpardonable piece of carelessness.

"I should never have believed it of Calvin," he thought. "The man must be in his dotage."

He lifted the lid of the unattractive volume, and discovered to his further surprise that it was a bound manuscript, written in a clear but spidery hand, with ink that showed a variety of discolorations, on paper brown and slightly charred at the edges. Apparently it had been saved from a conflagration; or perhaps someone had started to burn it and had changed his mind. After reading a few sentences here and there, Woadley was inclined to the latter supposition, but could not imagine why the burning had been prevented.

The manuscript was untitled, unsigned, and appeared to be a collection of miscellaneous notes and jottings, made by some eccentrically minded person who had lived in New England toward the latter end of the era of witchcraft. References were made in the present tense to certain notorious witches of the time. Most of the entries, however, bore on matters that were fantastically varied and remote, and which had no patent relationship to each other aside from their common queerness and extravagance. The erudition of the unknown writer was remarkable even if misguided: as he turned the leaves impatiently, the attention of Woadley was caught by unheard-of names and terms wholly obscure to him. He frowned over casual mentionings of Lomar, Eibon, Zemargad, the Ghooric Zone, Zothique, the Table of Mordiggian, Thilil, Psollantha, Vermazbor, and the Black Flame of Yuzh. A little further on, he came to the following passage, which was equally holocryptic:

"The star Yamil Zacra, which shines but faintly on Earth, was clearly distinguished by the Hyperboreans, who knew it as the fountain-head of all evil. They knew, moreover, that in every peopled world to which the beams of Yamil Zacra have penetrated, there are beings who bear in their flesh the fierie particles diffused by this star throughout time and space. Such beings may pass

their days without knowledge of the perilous kinship and
the awefull powers acquired by virtue of these particles;
but in others the evill declares itself variously. All who are
witches or wizards or necromancers, or seekers of any forbidden lore or domination, have in them more or less of
the seed of Yamil Zacra. Most mightily do the fires
awaken, it is said, in him that wears on his person one of
the black amulets which were brought to Earth in elder
time from the great planetary world that circles eternally
about Yamil Zacra and its dark companion, Yuzh. These
amulets are made of a strange mineral, and upon each of
them, as upon a seal, is graved the head of an unknown
creature. They were once five in number, but now there
are only two of them left on Earth, since the other three
have been translated with their wearers back to the parent world. The manner of such translation is hard to comprehend; and the thing can occur only to one who has in
himself the highest and most potent of the severall kinds
of atomies emitted by Yamil Zacra. These, if he wear the
amulet, may master within him in their fierie flowering
the seeds of all other suns, and, being brought by virtue
of this change beneath the full magneticall sway of the
parent star, he will see the walls of time and place dissolve
about him, and will walk in the flesh on the planet that
is near to Yamil Zacra. Howbeit, there are other mysteries concerned, of which nothing is known latterly: for this
lore was mainly lost with the elder continents; and lost
likewise are the very names of the three men who were
transported formerly from Earth. But Carnamagos, in his
Testaments, prophecied that a fourth transportation would
occur during the present cycle of terrene time; and the
fifth would not occur till the final cycle, and the lifting of
the last continent, Zothique."

Appended to this passage, in the form of a footnote, was
another entry. "The star Yamil Zacra is unnamed by

astronomers, and is seldom noted, being insignificant to the eye because of the brighter orbs that surround it. He who would find it must look midway between Algol and Polaris."

Woadley was unable to account for the patience he had shown in perusing this ineffable farrago.

"What stuff!" he exclaimed aloud, as he closed the volume and dropped it on the library table with a vehemence that bespoke his indignation. "I had no idea that Calvin went in for astrology and such rot. I must give him a piece of my mind about this damnable mistake."

His eye returned to the volume, noting with fresh displeasure that the somewhat shabby binding, which was plainly the work of an amateur, had cracked a little at the back from the violence with which he had let it fall. Gingerly he picked it up again, to examine the damage. Behind the rent in the shoddy leather, which ran diagonally down from the book's top, he discerned the rime of a small flat article, dark but scintillant, that was lodged in the interstices of the binding. Moved by a half-unwilling curiosity, he pried the thing very carefully from its hiding-place with a thin paper-cutter, without lengthening the rift.

"Well, I'll be damned," he said to himself, aloud. The profanity was almost without precedent for Woadley, but, in justification, the object that lay in the palm of his hand was nothing less than unique. It was a kind of miniature plaque or seal-like carving, little larger or thicker than an Attic mina, made of a carbon-black material which seemed to emit phosphorescent sparklings and was impossibly heavy, being at least double the weight of lead. Its outlines were unearthly, but, in the absence of any data to enlighten him, he assumed that the thing represented a sort of profile. This profile possessed a sickle-like beak and semi-batrachian mouth whose underlip curved down obscenely and divided into swollen wattles. Far back in the corrugated face, there was a round, protuberant eye that gave the uncomfortable illusion of revolving in its socket beneath the least change of light. Above this eye, the head rose in a series of bosses, each of which was armed with a formidable upward-jutting spike. The monster was neither bird, beast nor insect, and it seemed to express a diabolism beyond anything in nature or human art. A medieval gargoyle, or an Aztec god, would have been mild and benignant in comparison. Shimmering as if with black hell-fire, it appeared to twist and writhe in malign fury as it lay in Woadley's hand. He turned it over rather hastily, but found that the obverse side repeated the figure in every hideous detail, like the other half of a face.

Owning himself utterly at a loss, he put the thing in his coat pocket, with the intention of showing it to the curator of a local museum. This curator, with whom he was on friendly terms, would no doubt be able to identify it. Later, he would return it to the book-seller, together with the offensively substituted volume.

He looked at the clock, and saw that the closing time of the museum was nearly at hand. The curator seldom lingered after hours, and he lived in a remote suburb, so Woadley decided to defer his visit till the following day. It still lacked an hour of his customary dinner-time; and a curious languor, a disinclination toward any effort, either mental or physical, seemed to come upon him all at once. The annoyances of the book-dealer's error, the bothersome riddle of the carving, began to slip from his mind. He sat down to peruse the evening paper, which his manservant had brought in a little while before.

Amid the heavier head-lines of crime and politics, his eye was drawn almost immediately to an unobtrusive item relating to a new scientific discovery. It was headed:

INFRA-MICROSCOPIC SUNS
IN LIVING BODY-TISSUE

Woadley seldom read anything of the sort; but for some reason his interest was inveigled. He found that the gist of the article was in the following paragraph:

"It has now been proved that the human body contains atoms which burn like infinitesimal suns at a temperature of 1500 Centigrade. They stimulate vital activity, and many of their functions and properties are not yet wholly comprehended. In the most literal sense, they are identical with sun-fire and star-fire. Their arrangement in the tissue is like the spacing of constellations."

"How queer!" thought Woadley. "Bless me, but that's like the stuff in the astrological manuscript — the 'fierie particles', etc. What are we coming to, anyway?"

* * *

After dining with the moderation that marked all of his habits, Oliver Woadley was overcome by an unwonted and excessive drowsiness, which he could hardly attribute to his single glass of port. Being a respectable bachelor, he commonly spent his evenings in his own home, or else at one of the ultra-conservative clubs to which he belonged. In either case, with an unfailing punctuality, he was in bed by 10:30 p.m. This time, however, to the mild scandalization of his valet and house-keeper, he fell asleep in an easy chair among his books, after vainly trying to keep himself awake with volume I of *Sense and Sensibility* from the new and strangely incomplete set of Jane Austen. There was a feeling of insidious narcotic luxury, a dim and indolent drifting as if upon Lethean clouds or vapors or exotic perfumes. At moments he was vaguely troubled by this infinite relaxation, which seemed to have in it something of decadent sensuality and sybaritism. However, he quickly resigned himself, and slumber bore him away on a tide softer than drifted poppy petals.

His sleep was soon troubled by a feeling of vast subliminal unrest and activity. In a state midway between oblivion and coherent dream, he seemed to apprehend the muttering of myriad voices, the opening of many doors, the lighting of myriad lamps and furnaces in the secret subterranes of his mind,

that had lain dark and stirless heretofore. The muffled tumult
rose and grew louder, the flames brightened, as if a resurrection
of dead things were taking place. Then, like an ever-streaming
pageant called up by necromancy, the dreams began.

His dreams, as a rule, were no less ordinary, no less innocu-
ous, than the doings and reveries of the daytime. But now, with
no violation of congruity, and no sense of strangeness or revulsion, he found himself playing the chief role in dramas from
which the waking Woadley would have recoiled with horror.

In one of the dreams he was a medieval sorcerer taking part
in the gross abominations of the Sabbat, amid the hysterical
laughter of witches, the moaning of succubae, and the leaping
of flames that flung their bloody gules on the black enormous
Creature presiding over all. In a second dream, he was an
alchemist who sought the elixir of immortal life. He breathed
the vapors of poisonous chemicals, he delved in volumes of
unholy lore and madness, he tampered with the secrets of death
and mortality, in the effort to reach his goal. Then he became
an Atlantean scientist who had mastered the creation of living
protoplasm and the disintegration of the atom, and who, by
virtue of this knowledge, had attained tyrannic empire over the
peoples of the crumbling continent. He made war on rebel
cities with armies of artificial monsters; till, threatened in his
citadel by the deadly fungi sent against him by a rival savant,
he loosed the cataclysmic forces that would shatter the last
foundations of Atlantis and bring upon it the engulfing sea.
Subsequently, by turns, he was a shaman of some Tartar tribe,
performing rude sacrifice to barbarous gods; a Yezidee devil-
worshipper, serving the baleful Peacock; and a witch of Salem,
who called upon strange demons and hurled venomous male-
dictions at the bystanders as she was led to the stake.

Centuries, cycles of wild and various visions followed,
with no other thread of unity than the lust for unlawful
knowledge and power, or pleasure beyond the natural limits
of the senses, which was common to all the selves of the

dreamer. Then, with casual suddenness, the phantasmagoria took an even stranger turn.

The scene of these latter dreams was not the Earth, but an immense planet revolving around the sun Yamil Zacra and its dark companion, Yuzh. The name of the world was Pnidleethon. It was a place of exuberant life, and its very poles were tropically fertile; and the lowliest of its people was more learned in wizardry, and mightier in necromancy, than the greatest of terrene sorcerers. How he had arrived there, the dreamer did not know, for he was faint and blinded with the glory of Yamil Zacra, burning in mid-heaven with insupportable whiteness beside the blackly flaming orb of Yuzh. He knew, however, that in Pnidleethon he was no longer the master of evil he had been on Earth, but was an humble neophyte who sought admission to a dark hierarchy. As a proof of his fitness, he was to undergo tremendous ordeals, and tests of unimaginable fire and night.

There was, he thought, a terrible terraced mountain, lifting in air for a hundred miles between the suns; and he must climb from terrace to terrace on stairs guarded by a million larvae of alien horror, a million chimeras of the further cosmos. Death, in a form hideous beyond the dooms of Earth, would be the price of the least failure of courage or any momentary relaxation of vigilance. On each of the lower terraces, when he had attained it after incalculable jeopardy, there were veiled sphinxes and hooded colossi of ill to whose interrogations he must give infallible answer. Having answered them correctly, thus evading the special doom assigned for the ignorance or forgetful, he must commit himself to the care of those Gardeners whose task was the temporary grafting of human life on the life of certain monstrous plants. And after the floral transmigration, in which he must abide for a stated term of time, there were other transmigrations for the acolyte to undergo on his way to the mountain summit, so that no order of life and sentience should be foreign to his understanding.

In another dream, he had nearly gained the summit and the rays of Yamil Zacra were upon him like ever-falling sheets of levin-flame in the cloudless air. He had passed all of the mountain's guardians, except Vermazbor, who warded the apex, and was the most terrible of all. Vermazbor, who had no visible form, other than that derived from the acolyte's profoundest and most secret fear, was taking shape before him; and all the pain and peril and travail he had endured in his ascent would be nothing, unless he could vanquish Vermazbor. . . .

Chapter II

The Wearing of the Amulet

When Woadley awakened, all of these monstrous and outré dreams were like memories of actual happenings in his mind. With bewilderment that deepened into consternation, he found that he could not dissociate himself from the strange avatars through which he had lived. Like the victim of some absurd obsession, who, knowing well the absurdity, is nevertheless without power to free himself, he tried vainly for some time to disinvolve the thoughts and actions of his diurnal life from those of the seekers after illicit things with whom he had been identified.

Physically, his sensations were those of preternatural vigor, of indomitable strength and boundless resilience. This, however, contributed to his alarm and mental dislocation. Almost immediately, when he awakened, he became aware of the heavy carving pressing against him like a live and radiant thing in his pocket. It thrilled him, terrified him inexpressibly. An excitement such as he had never known, and bordering on hysteria, mounted within him. In a sort of visual hallucination, it seemed that the early morning room was filled with the lambence of some larger and more ardent orb than the sun.

He wondered if he were going mad: for suddenly, with a sense of mystic illumination, he remembered the passage in the old manuscript regarding Yamil Zacra and the dark amulets; and it came to him that the thing in his pocket was one of these amulets, and that he himself was the fleshly tenement of certain of the fiery particles from Yamil Zacra. His reason, of course, tried to dismiss the idea as being more than preposterous. The information on which he had stumbled was, he told himself, a fragment of obscure folklore; and like all such lore, was crass superstition. In spite of this argument, which could have seemed incontrovertible to any sane modernist, Woadley drew the carving from his pocket with a fumbling haste that was perilously near to frenzy, and laid it on the library table beside the dilapidated volume that had been its repository.

To his infinite relief, his sensations quickly began to approximate their normal calmness and sanity. It was like the fading of some inveterately possessive nightmare; and Woadley decided that the whole phenomenon had been merely a shadowy prolongation of his dreams in a state between sleeping and waking. The removal of the plaque from his person had served to dissipate the lingering films of slumber. Reiterating to himself this comfortable assurance, he sat down at once and wrote a letter of protest to the dealer who had mistakenly supplied him with the volume of ungodly and outrageous ana. Still further relieved by this vindication of his natural, everyday self, he repaired to the bathroom. The homely acts of shaving and bathing contributed even more to the recovery of his equanimity; and after eating an extra egg and drinking two cups of strong coffee at breakfast, he felt that the recovery was complete.

He was now able to re-approach the engravure with the courage and complacency of one who has laid a phantom or destroyed a formidable bogy. The malignant profile, jetty and phosphorescent, seemed to turn upon him like a furious gargoyle. But he conquered his revulsion and, wrapping it carefully in several thicknesses of manila paper, he sallied forth toward the local museum, whose curator, he thought, would be able to resolve the mystery of the carving's nature and origin.

The museum was only a few blocks away, and he decided that a leisurely saunter through the spring air would serve as a beneficial supplement to the hygiene of the morning. However, as he walked along the sun-bright avenue into the city, there occurred a gradual resumption of the dream-like alienage, the nervous unease and derangement that had pursued him on awakening from that night of prodigious cacodemons. Again there was the weird quickening of his vital energies, the feeling that the flat image was a radiant burden against his flesh through raiment and wrapping-paper. The phantoms of foundered and unholy selves appeared to rise within him like a sea that obeyed the summoning of some occult black moon.

Abhorrent thoughts, having the clearness of recollections, occurred to him again and again. At moments he forgot his destination . . . he was going forth on darker business, was faring to some sorcerers' rendezvous. In an effort to dispel such ridiculous fantasies, he began to tell over the treasures of his library . . . but the list was somehow confused with dreadful and outlandish volumes, of which the normal Woadley was altogether ignorant or had heard of but vaguely. Yet it seemed that he was familiar with their contents, had memorized their evil formulas, their invocations, their histories and hierarchies of demons.

Suddenly, as he walked along with half-hallucinated eyes and brain, a man jostled him clumsily, and Woadley turned upon the offender in a blaze of arrogant fury, the words of an awful ancient curse, in a rarely studied language, pouring sonorously from his lips. The man, who was about to apologize, fell back from him with ashen face and quaking limbs, and then started to run as if a devil had reached out and clawed him. He limped strangely as he ran, and somehow Woadley understood the specific application of the curse he had just fulminated in an unknown tongue. His unnatural anger fell away from him, he became aware that several bystanders were eyeing him with embarrassing curiosity, and he hurried on, little less shaken and terrified than the victim of the malediction.

How he reached the museum, he was never quite able to remember afterward. His inward distraction prevented him from noticing, except as a vague, unfeatured shadow, the man who descended the museum steps as he himself began to climb them. Then, as if in some dream of darkness, he realized that the man had spoken to him in passing, and had said to him in a clear voice, with an elusively foreign accent: "O bearer of the fourth amulet, O favored kinsman of Yamil Zacra, I salute thee."

Needless to say, Woadley was more than astonished by this incredible greeting. And yet, in some furtive, unacknowledged way, his astonishment was not altogether surprise. Recalled by the voice to a more distinct awareness of outward things, he turned to stare at the person who had accosted him, and saw only the back of a tall, gaunt figure, wearing a formal morning coat and a high-piled purplish turban. Apparently the man was some kind of Oriental, who had compromised between his native garb and that of the Occident. Without turning his head, so that Woadley could have seen his face or even the salient portions of his profile, he went on with an agile gait that appeared to betoken immense muscular vigor. Woadley stood peering after him, as the man strode quickly along the avenue toward the low-hanging matutinal sun, and, dazzled by the brilliant light, he closed his eyes for a moment. When he opened them again, the stranger had disappeared in a most unaccountable fashion, as if he had dissolved like a vapor. It was impossible that he could have rounded the corner of the long block in that brief instant; and the nearby buildings were all private residences, a little withdrawn from the pavement, and with open lawns that could hardly have offered concealment for a figure so conspicuous.

Two hypotheses occurred to Woadley. Either he was still dreaming in his arm-chair, or else the man who had spoken to him on the steps was an hallucinatory figment of the aberration that had begun to submerge his normal consciousness. As he climbed the remaining stairs and entered the hall, it seemed that circles of fire were woven about him, and his brain whirled with the vertigo of one who walks on a knife-edge wall over cataracts of terror and splendor pouring from gulf to gulf of an unknown cosmos. He fought to maintain corporeal equilibrium as well as to regain sanity.

Somehow, he found himself in the curator's office. Through films of dizzying, radiant unreality, he was conscious of himself as a separate entity who received and returned the greeting of his friend Arthur Collins, the plump and business-like curator. It was the same separate entity who removed the carving from his pocket, unfolded it from the quadruple wrapping of brown papers, laid it on the desk before Collins, and asked Collins to identify the object.

Almost immediately, there was a reunion of his weirdly sundered selves. The floors became solid beneath him, the webs of alien glory receded from the air. He realized that Collins was peering from the carving to himself, and back again to the carving, with a look of ludicrous puzzlement on his rosy features.

"Where on earth did you find this curio?" said Collins, a note of faint exasperation mingling with the almost infantile perplexity in his voice. The fresh color of his face deepened to an apoplectic ruby when he held up the carving in his hand and perceived its unnatural weight.

Woadley explained the circumstances of his finding of the object.

"Well, I'll be everlastingly hornswoggled if I can place the thing," opined Collins. "It's not Aztec, Minoan, Toltec, Pompeiian, Hindu, Babylonian, Chinese, Graeco-Bactrian, Cro-Magnon, mound-builder, Carthaginian, or anything else in the whole range of archaeology. It must be the word of some crazy modern artist — though how in perdition he obtained the material is beyond me. No mineral of such weight and specific gravity has been discovered. If you don't mind leaving it here for a few hours, I'll call in some expert mineralogists and archaeologists. Maybe some one can throw a little light on it."

"Surely, keep the thing as long as you like," assented Woadley. There was a blessed feeling of relief in the thought that he would not have to carry the carving on his person when he returned home. It was as if he had rid himself of some noxious incubus.

"You don't even need to return it to me," he told Collins. "Send it directly to Peter Calvin, the book-dealer. It belongs to him if to anyone. You know his address, I dare say."

Collins nodded rather absently. He was staring with open, semi-mesmeric horror at the baleful gravure. "I wouldn't care to meet the original of the creature," he observed. "The mind of its creator was hardly embued with Matthew Arnold's sweetness and light."

Toward evening of that day, Woadley had convinced himself that his morning experiences, as well as the dreams of the previous night, were due to some obscure digestive complaint. It was, he told himself again and again, preposterous to imagine that they were connected in any way with the star Yamil Zacra or a dark amulet from Yamil Zacra or any other place. By some kind of sophistry, the vague, elastic explanation had somehow included the disturbing incident of the curse; and he was willing to admit the possibility of an element of auto-suggestion in the strange greeting he had heard, or seemed to hear, from the man on the museum stairs. The foundations of his being, the fortified ramparts of his small but comfortable world, which had been sorely shaken in that hour of tremendous malaise, were now safely re-established.

He was perturbed and irritated, however, when a messenger came from the museum about sunset, with a note from Collins and a package containing the little plaque. He had thought him-

self permanently rid of the thing, but evidently Collins had forgotten or misunderstood his instructions. The note merely
stated, in a fashion almost curt, that no one had been able to
place either the material or the art period of the carving.

Leaving the package unopened on his library table, he
dined early and went out to spend the evening at one of his
clubs. Returning home at the usual hour of 10:30, he retired
very properly to his bedroom with the hope that his unholy
nightmares would not be repeated.

Sleep, however, betrayed him again to forgotten worlds of
blasphemy, of diabolism and necromancy. Through eternal
dreams, through peril, wonder, foulness, ghastliness and glory,
he sought once more the empire barred by a wise God to finite
man. Again he was alchemist and magician, witch and wizard.
Reviling and scorn, and the casting of sharp stones, and the
dooms of thumbscrew and rack and *auto-da-fé*, he endured in
that quest of the absolute. He dabbled in the blood of children,
in filth and feculence unspeakable, and the ultimate putrefaction of the grave. He held parley with the Dwellers in pits
beyond geometric space, he gave homage to hideous demons
seen by the aid of Avernian drugs that blasted the user. From
sea-corroded Atlantean columns, he gleaned a lore that seared
his very soul in the gleaning; on lost papyri of prehistoric
Egypt, and tablets of green brass from Eighur tombs, he found
the wisdom that was henceforth as a mordant charnel-worm in
his living brain. And great, by virtue of all this, was the reward
that he won and the masterdom he achieved.

His stupendous dreams of Pnidleethon were not resumed
on that night; but with certain other dreams the pristine tradi-
tion of Yamil Zacra and the five amulets was interwoven. He
sought to acquire one of the fabled amulets, seeking it through
his avatar as a Hyperborean wizard, in archetypal cities and
amid subhuman tribes. A lord of earthly science and evil, he has
aspired madly to that supreme evolution possible only through
the amulet, by which he would return through the riven veils

of time and place to Yamil Zacra. It seemed that he pursued the quest in vain through life after life, till the great ice-sheet rolled upon Hyperborea; and the sight of nescience came upon him, and he was swept away from his antique wisdom by other lives and deaths. Then there came darker visions, and more aimless seekings unlit by the legend of Yamil Zacra, in ages when all wizards had forgotten the true source of their wizardry; and after these he dreamed that he was Oliver Woadley, and that somehow he had come into possession of the longed-for talisman, and was about to recover all that he had lost amid the dust and ruining of cycles.

From this final dream, he awakened suddenly and sat bolt upright in bed, clutching at the pocket of his old-fashioned nightgown. There was a glowing weight against his heart, and the grey morning twilight about him was filled with an illumination of infernal splendor. In an exultation of rapturous triumph, no longer mingled with any fear or doubting or confusion, he knew that he wore the amulet and would continue to wear it thereafter.

Early in his sleep, he must have risen like a noctambulist to untie the thing from the parcel on the library table, where, later, he found the small cardboard box and crumpled paper in which Collins had returned it to him.

Chapter III

"'I am Avalzant, the Warden of the Fiery Change'".

In telling me his story, Woadley was somewhat vague and reticent about his psychological condition on the day following the second night of necromantic dreams. I infer, though, that there were partial relapses into normality, fluctuations of alarm and horror, moments in which he again mistrusted his own sanity. The complete reversal of his wonted habits of thought, the flight of his strait horizons upon vertiginous gulfs and far worlds, was not to be accomplished without intervals of chaos or conflict. And, yet, from that time on, he seems to have accepted his incredible destiny. He wore the amulet continually, and his initial sensations of vertigo and semi-delirium were not repeated. But under its influence, he became literally another person than the mild bibliophile, Oliver Woadley. . . .

His outward life, however, went on pretty much as usual. In answer to the vehement epistle of complaint he had written to Peter Calvin, he received an explanatory and profusely apologetic letter. The untitled manuscript had belonged to the library of a deceased and eccentric collector, which Calvin had purchased *in toto*. A new and near-sighted clerk had been responsible for the misplacing of the dark volume amid the set of Jane Austen, and the same clerk had packed the set for shipment to Woadley without detecting his error. Calvin was very sorry indeed and, he was sending volume X by express prepaid. Woadley could do whatever he pleased with the old manuscript, which was more curious than valuable.

Woadley smiled over this letter, not without irony; for the manuscript of obscure ana, which had outraged him on his first cursory perusal of its contents, was now of far more interest to him than Jane Austen. Living umbrageously, and avoiding his friends and acquaintances, he had already begun the study of certain excessively rare tomes, such as the *Necronomicon* and the writings of Hali. These he collated carefully with the *Testaments of Carnamagos*, that Cimmerian seer whose records of ultimate blasphemies, both past and future, were found in Graeco-Bactrian tombs. Also, he perused several works of more recent date, such as Vertnain's *Pandemonium*. How Woadley acquired these virtually unheard-of volumes, I never understood; but apparently they came to his hand with the same coincidental ease as the black amulet: an ease in which it is possible to suspect an almost infinitely remote provenance.

To these books, the darkest cabbala of human and demoniac knowledge, he applied himself like an old student who wishes to refresh his memory, rather than as a beginner. Their appalling lore, it seemed, was a thing that he remembered from pre-existent lives, together with the lost words, the primal arcanic symbols that had baffled their translators. The memory had been revived within him by the talisman. It was the flowering of the monads of Yamil Zacra, the eternal, unforgetting atoms which, before entering his body at birth, had been incarnate in a thousand sorcerers and masters of unpermitted wisdom. These esoteric truth, so difficult to believe or understand, he knew with a simple certainty.

His servants, or so it would appear, were not cognizant of any change in Woadley, and thought nothing of his studies, doubtless taking the tomes he perused so assiduously for quaint incunabula. A general impression that he was out of town seems to have been created in the small social circle to which he belonged; and, of a coincidence that suited well enough with his own inclination no one came to call upon him for a whole fortnight.

At the end of that fortnight, in the late evening, he received an unexpected visitor. His servants had gone to bed, and he was memorizing a certain ghastful incantation from the *Testaments of Carnamagos*: an incantation which, if uttered aloud, would cause the complete annihilation and vanishment of a dead human body, either before or after the onset of *rigor mortis* and the beginning of corruption.

Why he was so intent on learning this formula, he hardly knew; but he found himself conning it over and repeating it silently with a feeling of actual haste and urgency, as if it were a lesson important for him to master. Even as he came to the end, and made sure that the last abhorrent rune was fixed firmly in his mind, he heard the loud and vicious buzzing of the doorbell. No doubt the bell was like any other in its tonal vibrations; it had never impressed his ear unusually before; but he was startled as if by the clashing of sinister sistra, or the rattling of a crotalus. The electric warning of a deadly danger tingled through all his nerves as he went to open the door.

As if he had already begun to exercise the clairvoyant powers proper to his new state of entity, he was not all surprised by the extraordinary figure that stood before him. The figure was that of a Tibetan lama, garbed in monastic robe and cap. He was both tall and portly, seeming to fill the entire doorway with his presence. His level, heavy brows, his large eyes that flamed with the cruel brilliance of black diamonds, and the high aquiline cast of his features bore witness to some obscure strain of non-Mongolian blood. He spoke in a voice that somehow suggested the purring of a tiger; and Woadley was never sure afterward as to the language employed: for it seemed then that all languages were an implicit part of his weirdly resurrected knowledge.

"Bearer of the fourth amulet," said the lama, "I crave an audience. Permit me to enter thy lordly abode." The tone was respectful, even obsequious, but behind it, Woadley was aware of a black blaze of animosity toward himself, and a swollen venom as of coiled cobras.

"Enter," he assented curtly, and without turning his back, allowed the lama to pass by him into the hall and precede him to the library. As if to impress Woadley with his subservient attitude, the lama remained standing, till Woadley pointed to a chair beneath the full illumination of a floor-lamp. Woadley then seated himself in a more shadowy position from which he could watch the visitor continually without appearing to do so. He was close to the oaken library table, on which the *Testaments of Carnamagos* lay open at the lich-destroying formula, with the leaves weighted by a small Florentine dagger which he often used as a paper-knife. Before going to answer the bell, he had switched off the light that shone directly on the table, and the floor-lamp was now the only light burning in the room.

"Well, who are you, and what do you want?" he demanded, in an arrogant, peremptory tone of which he would scarcely have been capable a fortnight previous.

"O master," replied the lama, "I am Nong Thun, a most humble neophyte of the elder sciences. My degree of illumination is as darkness compared to thine. Yet has it enabled me to recognize the wearer of the all-powerful amulet from Pnidleethon. I have seen thee in passing; and I come now to request a great boon. Permit thy servile slave to behold the amulet with his unworthy eyes."

"I know nothing of any amulet," said Woadley. "What nonsense is this that you prate?"

"It pleases thee to jest. But again I beg the boon." The lama had lowered his eyes like a devotee in the presence of deity, and his hands were clasped together as if in supplication on his knees.

"I have nothing to show you." The finality of Woadley's voice was like a barrier of flint.

As if resigning himself to this denial, the lama bowed his head in silence. Apart from this, there was no visible movement or quiver in all his body; but at that moment the floor lamp above him was extinguished, as though he had risen to his feet and turned it off. The room was choked with sudden sooty darkness; there was no glimmer through the bay-window from the street-light opposite; not was there even the least glow or flicker from the table-lamp when Woadley reached out to switch it on. The night that enveloped him, it seemed, was a positive thing, an element older and stronger than light; and it closed upon him like strangling hands. But, groping quickly, he found the Florentine dagger, and held it in readiness as he rose silently to his feet and stood between the table and the arm-chair he had just vacated. As if from deep vaults of his brain, a low minatory voice appeared to speak, and supplied him with an ancient word of protective power; and he uttered the word aloud and kept repeating it in a sonorous unbroken muttering as he waited.

Apart from that sorcerous incantation, there was silence in the room, and no light rustle or creaking to indicate the presence of the lama. The unnatural night drew closer; it smothered Woadley like the gloom of a mausoleum, and upon it here hung a faint fetor as of bygone corruption. There came to Woadley the weird thought that no one lived in the room, other than himself; that the lama was gone; that there had never been any such person. But he knew this thought for a wile of the shrouded enemy, seeking to delude him into carelessness; and he did not relax his vigil or cease the reiteration of the protective word. A monstrous and mortal peril was watching him in the nighted chamber, biding its time to sprint; but he felt no fear, only a great and preternormal alertness.

Then, a little beyond arm's length before him, a leprous glimmering slowly dawned in the darkness, like a phosphor of decay. Bone by fleshless bone, beginning with the stalwart ribs, and creeping upward and downward simultaneously, it illumed the tall skeleton to which it clung; and finally it brought out the skull, in whose eye-pits burned like malignant gems; the living eyes of the lama. Then, from between the rows of yellowish vampire teeth, which had parted in a gaping as of Death himself, a dry and rustling voice appeared to issue: the voice of some articulate serpent coiled amid the ruins of mortality.

"Pusillanimous weakling, unworthy fool, give me the black amulet of Yamil Zacra ere it slay thee," hissed the voice.

Like a feinting swordsman who lowers his guard for a second, Woadley ceased for a second his muttering of the word of power which held the horror at bay as if a wizard circle had been drawn about him. In that instant, a long curved knife appeared from empty air in the fleshless hand, seen dimly by the phosphorescent glowing of the finger-bones, and the thing leapt forward, avoiding the chair, and struck at Woadley with a sidelong notice in which its arm-bones and the blade were like the parts of a sweeping scythe.

Woadley, however, had prepared himself for this, and he stooped to the very floor beneath the knife, and slashed upward slantingly with his own weapon at the seeming voidness of thoracic space below the ribs of the phosphor-litten Death. Even as he had expected, his dagger plunged into something that yielded with the soft resistance of living flesh, and the rotten glimmering of the bones was erased in a momentaneous darkness. Then the flame returned in the electric bulbs; and beneath their steady burning he saw at his feet the fallen body of the lama, with a long tear in the robe across the abdomen, from which blood was welling like a tiny spring. With a twisting movement like that of some heavy snake, the body writhed a little, and then became quiescent.

Briefly, while he stood staring at the man he had slain, Woadley felt the nausea, horror and weakness that his former self would have known under such circumstances.

The whole sinister episode through which he had just lived, together with his new self and its preoccupations, became temporarily remote and fantastic. He could realize only that he had killed a man with his own hand, and that the loathsomely inconvenient proof of his crime was lying at his feet with its blood beginning to darken the roses and arabesques of the Oriental carpet.

From this passing consternation, he was startled by a preternatural brightening of the light, as if an untimely dawn had filled the chamber. Looking up, he saw that the lamps themselves were oddly wan and dim. The light came from something that he could define only as a congeries of glowing notes, that had appeared in mid-air at the opposite side of the room, before his longest and highest bookcase.

It was as if the thickly teeming suns of a great galaxy had dwarfed themselves to molecules and had entered the chamber. The congeries appeared to have the vague outlines of a colossal semi-human form, wavering slightly, spinning, contracting and expanding through the ceaseless gyrations of the separate particles. These atomies were insufferably brilliant, and the eyes of Woadley soon became dazzled as he regarded them. They seemed to multiply in myriads, till he beheld only a blazing, fulgurating blur. Miraculously, his vision cleared, and the blur resolved itself into a figure that was still luminous but which had now assumed the character of what is known as solid matter. With reverential awe and wonder, wholly forgetful of the corpse at his feet, he saw before him a creature that might have been some ultra-cosmic angel of ill. The giant stature of this being, in the last phase of his epiphany, had lessened till he was little taller than an extremely tall man; but it seemed that this lessening was a mere accommodation to the scale of his terrene environment.

The quasi-human torso of the being was clad in laminated armor like plates of ruby. His four arms, supple and sinuous as great cobras, were bare; and the two legs, powerful and tapering like the rear volumes of pythons standing erect, were also bare except for short greaves of a golden material about the calves. The four-clawed feet, like those of some mythic salamander, were shod with sapphire sandals. In one of his seven-fingered hands, he carried a short-handled spear with a sword-long blade of blue metal whose point there streamed an incessant torrent of electric sparks.

The head of this being was cuneiform, and its massive flaring lines were prolonged by a miter-shaped helmet with outward-curving horns. His chin sharpened unbelievably, terminating in a dart-like prong, semi-translucent. The ears, conforming to the head, were pierced and fluted shells of shining flesh. The strangely carven nostrils palpitated with a ceaseless motion as of valves that shut and opened. The eyes, far apart beneath the smooth, enormous brow, were beryl-colored orbs that fouldered and darkened as if with the changing of internal fires in the semi-eclipse of their drooping lids. The mouth, turning abruptly down at the corners, was like a symbol of unearthly mysteries and cruelties.

It was impossible to assign a definite complexion to the face and body of this entity, for the whole epidermis, wherever bare to sight, turned momently from a marmoreal pallor to an ebon blackness or a red as of mingled blood and flame.

Rapt and marvelling, Woadley heard a voice that seemed to emanate from the visitant, though the seal-like quietude of the lips remained unbroken. The voice thundered softly in his brain, like the fire and sweetness of a great wine transmuted into sound.

"Again I salute thee, O bearer of the fourth amulet, O favored kinsman of Yamil Zacra. I am Avalzant, the Warden of the Fiery Change, and envoy of Pnidleethon to the sorcerers of outer worlds. The hour of the Change is now at hand, if thy heart be firm to endure it. But first I beg thee to dispose of this carrion." He pointed with his coruscating weapon at the lama's body.

Chapter IV

The Passage to Pnidleethon

Woadley's brain was filled with a strange dazzlement. Recalling at that moment the half-seen Oriental who had addressed him on the steps of the museum, he stared uncomprehending from his visitor to the corpse.

"Why this hesitation?" said the being, in the tone of a patient monitor. Were you not conning the necessary spell for the annihilation of such offal when the lama came? You have only to read it aloud from the book if you have already forgotten."

The runes of the lich-destroying formula returned to Woadley, and his doubt and bemusement passed in a flood of illumination. In a voice that was firm and orotund as that of some elder sorcerer, he recited the incantation of Carnamagos, prolonging and accentuating certain words with the required semi-tones and quavers of vowel-pitch. As the last words vibrated in the lamplit air, the clothing and features of the lama became mantled with a still, hueless flame that burned without sound or palpable heat, rising aloft in a smokeless column, and including even the puddled blood on the Persian carpet. At the same instant, flame clothed the blade of the bloody dagger in Woadley's hand. The body melted away like so much tallow and was quickly consumed, leaving neither ash not charred bone nor any odor of burning to indicate that the eerie cremation had ever occurred. The flame sank, flattened, and died out on the empty floor, and Woadley saw that there was no trace of fire, no stain of blood, to mar the intricate design of the carpet. The stain had also vanished from the dagger, leaving the metal clean and bright. With the pride and complacency of a past-master of such grammaries, he found himself reflecting that this was quite as it should be.

Again he heard the voice of his visitor. "Nong Thun was not the least of the terrestrial children of Yamil Zacra; and if he had slain thee and had won the amulet, it would have been my task to attend him later, even as I must now attend thee. For he lacked only the talisman to assure the ultimate burgeoning of his powers and the supreme flowering of his wisdom. But in this contest thou hast proven thyself the stronger, by virtue of those illuminated monads within thee, each of which has retained the cycle-old knowledge of many sorcerers. Now, by the aid that I bring, that which was effluent from Yamil Zacra in the beginning may return toward Yamil Zacra. This, if thou art firm to endure the passage, will be the reward of thy perilous seekings and thy painful dooms in a thousand earthly pre-existences. Before thee, from this world, three wizards only have been transported to Pnidleethon, and seldom therefore is my adventure here, who serve as the angel of transition to those wizards of ulterior systems, whom the wandering amulets have sought out and chosen. For know that the amulet thou wearest is a thing endued with its own life and its own intelligence, and not idly has it come to thee in the temporary nescience to which thou wert sunken. . . .

"Now let us hasten with the deeds that must be done: since I like not the frore, unfriendly air of this Earth, where the seed of Yamil Zacra has indeed fallen upon sterile soil, and where evil blossoms as a poor and stunted thing. Not soon shall I come again, for the fifth and last amulet slumbers beneath the southern sea in long-unknown Moaria, and waits the final resurgence of that continent under a new name when all the others have sunken, leaving but ocean-scattered isles."

"What is your will, O Avalzant?" asked Woadley. His voice was clear and resolute; but inwardly he quaked a little before the presence of the Envoy, who seemed to bear with him as a vestment more than the vertigo-breeding glory and direness of Death. Behind Avalzant, the shelves of stodgy volumes, the wall itself, appeared to recede interminably, and were interspaced with sceneries lit by an evil, ardent luster. Pits yawned in livid crimson like the mouths of cosmic monsters. Black mountains beetled heaven-high from the brink of depths profounder than the seventh hell. Demonic Thrones and Principalities gathered in conclave beneath black Avernian vaults; and Luciferian Power loomed and muttered in a sky of alternate darkness and levin.

"First," declared Avalzant, in reply to Woadley's question, "it will be needful for thee to doff this sorry raiment which thou wearest, and to stand before me carrying naught but the talisman, since the talisman alone, among material objects may pass with thee to Pnidleethon. The passage is another thing for me, who fare at will through ultimate dimensions, who tread the intricate paths and hidden, folded crossways of gulfs unpermitted to lesser beings; who assume any form desired in the mere taking of thought, and appear simultaneously in more than one world if such be requisite. . . . It was I who spoke to thee on the stairs before the museum; and since then, I have journeyed to Polaris, and have walked on the colossean worlds of Achernar, and have fared to outermost stars of the galaxy whose light will wander still for ages in the deep ere it dawn on the eyes of thy astronomers . . . but such ways are not for thee; nor without my aid is it possible for thee or for any inhabitant of Earth to enter Pnidleethon."

Submissively, while the Envoy was speaking, Woadley had begun to remove his garments. Hastily and with utter negligence he flung the dark, conservative coat and trousers of tweed across an arm-chair, tossed his shirt, tie, socks and under-garments on the pile, and left his shoes lying where he had removed them.

Presently he stood naked from heel to head before Avalzant, the amulet glowing darkly in the palm of his right hand. Only with the utmost dimness was he able to prevision the ordeal before him; but he trembled with its imminence, as a man might tremble on the shore of uncrossed Acheron.

"Now," said Avalzant, "it is needful that I should wound thee deeply on the bosom with my spear. Art fearful of this wounding? If so, it were well to re-clothe thyself and remain amid these volumes of things, and to let the talisman pass into hardier hands."

"Proceed." There was no quaver in Woadley's voice, though sudden-reaching talons of terror clawed at his brain and raked his spinal column like an icy harrow.

Avalzant uplifted the strange, blue-gleaming weapon he bore, till the stream of sparks that poured ceaselessly from its point was directed upon the bare bosom of Woadley. The neophyte was aware of an electric prickling that wandered over his chest as Avalzant drew the weapon in a slow arc from side to side. Then the spear was retracted and was poised aloft with a sinuous, coiling movement of the arm-like member that held it. Death seemed to dart like a levin-bolt upon Woadley, but the apparent lethal driving-power behind the thrust was in all likelihood merely one more test of his courage and resolution. He did not flinch nor even close his eyes. The terrible, blazing point entered his flesh above the right lung, piercing and slashing deeply, but was not deeply enough to inflict a dangerous wound. Then, while Woadley tottered and turned faint with the agony as of throbbing fires that filled his whole being, the weapon was swiftly withdrawn.

Dimly through the million-fold racking of his torment, he heard the solemn voice of Avalzant: "It is not too late if thy heart misgive thee; for the wound will heal in time and leave thee none the worse. But the next thing needful is irrevocable and not to be undone. Holding the amulet firmly with thy fingers, thou must press the graven mouth of the monster into thy wound while it bleeds; and having begun this part of the process, thou hast said farewell to Earth and has foresworn the sun thereof and the light of the sister planets, and hast pledged thyself wholly to Pnidleethon, to Yamil Zacra, and Yuzh. Bethink thee well, whether or not thy resolution holds."

Woadley's agony began to diminish a little. A great wonder filled him, and beneath the wonder there was something of half-surmised horror at the strange injunction of the Envoy. But he obeyed the injunction, forcing the sickle beak and loathsomely wattled mouth of the double-sided profile into the slash inflicted by Avalzant, from which blood was welling profusely on his bosom.

Now began the strangest part of his ordeal for, having inserted the thin edge of the carving in the cut, he was immediately conscious of a gentle suction, as if the profile-mouth were somehow alive and had started to suck his blood. Then, looking down at the amulet, he saw to his amazement that it seemed to have thickened slightly, that the coin-flat surface was swelling and rounding into an unmistakable convexity. At the same time, his pain had altogether ceased, and the blood no longer flowed from his wound; but was evidently being absorbed through what he now knew to be the vampirism of the mineral monstrosity.

Now the black and shimmering horror had swollen like a glutted bat, filling his whole hand as he still held it firmly. But he felt no alarm, no weakness or revulsion whatever, only a vast surge of infernal life and power, as if the amulet, in some exchange that turned to demoniacal possession, were returning a thousand-fold the draught it had made upon him. Even as the thing grew and greatened on his breast, so he in turn seemed to wax gigantic, and his blood roared like the flamy torrents of Phlegethom plunging from deep to deep. The walls of the library had fallen unheeded about him, and he and Avalzant were two colossi who stood alone in the night and upon his bosom the vampire stone was still suckled, enormous as behemoth.

It seemed that he beheld the shrunken world beneath him, the rondure of its horizons curving far down in darkness against the abyss of stars, with a livid fringe of light where the sun hovered behind the eastern hemisphere. Higher and vaster still he towered, and his whole being seemed to melt with insufferable heat, and he heard in himself a roar and tumult as of some peopled inferno, pouring upward with all its damned to overflow the fixed heavens. Then he was riven apart in a thousand selves, whose pale and ghastly faces streamed about him in the momentary flashing of strange suns. The sorcerers of Ur and Egypt, of Antillia and Moaria; necromancers of Mhu Thulan and shamans of Tartary, witch and enchantress of Averoigne, Hecatean hag, and sybil from doomed Poseidonis; alchemist and seer; the priests of evil fetiches from Niger; the adepts of Ahriman, of Eblis, of Taranis, of Set, of Lucifer — all these, resurgent from a thousand tombs in demonomaniacal triumph, were riding the night to some Sabbat. Among others, like a lost soul, was the being who called himself Oliver Woadley. Upon the bosom of each separate self, as upon that of Woadley, a talismanic monster was suckling throughout the blackness . . . flight on deeps forbidden save to the stars in their . . . .

Here Smith's text breaks off.

◎ ◎ ◎

Story Intros

By Robert Price

1. "The Ghoul"

Clark Ashton Smith finished "The Ghoul" on November 11, 1930 and was pleased with the result. He mentioned it to Lovecraft: "The legend is so hideous, that I would not be surprised if there were some mention of it in the Necronomicon. Will you verify this for me?" (to HPL, ca. November 16, 1930). Not surprisingly, Smith's instincts proved to be sound; Lovecraft reported thusly: "Oh, yes - Abdul mentioned your ghoul, & told of other adventures of his. But some timid reader has torn out the pages where the Episode of the Vault under the Mosque comes to a climax — the deletion being curiously uniform in the copies at Harvard & at Miskatonic University [*i.e.*, the only ones near enough for HPL to consult]. When I wrote to the University of Paris for information about the missing text, a polite sub-librarian, M. Leon de Vercheres, wrote me that he would make me a photo-static copy as soon as he could comply with the formalities attendant upon access to the dreaded volume. Unfortunately it was not long afterward that I learned of M. de Vercheres' sudden insanity & incarceration, & of his attempt to burn the hideous book which he had just secured & consulted. Thereafter my requests met with scant notice — & and I have not yet looked up any of the other few surviving copies of the Necronomicon" (November 18, 1930).

From here, Lin Carter took up the challenge, consulting the copy at Chicago's Field Museum, but it, too, had suffered the censorious violence. "However, the Dee Manuscript... is whole and unimpaired" (note to "The Fifth Narrative: The Vault Beneath the Mosque," p. 142 of *The Necronomicon*, Chaosium, 1996). And yet the text he supplies has nothing to say of Smith's ghoul from the remote era of the Caliph Vathek. Elsewhere Carter assures us that "The Ghoul's Tale" is a separate chapter of Alhazred, and this he identified with the text of Smith's "The Ghoul" itself. He had intended to include the story in his complete edition of *The Necronomicon*, just as he would have included the text of Smith's "The Coming of the White Worm" as a chapter of *The Book of Eibon* (as, of course, Smith himself clearly intended).

It is fascinating how Smith's original tale "The Ghoul," which did not see print until the January 1934 issue of Charles Hornig's *The Fantasy Fan*, a non-paying fan magazine, turned out to be the mere tip of the iceberg for a larger tale, in effect, a kind of round robin to which he, Lovecraft, and Lin Carter would all contribute.

2. *"A Rendering from the Arabic"*

Clark Ashton Smith wrote his friend Lovecraft concerning an idea for a horror tale involving "the piecemeal resurrection of a dismembered corpse" to seek revenge on its killer. At the time he called the gestating tale "The Return of Helman Carnby," a characteristic Klarkash-Tonian pun: the carnal remains of a man back from hell. At first the tale involved simple murder and revenge. Lovecraft suggested the use of magic: "Thanks for your suggestion about magical affiliations on the part of the deceased — I am making both the murderer and the victim practitioners in the Black Arts, and am also taking the liberty of introducing the *Necronomicon* — in its original Arabic text" (early January, 1931).

Smith would seem to have been inspired in part by the mention in Lovecraft's 1927 bibliographic history of the *Necronomicon* of "a vague account of a secret copy [of the Arabic original] appearing in San Francisco during the present century, but later perishing by fire." Smith sets his story in Oakland (home of Chaosium, Inc.!), just across the Bay from San Francisco. But Smith did not think the book was destroyed: "But of course, it is not likely that the Arabic version was left undisturbed in that awful mansion *after* the death of *both* wizards. There are too many persons and powers that covet its possession. We can only hope that it has fallen into the hands of those who do not design *immediate* evil toward the world, but whose plans involve a respite of years or cycles" (ca. January 27, 1931). Uh-oh!

Smith completed the story on January 6, 1931 (it was published not long afterward in the September 1931 issue of *Strange Tales*) and sent it to Lovecraft for comment. Smith then wrote, "I was greatly pleased and gratified by your reaction to 'Carnby' — a tale to which I devoted much thought. The more veiled ending you suggest as possible was my original intention - certainly it would have been the safest and most surely successful method. I think what tempted me to the bolder and more hazardous revelation, was the visualizing of the actual *collapse* of that hellishly reanimated abnormality. If the tale is rejected as too gruesome, I can try the other ending, and have the secretary unable to enter the room till *all* is over, and there are merely two heaps of human segments on the floor" (ca. January 27, 1931). Smith did opt for the off-stage version of the ending, and he seems not even to have waited for an editor's complaint. But the original ending survives among Smith's papers, and Steve Behrends has unearthed it. As the hitherto published version of "The Return of the Sorcerer" is readily available in all editions of *Tales of the Cthulhu Mythos*, I have elected to publish the version of the tale that Smith sent Lovecraft, with the original ending. The ending itself appeared in *Klarkash-Ton # 1*, June 1988, but this is the first publication of the story as Smith first wrote it. To avoid bibliographical confusion with the better-known version, I have gone back to one of the working titles Smith had written on the typescript: "A Rendering from the Arabic."

Yet a third version of the story is August Derleth's "Wentworth's Day" (available in the Arkham House collection *The Watchers out of Time*), which combines elements from "The Colour out of Space" and "The Picture in the House," but is essentially Derleth's own version of "The Return of the Sorcerer." And though the hefty element of borrowing is quite clear, it in no way diminishes Derleth's excellent tale, which is as effective in its own way as the Klarkash-Tonian original.

Finally, I must thank Mark Louis Baumgart for passing on to me a marvelous comic book adaptation (uncredited!) of "The Return of the Sorcerer" called "The Corpse That Wouldn't Die" which appeared in *Web of Evil # 2*, January 1952. There the grimoire is not named, and it must be translated not from Arabic, but from Sanskrit.

3. "The Hunters from Beyond"

Smith confessed that "The Hunters from Beyond" (finished on April 28, 1931; published in *Strange Tales*, October 1932) "doesn't please me very well—the integral mood seems a bit second-rate, probably because the modern treatment is rather uncongenial for me."

Perhaps better than "second-rate" as a characterization of the story would be "second-hand," since it is rather obviously an amalgam of more or less equal portions of Robert W. Chambers' "The Yellow Sign," Lovecraft's "Pickman's Model," and Frank Belknap Long's "The Hounds of Tindalos." Lovecraft's Pickman was a solitary artist like Lovecraft himself; Smith has taken his nude model/lover from the analogous character in Chambers' story, the Yellow Nineties decadence of which struck a more responsive note in Smith than it did in Lovecraft. Note, too, Smith's use elsewhere of the name "Hastane," recalling both Chambers' character "Castaigne" in "The Repairer of Reputations" and the Bierce/Chambers "Hastur."

The link with Frank Long's "Hounds of Tindalos" is therefore quite natural, too, since Long named his visionary "Halpin Chalmers," half for Bierce's "Halpin Frayser" and half for Robert W. Chambers himself. Smith has also combined Long's Tindalos Hounds with Lovecraft's canine-snouted ghouls. But the mix is fine alchemy! It is a gem of a tale and may have suffered in Smith's estimation simply because, as he himself implied, he preferred working in another, more stylistically exotic, mode.

"Cyprian Sincaul," CAS's version of Pickman (and, of course, himself), has a last name implying his second sight into the world of horror — he is able to lift the caul, or veil, of Sin and see the abominations and monstrosities that lie beyond it.

4. "The Vaults of Abomi"

Smith was working on this story from late August through mid-September, 1931. He deemed the result "a rather ambitious hunk of extra-planetary weirdness" (to August Derleth, September 6, 1931). But *Weird Tales* editor Farnsworth Wright had other ideas. He thought the story was too slow getting started and asked Smith to get the thing off the ground quicker. Smith's reaction? "I *would* have told Wright to go chase himself in regard to 'The Vaults of Yoh-Vombis', if I didn't have the support of my parents, and debts to pay off. . . . However, I did not reduce the tale by as much as Wright suggested, and I refused to sacrifice the essential details and incidents of the preliminary section. What I did do, mainly, was to condense the descriptive matter, some of which had a slight suspicion of prolixity anyhow. But I shall restore most of it, if the tale is ever brought out in book form" (to HPL, early November 1931). The abridged version, shorn of "one or two thousand words of carefully built atmospheric preparation" (to Derleth, October 23, 1931), appeared in the May 1932 issue of *Weird Tales*.

Steve Behrends has compared the published version with a copy of the original manuscript of the story and restored the material Smith was forced to cut, as well as restoring the Afterword from the *Weird Tales* version to its original position as a Foreword. The restored text first appeared as a booklet from Necronomicon Press in 1988. It is that version that appears here, under Smith's original working title "The Vaults of Abomi," to distinguish it from the more familiar version.

Smith had read Lovecraft's *At the Mountains of Madness* in manuscript just one month before commencing work on this tale, and the influence shows. The whole idea of discovering monsters during an archaeological excavation on an alien world comes directly from HPL, the Mars and Antarctica locations being semiotically equivalent (as Marc A. Cerasini and

Chales Hoffman pointed out in a film treatment of *At the Mountains of Madness*, which, updating it, they set on the moon). Not only this, but the device of the monsters beheading their victims would seem to come from the ravaging of the Old Ones by the shoggoths, and the terminal lunacy of one of the party after seeing more than the others did is familiar, too. "I read *[At the Mountains of Madness]* twice — parts of it three or four times — and think it is one of your masterpieces. . . . I'll never forget your descriptions of that tremendous non-human architecture, and the on-rushing *shoggoth* in an underworld cavern!" (early August, 1931).

5. *"The Nameless Offspring"*

This story appeared in *Strange Tales*, June 1932. Smith had initially plotted it out during January of 1931 and finished it on November 12 of the same year. In a letter to Lovecraft (ca. January 27, 1931) he noted having much enjoyed Arthur Machen's classic "The Great God Pan." "'Pan', by the way, has suggested to me an idea so hellish that I am almost afraid to work it out in story form. It involves a cataleptic woman who was placed alive in the family vaults. Days later a scream was heard within the family vaults, the door was unlocked, and the woman was found sitting up in her *open* coffin, babbling deliriously of some terrible demoniac face whose vision had awakened her from her death-like sleep. Eight or nine months afterwards, she gives birth to a child and dies. The child is so monstrous that no one is permitted to see it. It is kept in a locked room; but many years later, after the death of the woman's husband, it escapes; and, co-incidentally, the corpse of the deceased is found in a condition not to be described. Also, there are monstrous footprints leading *towards* the vaults, but not away from them. If I do this tale I shall head it with a text from the Necronomicon."

In a subsequent letter to HPL Smith supplies the *Necronomicon* passage and comments on it in striking phraseology that almost reads like a continuation of the text itself: "This dreadful passage from the Necronomicon (which one fears to ponder overlong) is the one that I shall use to preface 'The Nameless Offspring'. Personally, I think that some of Alhazred's most appalling hints are beyond anything that I can hope to write, in their endless reverberations of cryptic horror. Is nothing safe or indesecrate - when *They sleep beneath the unturned stone, and rise with the tree from its root?* Are the fountains all polluted, is the very soil pervaded with their poison? Do they veil their obscene entity with the mist, and mask themselves in the cloud of alabastrine whiteness?" (ca. February 15-23, 1931).

6. *"Ubbo-Sathla"*

"**Y**ou will have seen 'Ubbo-Sathla' by now. Wright returned it, to my disgust, seeming to think that it would be over the heads of his clientele" (to HPL ca. March 1932). Nonetheless, Wright eventually reconsidered his decision and accepted the tale, thereby lessening by a modicum his time in Purgatory. (By my reckoning, he is nonetheless still there today.) "Ubbo-Sathla" finally appeared in the July 1933 *Weird Tales*.

Smith had finished the story on February 15, 1932. I do not know for sure what inspired it, but I am willing to wager that, like "The Nameless Offspring" and "The Beast of Averoigne," "Ubbo-Sathla" was based on Machen's "The Great God Pan." The backward slide down the evolutionary path to the primordial ooze seems to recall the final desuetude of Machen's Helen Vaughan. And the whole notion of the primordial Chaos from which all ordered organic life stems being terrible and unthinkable is the central premise of "The Great God Pan."

As for the name "Ubbo-Sathla" itself, I believe Smith derived it from the Buddhist term *Uposatha*, which Christmas Humphreys defines as "The 1st, 8th, 15th and 23rd days of the lunar month; i.e., Full Moon, New Moon and the days equi-distant between them. They were kept as fast-days in pre-Buddhist times, and were utilized by the early Buddhists as days for special meetings of the Order and for recitation of the [227 disciplinary rules binding on the monks]. They became recognized as 'sabbath' days, for expounding or listening to the *Dhamma*, for keeping special Precepts, etc." (*A Popular Dictionary of Buddhism*, Citadel Press, 1963, p. 207).

Two of the mewling efts proceeding from Smith's "Ubbo-Sathla" are Lin Carter's Lesser Old One "Ubb, Father of Worms," and Brian Lumley's "Sathlattae" incantations. It is worth noting that, despite Smith's plain statement in this story that Ubbo-Sathla was already here on earth when the extra-cosmic Old Ones descended from the stars, Lin Carter made Ubbo-Sathla one of the Old Ones, as he did Henry Kuttner's Zuchequan, whom Kuttner, too, had explicitly differentiated from the Lovecraftian pantheon in "Bells of Horror." Another egregious goof regarding poor Ubbo-Sathla was Derleth's repeated reference to Ubbo-Sathla as "the un*for*gotten source," rather than "the un*be*gotten source"!

7. *"The Werewolf of Averoigne"*

*W*eird Tales rejected "The Beast of Averoigne" (completed June 18, 1932) the first time Smith submitted it. Shortly thereafter, Smith sent it to August Derleth, speculating that "the documentary mode of presentation may have led me into more archaism than was palatable" (July 10, 1932). Derleth suggested a few changes, and Smith made them, submitting the new version, which appeared in the May 1933 issue of *Weird Tales*. What had Smith done to the story to reverse the editorial verdict? "I reduced 'The Beast of Averoigne' by 1400 words, left out the abbot's letter entirely, and told Gerome's tale in Luc le Chaudronnier's words. I think the result is rather good—terse, grim, and devilishly horrible" (to Derleth, August 21, 1932).

Rather than reprint the *Weird Tales*/Arkham House version, I have thought it better to return to Smith's original text, the one inspired by the dictates of the Muse rather than those of Mammon. Luckily, the original survives among Smith's papers, where text critic Steve Behrends found it and published it in *Strange Shadows: The Uncollected Fiction and Essays of Clark Ashton Smith* (Greenwood Press, 1989). To avoid bibliographical confusion with the better-known version of "The Beast of Averoigne," I have gone back to an earlier title Smith considered.

As Steve Behrends points out, the scene of the Werewolf's transformation is based on that of Helen Vaughan in Machen's "The Great God Pan," a story that influenced at least three of Smith's tales.

8. *"The Eidolon of the Blind"*

Smith regarded this story as "a first-rate interplanetary horror, sans the hokum of pseudo-explanation." He had finished it in August 1932 and sent it to *Weird Tales*, but Farnsworth Wright bounced it, on the grounds that it was sure to "sicken" many of his readers. Wright had apparently forgotten he was editor of *Weird Tales* and thought he was at the helm of *Ladies Home Journal.*. As Smith himself summed it up, Wright saw the story as being "too terrible and horrific for his select circle of Babbitts and Polyannas" (to August Derleth, September 20, 1932)! He next submitted the story to his "rebound" market, *Strange Tales*, but it ceased publication the very next month! He changed the title to "The Dweller in the Gulf" and proceeded to cast the pearl before another swine, Hugo Gernsback at *Wonder Stories*, who sent it back, saying he might take it if Smith did after all lard it with some rationalizing hokum.

He decided to run it by Farnsworth Wright again, hoping to catch him in "a semi-rational mood" (to Derleth, November 15, 1932). When this effort availed naught, Smith swallowed hard and decided to accommodate Gernsback's demands, adding the John Chalmers character "to offer some kind of semi-scientific explanation of the phenomena in the story" (to Derleth, November 24, 1932).

To make things even worse, when the story appeared in the March 1933 issue of *Wonder Stories*, Smith was aghast to discover that, first, the title had been changed to "The Dweller in Martian Depths," second, whole paragraphs of description had been chopped, and, third, his "magnificent Dantesque ending" had been rewritten, all apparently, by a "semi-illiterate office boy" (to Robert H. Barlow, February 8, 1933). He was right. "I have had a letter of apology from David Lasser, managing editor of *W.S.*, saying that he made the alterations only at Gernsback's express order. Gernsback must be loco to have a story spoiled in that fashion. I judge that the idiotic revision has cooked it with readers who might have liked it otherwise. Oh, phooey" (to HPL, March 1, 1933).

In 1987 Necronomicon Press published a better text of the story. Steve Behrends restored Smith's text by collating two manuscripts, one of the first draft, "The Eidolon of the Blind," the other of the second, "The Dweller in the Gulf." Behrends' text is eclectic, retaining Smith's stylistic polishing and title from the second draft, but removing the alterations Smith made at Gernsback's direction. The mutilations made by David Lasser had already been restored in the Arkham House publication *The Abominations of Yondo* (1960). What you will read here is the straight text of the first version, "The Eidolon of the Blind," presented here for the first time, again thanks to the spade work of Steve Behrends.

One final note: in "The Whisperer in Darkness" Lovecraft may be referring to Smith's Martian entity in the overheard litany of the Yuggoth-spawn who offer "(tri)butes to Him in the Gulf, Azathoth, He of Whom Thou hast taught us marv(els). . . ." Nyarlathotep has donned the Pallid Mask to "go out among men and find the ways thereof, that He in the Gulf may know." It is interesting to speculate whether Ramsey Campbell may have made this connection, identifying Azathoth with Smith's monster-deity with the ankylosaurus-like carapace. In this event, we might have the origin of Campbell's enigmatic references to Azathoth's original "bivalvular form." Ramsey tells me he doesn't remember, but says it's possible!

9. "Vulthoom"

Begun sometime in October of 1932 and completed on Valentine's Day, 1933, "Vulthoom" appeared in *Weird Tales*, September 1935. Smith made no bones about it, admitting that it "fails to please me" but "seems to have pleased [Wright] for some ungodly reason; but after all it's a cut or two above Edmond Hamilton." Hamilton was Lovecraft's and Smith's favorite whipping boy when it came to space-opera fiction, though Otis Adelbert Kline came in for a few strokes of Lovecraft's birch as well from time to time. Here, Smith is guiltily conscious of having approximated Hamilton a bit more closely than usual. He chides not only himself for writing it, but Wright as well, for making the mistake of accepting it! Poor Farnie! Damned if you do, damned if you don't! Of course, there is nothing stop-

ping us from dissenting from Smith's perhaps excessively severe self-judg-
ment and making our own estimate of the story.

In various lists of the Old Ones he gives in his stories, Lin Carter clas-
sifies Smith's Vulthoom among their ranks, but it is interesting to see that
in his early glossary "H.P. Lovecraft: The Gods," he had not yet enrolled
him. Still, the connection is natural, even inevitable, given the way Smith
describes the entity Vulthoom as an ancient space being opportunistically
fostering a cult among the puny inhabitants of his adopted world, just like
Cthulhu.

10. "The Treader of the Dust"

Smith's magic of names does the trick again in "The Treader of the
Dust." First, the excellent Hellenophonic name "Carnamagos"
seems intended to denote "carnal mage," reminiscent of C.S. Lewis'
"materialist magician" whose advent the demon Screwtape anticipates.
The Testaments of Carnamagos are a medieval-era doublette of Smith's own
Book of Eibon."Quachil Uttaus" plays on several associations in the text
such as the "chill" that is twice said to overtake John Sebastian, as well as
the general impression of tomb-like quiet overlaying the mansion. We
read of "utter, utmost," and "ultimate" desolation. The old butler
Timmers is apparently both timorous and subject to tremors, to say nothing of the fact that he crumbles into a pile of dust like the rotting "tim-
bers" Sebastian eventually hears collapsing. John Sebastian wonders why
doom has befallen him, since he has never called up the demons of evil
magic; he is as pious as his name, which is Greek for "religious, holy." In
this he resembles Lovecraft's pious farmer Nahum Gardner ("The Colour
out of Space") who also falls to disgusting dust as a result of an encounter
with alien forces and imagines it to be God's (unmerited) punishment.

The story fairly sighs with dusty desolation. It is a Poesque masterpiece
where the form matches the substance perfectly, down to the final wordless
epiphany of the terrible corruption elemental himself, the perfect embodi-
ment of premature aging: a fetus aborted by the onset of old age already
within the womb (perhaps a wry jibe at the Taoist legend that Lao-tsu
emerged from his mother's womb already an old man of seventy years).

Smith finished this story on February 15, 1935, and it was published in
Weird Tales for August 1935.

11. The Infernal Star

"*The Infernal Star*. . . I began a number of years back as a prospective
three-part serial for *W.T.* I drafted the first part (around 12,000 words)
but somehow never went on with it. The hero was an innocent bibliophile

who, through an amulet found behind the cracked binding of a volume of Jane Austen, was drawn into a series of wild and sorcerous adventures leading to a world of the star Yamil Zakra, the center from which all cosmic evil, sorcery, witchcraft, etc., emanate. I'll try to finish it if I can sell enough shorts to finance myself for a while" (to L. Sprague de Camp, October 21, 1952).

Smith fans drooled for many years over "The Infernal Star," since it seemed they had about as much chance of seeing it as they did the Arabic *Necronomicon*! But, thanks to Steve Behrends, "The Infernal Star" did finally see print in *Strange Shadows: The Uncollected Fiction and Essays of Clark Ashton Smith* from Greenwood Press in 1989. This book was not the easiest for fans to obtain, so many have still not laid eyes on the fragment. What you will read here is not, however, simply a reprint of what appeared in *Strange Shadows*. It turns out that that version was one Smith had retouched in accord with some suggestions of August Derleth, and by that time, Smith's style had become rather less ornate than when he had first written the fragment. Again, thanks to Steve Behrends, we are able to present here Smith's original 1933 version of as much of "The Infernal Star" as he wrote.